THE FURY OF A STORME

The Storme Brothers
Book Six

Sandra Sookoo

ARE YOU SIGNED UP FOR DRAGONBLADE'S BLOG?

You'll get the latest news and information on exclusive giveaways, exclusive excerpts, coming releases, sales, free books, cover reveals and more.

Check out our complete list of authors, too!

No spam, no junk. That's a promise!

Sign Up Here

www.dragonbladepublishing.com

Dearest Reader;

Thank you for your support of a small press. At Dragonblade Publishing, we strive to bring you the highest quality Historical Romance from some of the best authors in the business. Without your support, there is no 'us', so we sincerely hope you adore these stories and find some new favorite authors along the way.

Happy Reading!

CEO, Dragonblade Publishing

Dedication

To M. You know why.

Acknowledgements

I'd like to thank the following people who helped in my research by giving me a snapshot of daily life living with dyslexia and its many forms.

Cecilia R. Rodriguez

Christa Paige

Nicole Stein

CHAPTER ONE

September 1, 1818
London, England

THE HONORABLE CAROLINE Storme huffed in annoyance when a couple drops of rain splattered the page of her drawing notebook. One of them stained the ivory paper while the other smeared the charcoal she used to sketch. It made a few lines of the drawing out of order, and in some irritation, she dabbed at the spot with her sleeve. That, of course, made an even bigger mess of things, so she furiously frowned at the page in disgust.

Though she forgot names with alarming regularity, she never forgot a face, and for the past few months, the subject of her drawings—when she did them of people at all—had been the same man: barrel chest, big frame, golden brown hair that curled just above his collar, tawny eyes like a lion, and a sensual mouth that when curved in a specific grin had the power to flutter her heartbeat. Which was odd because she was never allowed to be in the same room with a man alone... not that any had shown interest in her. Sometimes she would sketch him in wintertime clothing. At others, she would portray him rigged out in ballroom finery. Every once in a while, she portrayed him shirtless to the waist, but that wasn't an accurate depiction, for she'd never seen any man in such a state of undress. Long ago her mind had buried his name, but her heart never wished to give him up.

Not that she minded. Once she'd done the preliminary sketches and she deemed them worthy enough, she took to her canvas and recreated the art using oil or watercolor paints depending on where the whim took her. Already, she had three such portraits hanging in the rooms of her London townhouse. Her cousin Andrew's to be precise, and when that same cousin had questioned her as to who the man in the paintings was and she couldn't say, he'd ordered her to cease drawing him.

She hadn't followed through with that order. Instead, she'd merely moved the paintings into her dressing room and made certain they were hidden away from his prying, judgmental eyes. The man in her paintings gave her a sense of peace and calm; she had the impression that she'd met him somewhere before, but since her mind often jumbled things up—people, places, things, locations—she had no idea where to put him in those recollections. Perhaps if she ever saw him again, the memories would float to the forefront, and everything would make sense again.

Not that anything made sense. Or rather, it made sense to a point in her mind, but not to the people around her if she should try and explain.

It made for a lonely world.

Another few drops of rain fell to further mar her sketch. Giving into the ever-present anger that simmered in her chest, she ripped the page from her drawing pad, wadded it up, and then hurled it with a cry into the Serpentine River from her position on a large boulder in Hyde Park. It bobbed upon the constantly moving water and the current carried the paper away from her, only to become snagged in a cluster of water plants. A pair of ducks came over to investigate but eventually grew bored.

Caroline sighed. She'd come here to paint in the relative privacy and quiet of the park, for Andrew's home was often mired in chaos and noise now that he had an infant daughter.

Not that he wasn't loud on his own—he often reminded her of a bull stomping his way through London—but he'd been the one to remove her from the institution for the insane when no one else in the Storme family had cared. Odd, that, for she'd always thought of him as quite selfish. She'd spent twenty long years there, for her mind didn't work like other people's and her parents hadn't known what to do about that. Twenty years of her life had been locked away from society, from her family, from anything that would have brought her joy, but now she lived in London, at a Mayfair address in her cousin the earl's home, yet it still felt as if she were a prisoner, still waiting on the day when someone—anyone—would rescue her and set her free.

Like in the storybooks Isobel used to read her.

Were there such things as heroes and knights of old in the modern age?

When the rain began in earnest, Caroline closed her notebook and then slid from her perch on the boulder. *Drat, drat, drat.* Perhaps it hadn't been the wisest decision to send the Hadleigh carriage back to the house, but she'd been intoxicated with a freedom of sorts, for her cousin had finally consented to let her take an outing by herself. Of course, she would not say no to being out of the townhouse. Andrew had been distracted with his babe as well as demands to his title, which had no doubt precipitated the decision, and truly, she was always someone's responsibility.

Which never failed to annoy her. But she'd declined the accompaniment of her maid, and her cousin would bluster once he discovered that. There was too much pressure to talk and make her mind work correctly when others were with her. So, she'd come to Hyde Park alone, for it had sounded thrilling, and there'd be inspiration everywhere.

After a couple of hours wandering the grounds in unabated solitude, she'd decided to sketch for a bit. Then the dratted rain had ruined a perfectly good afternoon, and that meant a return to her gilded prison.

With another huff of annoyance, Caroline reached into her reticule. She yanked out a map of the area she'd drawn to help jog her memory and remind her of where she'd been and where she needed to go. Though she'd thought she had put clues and landmarks onto the paper to encourage her broken brain to identify her location, they were nowhere to be found on the map now. Perhaps she'd been distracted when she'd drawn it, or perhaps she was too flustered by the unexpected rain to locate them on the drawing.

Oh, yes, that was it. There'd been a pair of white swans on the water, and she'd wanted to sketch them. Then she'd let her mind wander back to her childhood when her sister Isobel would read fairy stories to her about brave knights who'd rescue trapped princesses from high towers and such. Sometimes there'd been swans in those stories. And then she wondered where the swans had spent their days when not on the water…

But none of that helped her now. The rain-spotted paper quickly lost its integrity, so it too was wadded up and hurled into the river.

"Why I cannot normal be?" she asked of no one in particular as the rain came down in earnest. Caroline cried out in frustration, for once again, the words that came out of her mouth had arranged themselves into an awkward pattern.

But she wasn't and she never would be.

Having no choice except to run along the many pathways that intersected and crisscrossed through the park, all too soon Caroline was lost and disoriented. The rain had seeped through her spencer. The sensation of wet cloth against her skin wasn't pleasant, and it took every shred of control not to rip the clothes from her person. Every direction she looked seemed unfamiliar. There was no clear way to proceed. Hot panic rose in her throat, for she didn't know what to do.

And the rain kept coming down. Being wet had knots of worry pulling in her belly. Water had the tendency to bring on terror, for in the asylum they often dunked patients' heads into tubs full of it in an effort to gauge their reactions and emotional responses for no reason Caroline could fathom. She was fine looking at water, but the second too much of it touched her skin, memories assailed her and often brought more confusion with them.

The panic intensified until it threatened to choke her. Blindly, she ran down paths and indiscriminately through shrubbery and landscaping in an attempt to find her way out of the park. As she spared a second to glance back over her shoulder, her forward momentum was abruptly halted when she ran bodily into the chest of a large man who promptly enclosed her into a protective embrace.

"Oh!" Immediately, the comforting scents of salt, sun, a breeze laden with exotic things, and beneath that leather and man. *I've smelled that before.* Some of her anxiety calmed. When she curled her fingers into his lapels, determined to hang on until the memory could surface in her brain, the man moved his hands to her shoulders to steady her.

"My apologies, miss. I sometimes need to be more careful as to where I'm going, but in an area as beautiful as Hyde Park, that's a difficult endeavor."

As much as she didn't want him to talk and disrupt a delve into her mind, the rumble of his deep voice paired with that scent and the golden-brown eyes she stared up into yanked them from the jumbled attics of her mind. Excitement shuddered down her spine while at the same time, an odd sort of awareness prickled over her skin. Of course! "Mr. Butler, correct?" He was the man she'd met while at a Christmastide house party for the Stormes in the Derbyshire countryside, the man who had treated her with kindness and respect.

And he was the man she couldn't stop painting. Perhaps now she would discover the answers as to why.

"Yes!" He bent his head and peered into her eyes, and she knew a moment of profound peace in those golden-brown— almost tawny—pools. Oh yes, she remembered those eyes! "Well, if this isn't providential, I don't know what is." As his lips curved with a wide grin, butterflies set up a ballet in her belly.

"Miss Storme. Imagine that." Though the rain fell steadily onto both of them, he didn't seem to mind. Neither did she, not now that he was there. The prickling panic regarding water wasn't as prominent now that she could concentrate on something else. "How are you, aside from being wet and from the looks of it, frightened?"

When she'd seen him at Christmastide, he'd taken the lead in whatever situation where they were both together. His big, commanding presence meant that she was never disrespected or ignored, and then just as now, she felt safe with him, as if he were a calm harbor to her storm-rocked boat. Giving him a small, tight smile, Caroline nodded and concentrated on her next words. "I am well." Her throat was entirely too dry. She gripped the edge of her sketchbook. "Passing time. Painting is how I've been."

Of course, her mouth wouldn't say what her brain wished to convey. They never worked in tandem, and it was maddening, which was why she seldom talked in public if she could help it.

Mr. Butler didn't seem to mind. Rain dripped from the brim of his beaver felt top hat. It also seeped into her hair. Only then did she realize she had forgotten her dratted bonnet. Such trivial things, fripperies like hats and gloves. They served no purpose except to be silly... or set her apart from others. Neither did he make jest of her, much like he'd been all those months ago. When he didn't immediately attempt to usher her away, some of the tenseness left her shoulders. "That's wonderful, Miss Storme. I knew you could draw, for I'd seen some of your creations at Christmastide, but I wasn't aware your talents went to painting too."

"Yes." She nodded. What would he say if he knew *he'd* been the subject of far too many of her pieces in ways she couldn't quite fathom?

As if realizing it wasn't quite proper to keep standing there with his hands on her person, he backed away, and as he did so, some of the cozy protectiveness went with him. How she despised that widening gap between them. It felt much like he would vanish into the mist surrounding her mind and she might never see him again.

Threads of panic began to return. "Don't go."

"I won't." Again, he grinned. "Continuing to talk about your drawings, I admire people who are artistic. It's not something I've been blessed with."

Caroline lifted her face to the rain. Perhaps it would cool her overheating cheeks. "It is nothing." When she transferred her attention back to him, the sapphire blue color of his jacket stirred her muse. Could she capture that exact hue for her next painting? How much of each paint would she need to blend? It would be nice for the color of a midnight sky sprinkled with stars…

"So says the woman with natural talent." His grin never faded. "You wouldn't say that if you could see my pathetic attempts at drawing of any kind. Imagine being surrounded by your creations, to look at them and study them whenever one wished."

"Oh?" He liked them that much?

"Damnation." The jovial attitude vanished under a cloud of concern. "I beg your pardon, Miss Storme. What a nodcock you must think me for keeping you out in such dismal weather."

She snorted. "I enjoy the rain." Until she didn't because it touched her skin, wet her clothing, or ruined her sketches. Oh, thank goodness the words were in the correct order. "When it ruins except my drawings." And her mind was back to mucking things up. "I had a map but turned around was from fright." Annoyed at the disconnect of her mind, she plunged onward. "You can help me at home?"

Mr. Butler frowned. Though it took him a few seconds, he managed to puzzle out her intent. For that she was grateful. "Of course I'll take you home."

Caroline almost sagged with relief when he didn't correct her speech. Her siblings and cousins meant well—probably—but they didn't need to keep telling her that she'd put together a sentence wrong. Every minute of every day, she was already well aware of her speech patterns. Lady Jane was worse than all of them, but she was so nice it didn't rankle that much. Usually. "Thank you." She wiped the moisture from her forehead.

"Where is your carriage? I rather doubt Hadleigh would have let you walk or hire a hack."

"I don't know." She shrugged.

"Never mind. The earl will have my head in any event once you arrive wet and bedraggled and in my company." He huffed with apparent frustration. Caroline didn't like it when he wasn't smiling. "My vehicle isn't far from here." Then he offered an arm bent at the elbow. "Once you're safely inside and out of the rain, you can tell me your favorite spot in the park. I don't get up to London much, but the next time I do, I'll visit Hyde Park again. It's a wonderful place for reflection."

He would find no argument from her on that count, but she would rather not talk at all. Not even to him. Though as she walked briskly beside Mr. Butler—his long-legged stride meant she had to hustle to keep up—she marveled that she wasn't so nervous in his company as she was with many other people.

Why? What difference did one person's presence make?

They soon reached a sleek black carriage that bore a pretty crest done in silver paint on the door. Caroline traced the swirls and rampant lion artwork with a fingertip. The speckling of raindrops on the door formed an interesting pattern that might provide a new texture if she could reproduce it just right.

"Miss Storme?" Mr. Butler had opened the door and was waiting politely to one side. "May I help you up?"

"Yes." When she slipped her hand into his and his other briefly touched her waist as he assisted her into the carriage, warmth tingled through her lower belly. How exceedingly odd. She'd never felt that whenever her cousin handed her into a vehicle. With a tiny sigh, she settled onto one of the squabbed benches. As much as she liked the rain, she was glad to be out of it.

Seconds later, Mr. Butler came into the carriage after giving his driver an address. He closed the door and had no sooner sat heavily on the bench across from her than the vehicle lurched into motion. "It's unfortunate the weather didn't cooperate. I would have liked to stroll through the park with you a while. That Christmastide house party seems a million years from now." His grin returned and his eyes were kind. "I've often wondered what became of you after that."

"I have been… hiding." For lack of a better word. But that's what it felt like. Cousin Andrew kept her inside the townhouse. Did he fear that she would harm herself or others? Or was it that he didn't quite know what to do with her? Perhaps she caused him too much embarrassment. In many ways, it was little better than the institution, for she was allowed outside, but…

When Mr. Butler removed his hat and set it on the bench beside him, she eyed his hair, slightly longer than fashion demanded, with an artist's eye. Did she have enough yellows and browns to recreate that exact shade? A thin enough brush to make those slight waves? What would it feel like? She needed to know that to better understand how to sketch him.

"Why are you hiding?" The rumble of his voice in the small, enclosed space reverberated within her chest.

"I am different." That was the truth. Ordinarily, she didn't enjoy traveling with other people, but with Mr. Butler, his big presence brought comfort and calm. As if he would protect her from all the horrors and slights in the world, as if he would never judge her because of her failures. In his company, there was a peace she'd not known before, and it was slightly addicting.

"We are all different, Miss Storme. That doesn't mean you should hide away." He nodded with encouragement. "With your talents, you should be lauded and admired in society. Your paintings should hang in the most popular drawing rooms."

Oh, dear heavens. She shuddered. "Society wants perfection. I am broken." Relief shivered down her spine, for the words weren't mangled this time.

"Bullocks." He regarded her with pursed lips and bushy eyebrows that dipped in confusion. "Why do you assume so?"

Caroline wasn't in the mood for games or being analyzed, and she certainly didn't want him to think poorly of her. She thought of the words she wanted to say before she spoke them slowly. "Why are you here?"

His eyes twinkled with amusement as he observed her. "In Hyde Park or in London?"

Too many questions! Her confusion or panic must have shown on her face, for he made soothing sounds and held up a gloved hand. Caroline frowned. Where the devil had she left *her* gloves?

"Settle, Miss Storme. I like to walk in the park. Somehow, it makes me miss the sea less, and as long as I can see the water of the Serpentine, my homesickness isn't as acute."

Ah, a connection she understood. "Cousin Brand is on the sea."

Mr. Butler nodded. "He was, but now he's in London too, for a bit. He and I sailed in together."

"Why?"

"Brand wished to see his family and meet with prospective clients. I am here to see my father." He blew out a breath. "My father is a baron. He's in Town for the Season and Parliament's start." Emotions she couldn't read lined his face. "I'm on my way to see him, but wished for the calm of Hyde Park before I called."

"Oh." His tone was so deep and delicious; she could listen to him for hours. Caroline let her imagination run away with her. So easily she could imagine him as a knight of old, riding off into battle for a chance to win the hand of his lady fair, just like in the stories Isobel used to read to her, the stories she had memorized and could pretend to read for herself. "I am glad."

"Why?" He followed the inquiry with a wide grin that revealed straight even white teeth except for the left upper incisor, which was slightly crooked. Like his nose. Had it been broken at one time? Did he know how to fight? Those flaws made him that much more approachable, but he was still more perfect than her.

With heat in her cheeks, she shrugged. "I am here too. In London."

"Again, it's providence, I say." He sat back against his bench while resting an ankle on a knee—the picture of relaxed, English elegance. Her fingers itched to sketch him. As his golden-brown gaze held hers, he asked, "How is life with your cousin the earl?"

"Cousin Drew?" For a moment, she froze. No one was ever interested in any aspect of her life. They only assumed she was doing well within the family fold. A shaft of anger speared through her chest. People never really *saw* her. Except Mr. Butler, but then, perhaps he was only being polite. What was there to say, after all? The truth, of course. "The babe is noisy. Cousin Drew is so too." *Drat.* More of a jumble. Another round of heat filled her cheeks.

"That's what I've heard. Is he still riddled with anger and anxiety over his title?"

"He is better sometimes. Helps him, Sarah." A wave of confusion smacked her in the chest. "My mother. Dead." The more emotional she was, the less her syntax made sense, and the more her sentences broke down. And why did she share that with him?

Compassion lined his expression. "You have my condolences, Miss Storme. I was desolate for a time when I lost mine. You must be devastated."

How... odd. Why *must* she? Her relationship with all of her family members was complicated. Since she'd been separated from them for so long, the bond she should have had with them simply wasn't strong.

"No?" Caroline shrugged. "I don't know?" For she truly didn't. Everything that had to do with the Stormes was a murky maelstrom she couldn't make sense of but felt caught up in that vortex. Most of the time, she was angry, so very angry because they'd sent her away when she'd needed them the most. And now that she was back in London, kept like a prisoner in a gilded cage, away from anything that might prove an embarrassment, she still needed their permission to do almost anything. "I want freedom... John." Yes, that was his given name, and he'd asked her to call him that so long ago at Christmastide.

His expression brightened. "I'd hope you would have remembered… Caroline."

Oh, the way he said her name! The way it made her feel as if she were special and valued. It took the fury out of the storm brewing inside her spirit, if only for a time. She clutched at the strings of her reticule, for she yearned to draw exactly what she was feeling, how the emotions swirled around her like a cyclone, unable to be contained.

"It's all right, you know." He leaned forward, planted both boots on the floorboard, and then briefly touched her knee. A jolt of heated energy zipped up her leg to glance through her lower belly. "There is no correct way to feel about anything. The path through life is different for everyone; no two people walk it the same way."

For the first time in her existence, she was given affirmation to manage things in her own way. It was overwhelming and a rush. So much so that she wanted to experience more of that. "Thank you." She wiped the raindrops from the cover of her sketchbook. As the carriage rocked to a halt in front of Hadleigh House, she sighed. "Cousin Drew mad will be."

John snorted. "Isn't he always?" He shot her a mischievous glance. "I have time to linger if you'd like me to stay and explain your wet state and my escort."

How was it possible this man was completely different than her family? "Yes." She shook her head, but lingering meant he wouldn't stay permanently, and that brought panic rushing back into her throat. Once he left, she would return to that gilded cage with clipped wings.

He winked. "Never fear. I'll do my best to head off the storm that is your cousin."

But what about the storm brewing within her, the one she feared would soon consume her and carry her off into real madness?

CHAPTER TWO

Mr. John Butler, only remaining son of Baron Westfield, couldn't believe the boon he'd been given of Miss Storme popping back into his life. When he'd last seen her at that Christmastide house party the previous December, they had also met under extenuating circumstances. She'd needed help then just as she had now, and he'd been fortunate enough to provide it twice.

Like the other time, he had the sense she was on the verge of doing great things if only someone would give her half the chance.

A sigh from Caroline at his side as they entered the house ramped his protective instincts, for a din of chaos erupted from somewhere along the corridor—a study most likely. The Earl of Hadleigh's voice was raised, not in anger, but at a volume he probably used when excited about something. While John and Caroline gave the butler their dripping outer things, the earl exited a room down the hall, quickly followed by another, smaller man who was no doubt his man-of-affairs, if the armful of paperwork and ledgers was any indication.

"And make certain everyone on the committee knows of the changes," Hadleigh said from over his shoulder. "This could very well have fantastic implications for us all."

"Of course, Your Lordship," the other man said with a nod.

"I'll submit your proposal to the printer this afternoon." Then he scuttled past John, who looked at him with a faint grin. There was always something going on in the Storme family.

He glanced at Caroline. Her hair had mostly tumbled from its pins. The heavy dark brown mass fell down her back in long curls. It softened her face and made her appear less severe. "Is this the climate you live in all the time?"

"Yes." She shook her head. A damp curl fell over her forehead. "Loud. Always. My painting interrupts."

"Ah." John frowned. Though she had some difficulty speaking words or phrases in the correct order, it wasn't bad enough that he couldn't understand her, and she certainly shouldn't be berated or corrected for it. Perhaps her brain and higher consciousness had more important things to do than concentrate on speech. He'd seen a few of her sketches at Christmastide to know she was near a genius in that regard. And Brand had told him she could play the pianoforte with such talent that she only needed to look at sheet music once to memorize it.

Would that he were fortunate to bear witness to that.

Then Hadleigh was upon them, his frown fierce. For the moment, he ignored John to focus on his cousin. "Caroline, where have you been? We've been worried sick that something untoward had occurred when the carriage came back empty."

A huff of annoyance escaped from her. "I wanted to Hyde Park walk alone." A pink flush rose into her cheeks. "Was confused in the rain." She gestured to him. "John was there."

Hadleigh's eyes widened. "Is that why you wished to visit the park? You had an assignation?" His voice rose with each question.

"Good God, man, of course not," John interrupted. "I was simply there at the same time and had no idea she would be too." He gave her a reassuring grin. "However, it was pure good fortune that I was, for she became turned around and panicked. I escorted her home without incident. No need to come the crab."

A snicker issued from Caroline while Hadleigh's face took on the appearance of a summer thunderstorm. Once more he dismissed John. "I should never have let you convince me going out of the house was a good idea." The earl shook his head. "You simply aren't meant to go it alone, Cousin. Though you are a woman grown, next time, you'll have an escort. No more arguments. You're much safer here."

As if she were an oddity or monster who needed a keeper. Or too complicated that the best course was to shut her away. It was unfair. And quite harsh. John narrowed his eyes when disappointment shadowed her eyes. Hadleigh apparently wished to keep her tucked away without trying to understand her or let her spread her wings to discover who she was outside of the stifling confines of the Storme connection.

"Actually, Lord Hadleigh, Caroline is quite intelligent. Give her the benefit of the doubt. Let her learn as she interacts with the world around her."

"You know nothing about it." The earl stared him down.

A flash of color tugged John's attention away. Caroline had wandered down the corridor toward the grand staircase. Had she tired of the scene or of his presence? He didn't know but he did wish to tell her goodbye and let her know he'd enjoyed their brief outing. By the time he focused upon the earl, annoyance roiled in Hadleigh's stormy eyes, but John stood his ground.

"Mr. Butler, I would appreciate it if you would attend me when I'm speaking to you."

"Then perhaps you should say something worth hearing." As a mottled red color crept up the earl's face, John sighed and tamped down the urge to roll his eyes. Such dramatics. Brand had been quite correct when he said his older brother was often over the top. "I beg your pardon, Lord Hadleigh, but I'm still concerned about Caroline, er, Miss Storme. Might I see that she's properly settled before I leave?"

"My cousin is not your responsibility."

"I never said she was, and by that way of thinking, a woman should never be considered a responsibility to begin with. She is not something one owns or has an obligation to, and she certainly shouldn't be kept as an oddity or a china doll."

The corner of the earl's right eye twitched. He crossed his arms at his chest and glared. "She is, and my word is final."

Spare me the arrogance.

This was why he missed the simple life he had in Ipswich. Every time he came back to London and added members of the *ton* to his interactions, his patience was tried, and a foul taste lingered in his mouth. Truly, he had no use for such people. "It seems I must beg your pardon again, but I suspect she is not. Miss Storme is her own person, and she's largely been ignored here." He didn't know that for a fact, but from everything he'd heard and seen, now and during that Christmastide house party, the behavior pointed to it.

"Enough!" The earl's face turned an alarming shade of reddish-purple, but before he could explode, the sound of a female's voice floated down to their location.

"Andrew, dear, remember your breathing exercises, and if we have a guest, please bring them up to the drawing room. I fancy socializing a bit."

Ah, that must be the countess. John stared at the earl with a faint grin. When Hadleigh's shoulders drooped and his color returned to normal, he sighed, followed that with a few deep breaths.

"Please, join Lady Hadleigh and me in the drawing room so we might discuss this calmly and rationally."

"Thank you." Had no one challenged the man on the subject of Caroline's care or future? She couldn't very well be kept a pampered prisoner. As he climbed the stairs behind the earl, he widened his grin. Now he remembered how fun it had been to tease Brand's brother. Really, the man took life entirely too seriously. Upon entering the drawing room, he paused to enjoy the domestic scene.

The countess sat with her feet propped on an embroidered foot stool. Her spectacles were perched low on her nose while she read a book. A younger lady with the same features and hair color of all the Stormes sat across from her, knitting. That must be Brand's youngest cousin, Isobel. She'd married Doctor Marsden not long ago. They both looked like summer flowers in yellow and green muslin, respectfully. Near one of the tall windows, a baby cradle rested. Caroline peered into it, her expression full of speculation and longing while her curls tumbled over her shoulder like a mysterious waterfall. Then she retreated to a chair farther away from the other ladies.

"Good afternoon, Countess. Mrs. Marsden." At the back of his mind, he realized she was also a countess, but he couldn't recall the title's name. He paid the proper respect to the ladies, going for the theatrics of bowing over their hands while the earl emoted dislike and disapproval in waves. "It's been an age since I've seen either of you."

Lady Hadleigh looked up from her book with a smile. "Ah, Mr. Butler. You're Brand's best friend, correct?"

"I am. He tells me every chance he gets I'm an honorary Storme." Closer to him than his own blood brothers.

"He talks about you all the time and is quite fond of you, as are we all." When her husband snorted, she waved at him. "It's wonderful you're in London with Brand. I hope before the two of you go back, you will join us for dinner one night. Finn would love to see you, since his wife is in Ipswich presently."

"I wouldn't dream of disappointing you, my lady." Though he and Brand had sailed to London for various reasons, his best friend had a new baby at home, which had prompted a visit from the dowager countess as well as Finn's wife, Lady Jane.

"You are quite charming, Mr. Butler." She flashed him a grin. The countess was a breath of fresh air and a perfect foil to her husband. "How have you fared this year?"

"Not too badly. The shipping business I run with Brand and the others is doing well for being so new." He glanced at Caroline who stared back at him with mild interest. "I look forward to seeing where and how we can grow."

"Marvelous." The countess nodded. "Are you in Town to

visit with Brand?"

"Yes, and to meet with potential clients, though he's the face of the company, as it is. I'm mostly here to see my father." All his previous joviality left him. "It's a bit of an unsavory chore."

"Family sometimes is." There was no censure in her tone. "You must do what you feel is best."

"Yes." His gaze again jogged to Caroline. "I ran into Miss Storme while at Hyde Park today. It cheered me considerably."

The earl harrumphed.

His wife ignored him. "How fortunate. Andrew mentioned you'd brought her back home. We were worried when the carriage returned empty." She sighed. "Caroline doesn't have enough experience in going about alone or even knowing what's dangerous or not. My heart aches for her each time she leaves the house."

Though he believed the countess was truly concerned, the remainder of her statement sent a stab of irritation through John's chest. The household at large was smothering the woman. "So, then, Miss Storme has been allowed to go where she wishes when she wishes?" When the countess exchanged a glance with the earl, he continued. "Perhaps she should visit the Tower, see the menagerie, or even drop by the museum and take in the Elgin Marbles. Any of these places would inspire her creativity, I should think."

"While that does sound exciting," the countess said with some hesitation while she again looked at Hadleigh, "we prefer to have Caroline close. Besides, I rather think she wouldn't have an interest, for she keeps mostly to herself regardless."

"Exactly." The earl moved closer to the cradle. When he peered at the sleeping baby within, his whole expression softened. "My cousin prefers to stay in her room and paint."

The countess nodded. "She doesn't enjoy socializing."

As the conversation progressed, John observed Caroline. Her hands were curled into fists while her lips moved but no sound came forth. Was she simple like they assumed? Or perhaps insane? He'd not seen any sign of either during his meetings with her. However, if he had to wager, he'd put coin down on anger—fury really—and partial hatred. What had her life been like in that asylum? He didn't know but he desperately wished to, so that he might understand her better.

Even help her.

"Excuse my ignorance, but has anyone thought to ask the lady what *she* wants from her life, or even from day to day?

The earl scoffed. "The world is too dangerous for Caroline, as evidenced by the afternoon's incident."

John narrowed his eyes. "But if someone wished to visit or accompany her out, she has every right to indulge in these things. And I will remind you that no harm befell her."

They both exchanged glances once more. "That depends," Hadleigh finally said.

"On?" Why he kept picking at this topic, he couldn't say, but it wasn't right that Caroline was kept a prisoner and not given a chance to grow.

"Many factors."

From across the room, Caroline huffed.

John shared in her frustration. "So, then, that's a no." He glanced at her. She trained her gaze out the window and at the rain. "What are you afraid will happen if you give her the same freedoms you currently enjoy?"

"Exactly what happened today," Hadleigh said, and there was a growl in his voice. "She found herself lost with no conveyance as well as was escorted home by a questionable person." His eyes narrowed. "You could have molested her."

The effrontery of the man! "But I didn't, and she knows me." This family got under his skin and drove him mad all too quickly. "Obviously, there is no point in discussing this further, and I have an appointment yet this afternoon. How long is Brand expected to be out?"

"He won't return until dinner." The countess gave him a tight smile. "Come to our rout in a few days. You can talk to him then."

"Very well." John gave a terse nod. "My father is expecting me."

"No!" Caroline's exclamation was so soft he almost missed it. She threw him a look of panic. "Talking stay and tea?" She huffed, for it no doubt frustrated her when the words were jumbled. "Will you stay for tea and conversation?" When she slowed her pacing, the speech was flawless.

Isobel snorted. "Dear Caroline, you cannot manage to talk while company is underfoot. It's best we keep that to the family."

Damnation. It seemed they all treated Caroline as if she were something to be avoided. Which was sad because they were missing out on the best parts of her. His chest tightened. "Not today, Miss Storme, but I will come for the rout."

Would she also attend?

She nodded but remained silent, once more turning her attention to the window.

"Do enjoy the rest of your day, Your Lordship, Ladyships." Then he took his leave, but Caroline's situation was never far from his mind.

⤜⤜⤜✖⤛⤛⤛

THIRTY MINUTES LATER, he entered his father's study at the Grosvenor Square residence.

"Good afternoon, Father."

Over the years, his sire had grown older and more frail than he'd been since the last time John had seen him, but he was still a powerful man. Thinning gray hair, sallow cheeks, bloodshot eyes completed the picture of destruction. A half-filled bottle of brandy sat on his desk, resting next to a snifter that retained a measure of the amber liquid. The stink of liquor and stale cigar smoke clung to the room.

"You are not looking well." Living that dissolute lifestyle

would hasten him to an early grave, and frankly, John wasn't ready for that.

"Who are you to say when I haven't seen you for years?" Tension brewed between them, compounded by the fact the baron continued to regard his account ledgers instead of giving John his full attention.

"I merely showed concern for your health." No, his father hadn't changed, and at this late date, it was doubtful he ever would.

"Bah." The baron took a sip of his brandy. "Why are you in London? Thought you'd washed your hands of life here to be a layabout in Ipswich."

"I'm hardly that anymore." John tamped the urge to bit off a snippy reply. "I came to see you as well as meet with prospective clients." His father didn't deserve to hear anything about his life and the success he was finding. Respect begat respect. This man hadn't earned even a drop of it. "You should stop drinking, Father."

"Why do you care?" He waved a hand. "You've not been around. I don't need to extend my miserable existence for you."

"So I can see, and you're certainly intent to destroy the title while you have it." Damn, he'd let his father irritate him. "And why should I be in your company after the way you treated Mark and me over the years?"

He hadn't meant to mention his brother, but that was still a very open wound, further ripped wide by seeing his sire.

With a definite glint in his eye, the baron lifted his snifter and then drained it. "Ungrateful boy. What do you know about it?"

"At least I'm not a drunkard." It was one of the things he detested about his father, and the more the man drank, the more angry and violent he grew. When John drank, he knew his limits and stopped there. It had taken many years to learn, but he had.

Silence reigned in the room.

Finally, John sighed. "You're killing yourself."

"That is my prerogative."

"You're a selfish blackguard. Always have been. I've tried over the years to make amends with you, but you're incapable of apologizing."

His father shrugged. "I've done nothing I'm ashamed of." He poured out another measure of brandy into the snifter. "And you're the selfish one. You've not deigned to learn anything about the title or the life you'll need to lead here."

Knots of worry pulled tight in John's gut. "I don't want the title or anything that comes with it. Besides, you've ruined it, run everything into the ground, buried the rest beneath a mountain of debt. Where is the pride in that?"

"It was mine to do as I pleased." He narrowed his eyes and his voice increased. "It has always been mine. You and your brother had no right to try to dictate to me how I should live."

"Your lifestyle killed Mother." Damn, but he hadn't meant to mention that, but he might as well air out all the laundry.

"Your mother was weak!" He slammed a hand down on the desk. The glass rattled against the bottle of brandy. "Never marry beneath your position, boy. The *ton* will tear those types to shreds, and we are better than that."

"She died from a broken heart. Status and titles can't prevent that." John rubbed a hand along the side of his face. It was good he hadn't taken a seat in one of the leather chairs that faced the desk, for he despised being in the same room as this man. "But take heart. I don't intend to marry, for one reason only. I refuse to follow in your footsteps."

For a few seconds, he thought his father would hurl the brandy bottle at him, but the baron merely downed the glass he'd poured and repeated the action. "You know nothing about the tolls the title takes, about how much blunt keeping up the Surrey manor house costs. The coffers are running bare, not due to my drinking, but because there are no rents coming in. The estate can't be turned about." His father tossed the ledger his way. It bounced off John's chest and thudded to the floor.

No doubt they could if his father had been a better manager.

"I'll wager it would be a lot less stressful if you gave up the vices. I'm told mistresses don't come cheap." He didn't care any longer if he angered this man. "At least attempt to reconcile with me and Mark."

"Why? When your mother died, you took off for the Navy. You left your brother behind. There's no love between any of us, and you know it."

"True, but I don't want guilt when you pass." And that's what would happen. That emotion would cripple him, for it was *his* fault that he'd left his younger brother behind to bear more abuse at their father's hand. But he'd had to get out, to move on, to survive. He'd hoped Mark would have done the same.

"That is your problem, not mine. True Englishmen don't let emotions rule their lives." He cackled and reached for the bottle again. "You're weak, just like *her*."

"And it's glad I am, for that means I'm not like you." John curled a hand into a fist at his side. "You're impossible. I should never have come."

"Agreed, and I have every right to be that. You've been too noble, lording your naval career over me." His father glared, his eyes even more bloodshot. "Yet you come swaggering in here with lectures on your lips, and why should I care?" He was nearly yelling now. "You've not made a name for yourself. No wife with a large dowry to help turn the estate solvent, no brats to carry on the name. No fortune, just carousing and drinking with your mates." His grin was cold. "Just like me after all."

The heat of embarrassment and anger swept through John. Perhaps that was partially true, but he had the chance to do well for himself now with the shipping outfit. "I'm turning my life around. That's more than I can say for you."

"Bah." The baron waved a hand. "Come back when you have something to be proud of."

It was like all the other times he'd ever tried to talk with his father. Here he stood, annoyed and irritated yet still wanting this man's damn approval. He shook his head. "I've wasted my time coming here."

"Agreed. When you have something worth saying, I'll see you then." He lifted the brandy bottle to his lips, clearly dismissing John.

"I'll be the first person to dance on your grave." Without another word, he turned and strode from the room. Nothing he did would be good enough for his father.

And, by God, he refused to sink to that man's level. Even slow progress forward was progress just the same. He was proud of the man he'd become over the years.

I am not like him.

CHAPTER THREE

September 4, 1818

CAROLINE RESISTED THE urge to clamp her hands over her ears like she'd done as a child when the noise that filled the room clanged through her head like a wild cacophony. She'd only consented to join her cousin's rout due to the fact that Mr. Butler—John—might be there. It had been three days since he'd come upon her at Hyde Park, and she'd rather missed having him around. The peace and safety he made her feel would be most welcome now.

And still, her muse had dictated that she continue to sketch and paint him, much to her maid's amusement and Cousin Andrew's consternation. Her dressing room was rather crowded with paintings.

Dinner had been a trial and a form of torture, for she didn't wish to talk and the men on either side of her weren't the slightest bit interesting. Even if she *had* wished to add to the conversation, they talked incessantly of themselves or conversely, they ignored her to blather about politics. There was simply no beauty or inspiration in that; it only inspired arguments and hurt feelings. She'd picked at her food, the meal more daunting than it should have been due to the fact she disliked her foods to touch each other.

And though she enjoyed perusing the ladies' dresses and jewels, perhaps making up stories about them to pass the time, John hadn't arrived at the meal, which left her feeling an odd sort of emptiness she couldn't explain.

Now, she slowly edged around the perimeter of the drawing room. People filled the space, all laughing and talking until the noise gathered into a loud, clinging wad of sound that threatened to steal her peace of mind and her ability to think. For far too many years, she'd spent the bulk of her life alone in that asylum, confined to her room, only seeing the doctors and nurses when they deigned to visit or remove her from said room when they wished for experiments. She'd taken meals alone, trays brought to her room, for she'd been deemed too volatile to partake of such in the dining room. Occasionally, she'd been granted an escape to a courtyard, but was always accompanied by a member of the staff.

And the silence had been deafening until she'd become used to it.

Now, the unrelenting noise found within the society of London threatened to drive her truly mad. And everyone sent glances her way: questioning, judging, wondering. She detested feeling as if she were in a fishbowl without escape from the scrutiny. Yet the absence of one man pushed her toward the depths of despair.

What the devil for? It was ineffable.

Cousin Brand caught her eye, and with a grin, he moved toward her. Caroline frowned, for she wasn't certain how to interact with him. Even though he was her family, he was much a stranger, and the need to do the pretty with anyone left her gasping and uncomfortable, for the chance for a misstep or to make a fool of herself remained high.

"Good evening, Cousin," he greeted with the wide grin she was beginning to associate with him. In his dark evening clothes and with the eyepatch he'd acquired when he'd returned from the war, he resembled a wayward pirate. A reformed one, to be sure, but a pirate, nonetheless. His expression contained a hint of amusement, as if he were laughing up his sleeve at all these people. "How do you fare tonight?"

"Overwhelmed." What she wouldn't give to escape the drawing room and hide away in her room, or better yet, run from the house entirely merely for the opportunity to revel in the quiet. Since she'd been taken from the asylum, this was the second society event she'd attended, and she didn't enjoy it any more than the first.

"I can understand that." He gently touched her arm. "You look nice tonight, though. That color suits you."

"Thank you." Caroline glanced down at her gown. Done in a light blue almost periwinkle silk, it was the most ethereal garment she owned. Silver embroidery lined the bodice—that she considered entirely too low—as well as the hem of the skirt. It felt cool and sophisticated against her legs every time she moved and helped her to pretend she might be a long-lost princess. It might sound immature if she uttered that thought aloud, but she adored fairy stories and secretly wished to live one out. "It's pretty."

"Oh, indeed." His grin faltered. "I haven't seen you since Christmastide last, but I hope you don't hold that against me. I…" The muscles in his throat worked with a hard swallow. "I was working through my own demons and emotions that stemmed from growing up in the Storme family as well as things I assumed were failures on my part."

Caroline's eyebrows raised. Was it possible her cousin had been as confused and angry at the family as she? "Troubled, too, you were?" Heat sank into her cheeks, for once more the words were jumbled.

"Yes." He nodded. "Troubled is an understatement. In fact, I was mad at the world, bent on destructive behaviors, but then I met Elizabeth. Everything changed then. She helped me let go of things that didn't matter." Longing clouded his eyes. "I miss her," he added in a soft voice. "And the baby."

Everyone in the family was starting their nurseries or had someone in their lives that made them… better. Jealousy speared through her chest. She couldn't help it. Never had she given much thought about a future containing those things, but then, she'd not been afforded chances to capture any of that. With great concentration, she asked, "When you married, was it a happy time?"

"God, no." Brand chuckled. "It was confusing and difficult and sometimes painful." His levity sobered as he met her gaze. "There at the end, when I thought I'd hurt Elizabeth beyond repair—nearly lost her—I figured out that my only obstacles to the future I wanted were put there due to my own hand."

"You acted as a hero though." She'd heard enough snatches of the story to know it had been a romantic affair.

"I suppose if you mean my actions toward the end, when I finally won her heart." Brand shrugged. "But I was a different person then. *I* had to change to be worthy of her—of the dream of us together."

"A storybook romance." Caroline sighed. She offered a smile to her cousin. "I want that too." Of course, she had no experience around men, to say nothing of the fact that most shied away from her once they realized who she was and her history. No amount of Cousin Andrew's influence could help that, and it was an oddity that she was even here tonight at all. One couldn't meet others if one kept to their rooms.

Shock filtered through Brand's expression. "You *want* a husband." It wasn't a question.

"No." She shook her head. "A *romance*. Like in fairy stories." She wouldn't know the first thing about how to behave in a marriage, and even more to the point, if she were well and truly mad, any children she might have didn't deserve that.

"Oh, my dear girl." Brand put an arm about her shoulders. She stood stiffly at his side, for she wasn't in the habit of being touched by people. Not even her family. The only person with whom she felt comfortable in close proximity was John. "I'm not sure you can have one without the other."

She frowned. "Princess and tiara I want to have. Hand kisses too. And kindness." Was that too much to ask? When she glanced about the crowded drawing room at the people assembled there who paid her no mind, perhaps it was. "Men are selfish."

"Yes, they are." He leaned in and bussed her cheek. "Perhaps you should stay far away from them. You needn't put yourself into possible scandal, for you are doing well enough alone."

Alone. Where she always was.

Bubbles of anger danced through her blood. She shook off her cousin's arm. Once more, someone in her family thought to make decisions on her behalf. "Not good enough am I for romance? You assume I am a freak." That last bit came out loud and clear as a bell.

A few heads turned their way. Across the room, Cousin Andrew frowned. Brand held up a hand, presumably to tell his brother all was well. "Of course I don't think that." His tone was low, in an attempt to soothe. "I'm merely saying that you are innocent in all things romantic or smacking of match making."

"Whose fault is that?" Her voice rose. "Family left me to asylum in that! No one cared."

Brand's eye widened. "Calm yourself, Caroline. I don't want to see your heart broken or you hurt. I meant no offense."

This was why she despised mingling with others. It never ended well. Everyone wished her calm, yet not one of them acknowledged that their behavior was what had irritated her to begin with. Calm, which assumed any other feelings she might have were wrong.

"But you don't think I can try. No one wants to see what I can do. You don't let me be me." Was she too broken for all of that? Did it show in her face? Panic rose in her chest. The room and its inhabitants seemed to close in on her. "That no man will have me due to my fractured mind."

"Pardon me, but is there an issue here?"

Caroline's heart beat a bit faster at the sound of *his* familiar voice. She whirled around in time to meet John's gaze. Concern clouded those golden-brown depths. Immediately, his presence was like a warm, heavy blanket around her. "John. You came." At the back of her mind, she recognized that she should probably address him formally when in public, but that seemed a waste of time. He was John regardless of where they were.

"How could I not when you're dressed like a vision?" He took one of her gloved hands and placed a kiss upon the back, and her heart beat even faster. A hand kiss! Then he glanced at Brand. "Good evening, Captain."

"It's good to see you, John." There was such relief in her cousin's face that she narrowed her eyes, and when John released her hand, she almost cried out from the break of connection.

"The two of you seemed about to have an argument," the big man continued. The rumbling sound of his voice washed over her, scrubbing, cleansing, pushing the animosity to the sides where it couldn't harm her. "Is there something I can assist with?"

"No." Brand shook his head. "It was nothing. I shouldn't have said anything, for it upset Caroline." Then he looked at her. "Perhaps you should go lie down."

Some of her simmering anger boiled over. "Not an invalid I am!"

"All right." Brand held up a hand. "Again, no offense meant. I'm merely trying to look out for you."

"Didn't ask me what *I* wanted," she hissed as her chest tightened. "No one ever does. I can think for myself." That was one of the biggest problems she faced. Her thoughts were quite clear, but conveying them to others was what made her look like an idiot.

When someone in the room called for dancing and Cousin Andrew ordered the furniture put to the sides and the rugs rolled back, John drew him a few steps away. "Perhaps I can talk to her somewhere quieter. Your cousin doesn't enjoy crowds of strangers."

Brand snorted. "If you ask me, she doesn't enjoy people in general."

"You simply need to show patience, my friend, and compassion." He clapped her cousin on his shoulder. Each movement showed his big body to advantage. In his formal clothing, he was no less rugged, but he looked a tad uncomfortable, as if he weren't sure of his own place among these glittering allegedly perfect people. "Go enjoy yourself. Too soon you'll return to Ipswich and this world will be but a memory."

"Thank you." He nodded then left to assist with the rugs.

John returned and offered her his arm, bent at the elbow. "Would you indulge me in a walk this evening, Miss Storme? I find all this falderol bothersome."

"Where?" She didn't trust most people, but whenever this man came near, it was much easier to do.

"Wherever the wind takes us." He grinned, and flutters danced through her belly. "It's a fine evening. The stars are out. The gaslights are glimmering, and there's the veriest hint of autumn in the air. And you look like a fallen moonbeam. What else could we possibly need?"

Oh, his words were poetical and smacked of romance. They painted a picture in her mind that made her wish to run upstairs and grab her sketch pad, but he might vanish if she delayed. "I wanted my magical wand and tiara."

"The ones you received at Christmastide?"

"Yes." He remembered!

"They would make a fine addition to the magical gown."

"Sarah said no, that I wasn't a child." Tears threatened. Why could she never enjoy things that brought her happiness? She'd had enough of that stolen when in the asylum.

"I'm sorry to hear that. If it were up to me, you could wear the damned tiara whenever you wished."

"You are a good man." Caroline nodded and laid a hand upon his sleeve. He offered a respite from the storm she'd landed into. "Often do you gaze at the stars?" In his company, it didn't matter overly much that her words were jumbled or out of order. He never made her feel that she was an idiot for not speaking as well as others.

"Every chance I have, Miss Storme." He smiled down as her as he led her around the perimeter of the room to the open terrace doors. "The skies hold many mysteries, and the stars tell more stories than a library full of books."

"I adore books."

"Ah, then you must also adore reading. I believe you are highly intelligent."

She frowned as she kept pace beside him, but he didn't stop on the terrace where a few other couples lingered. "Reading is… difficult."

"How so?"

"It leaves me quite tired," she said slowly so the words would align themselves properly. "It frustrates me, not because it is a hard task but because I can't grasp it. Words jump over the pages." Even talking about it made her huff with annoyance. "Words move between the type and rearrange themselves into a jumble, so much that I can make no sense of them."

"I'm sorry to hear that. It must cause you grief to so love literature but seem so far from it." He guided her down the few steps that led away from the terrace then continued through the garden and eventually off the property, where he encouraged her onto a walking path that went around the square at the rear of the three long rows of townhouses.

"Yes." How was it possible this man, a veritable stranger, understood her more than her own family? "My sister and aunt used to read me stories. Long ago, before…"

He patted her hand. "Before you were sent away." It wasn't a question.

Caroline nodded. "I memorized the words." Her mind skipped backward to those times when she'd felt a smidgeon more accepted than now. Before it was difficult to communicate, before she became painfully aware of how awkward and odd she was. Before her parents sent her away. "Isobel was angry when reading so much to me so I could learn." She allowed herself a small smile. "Favorites are fairy stories." Beneath her gloved fingertips, the muscles in his arm tensed. He was strong, solid, like a great oak tree, one that wouldn't break in the face of a storm. Awareness of him as a man tingled over her skin. "Now I can pretend to read the books."

"Why, Miss Storme, how ingenious you are."

His response pulled out another grin, and a sigh of relief shuddered from her. How lovely it was not to gain yet another rebuke for something she couldn't do well. "I have learned to hide… many things of myself."

"I'm sorry to hear that." He frowned. "Who you are is unique. Never hide your special sun because others prefer the shade."

Her lower jaw dropped slightly. "Th… thank you, John." His perspective on things ripped open a hole in her dark existence. It allowed light to filter in and illuminate a new path and oh how she craved more of that.

"I only speak the truth." Carefully, as she were made of the finest porcelain, he escorted her to a dear little duck pond, the same one she saw out her bedroom window. "If you wish it, we can sit on the rim here and take in the night air."

"Yes." Quickly, before he could change his mind, she sat on the relatively cool stone. "Affinity I have at night." Why couldn't all her words come out right?

"Because you can better hide at night?" he asked softly as he sat beside her, not close enough to touch but close enough that the heat of him seeped into her arm and shoulder.

It was oddly comforting he knew her—or guessed—so well. "No one stares or whispers about me in the dark."

"Then you don't know the right people, my girl, for there are times when stares and whispers in the dark are quite delicious." The tone of his voice, combined with a twinkle she could only describe as wicked worked at freeing another few butterflies in her belly. "But I know what you mean. People stare at me when I'm forced into society as well."

"Why? You are not broken or suffer from insanity."

"Ha!" He turned more fully toward her. When their knees bumped, warmth emanated up her leg from the point of contact. "I suspect we are all broken in our own ways, but one thing I *am* certain about. You do *not* suffer from insanity."

Slowly, she smiled. No one had ever said something as sweet as that to her. In her mind, there was the distinct clank of an invisible chain breaking. "Agreed. I am *not* mad, but I *am…* different." For lack of a better word.

"Oh, indeed, but why do you assume different isn't a fine attribute? Sharks and dolphins are very different from each other, but the sea needs them both." With the starlight reflected in his eyes and the formal clothes stretched on his frame showing his powerful body to advantage, it was easy to see him as a hero of old, clad in armor, riding to the rescue of a damsel in distress. Additionally, with his kind heart, any lady would snatch him up. "Regardless, people stare for the simple fact I don't belong here."

She frowned. "At Cousin Andrew's house?"

"No, in society in general." He shrugged, and she would give anything to watch the play of muscles beneath that fabric. "I'm big and rugged, not refined like most men of the *ton*. My hands are rough with callouses, given to me from hard labor on the sloop or schooner. I toil for a living instead of using family coin." Sadness scudded through his eyes, gone at his next blink. "I like to curse and drink ale more than I probably should; brandy and wine aren't for me. Neither is inane small talk confined to stuffy drawing rooms."

"Does it make you angry, being different?"

"No. In fact, I'm glad for who I am." He glanced across the green at the row of townhouses. Golden illumination spilled from many of the windows, and if she held her head just so, the whispers of laughter drifted to her ears. "I don't aspire to be one of those fancy lords, especially since I'll have that title soon enough."

What did that mean? "You are a sailor, like Brand."

"Aye, for the time being." For the space of a few heartbeats, a certain hardness took possession of his eyes, and the delicate skin at the corners of his eyes didn't crinkle with a grin. "My father is a baron, and one who is apparently hell-bent on drinking himself into oblivion."

"That makes you angry." Some of it rolled from him in waves. It stirred her own ire, but not in a bad way and left her confused.

"At times, on many counts." John met her gaze, and when he did, his grin had returned. "However, I'm choosing not to think about that just now. Once my father passes, the damned title will go to me, and I want no part of it." He heaved a heavy sigh. "I am not like the other men in the *ton*, and I certainly don't aspire to anything that comes with it." With a wry expression, he shrugged again. "I'm a simple man who wishes for a simple life. I feel I can do more for others as the man I am instead of the man I'll have to become."

How completely refreshing he was! Caroline smiled. Sitting here beside him, listening to him talk, trying to understand what drove him made her feel that perhaps being broken wasn't a cross to bear after all. He wasn't like a knight as she'd assumed, but more the reformed scoundrel who can't help but go about the realm and perform acts of daring and kindness because he knew what it was like to feel helpless.

"I rather think you don't *have* to become anything you don't want." Daring much, she briefly rested a shaking hand upon his knee before drawing it away. Never had she wished to touch anyone as much as she did him. If she wasn't careful, it would change into a craving, one he wouldn't understand, for the absence of connection in the asylum would bring her to desperation soon, and if it was rebuffed, it might break her further.

"You are wise, Caroline. I appreciate your insight." He said nothing else. Neither did she. Instead, they watched the stars or the lights of the townhouses for long moments. Eventually, he stirred and gained his feet. "Thank you for the reprieve. It's nice to know that not everyone has leveled untenable expectations on my shoulders."

She slipped her fingers into his palm when he offered a hand. "I like you as you are." As their gazes met, a blush jumped into her cheeks. Why, she didn't know, but he made her feel like falling and flying at the same time. "You be myself let me over others more than." *Well, drat.* That was a terrible jumble, but before she could attempt the sentence a second time, he squeezed her fingers.

"I completely understand." He pulled her hand through the crook of his elbow. "You deserve respect and praise for all the things you are instead of criticism for all you are not. In fact, you should be afforded the freedom and the time to discover everything you wish to be in this life, Caroline."

She giggled. Tingles danced down her spine, for what she couldn't say. "Sweep me away and carry me off like a storybook hero?"

A thoughtful look crossed his face. "Let me ponder that possibility."

Did that mean he would? Her heart beat faster.

When he set them into motion, she sighed, for the brief respite from anxiety was over. "I hope you'll come to realize that and use it to help you discover your strength."

"I hope so too," she answered in a barely audible voice.

If she did, then it might lead to freedom, a place where she could be anything she wanted without limitations and constraints.

CHAPTER FOUR

September 6, 1818

I T HAD BEEN two nights since the rout when he'd talked to Caroline beneath the stars as she'd worn the gown that had reminded him of moonbeams. Damn but she'd been a tempting vision. Two nights since he'd observed her within a society event. Two nights since an idea had occurred to him that might see her able to shine, yet that notion was also complete madness. No way would the Storme family would agree to such a thing.

Yet, the thought persisted. Especially since he'd witnessed Caroline's return from an errand with the countess. They'd apparently been shopping on Bond Street and the afternoon crush of people in the shops, to say nothing of the usual traffic on Rotten Row, had brought about what the countess delicately called an "episode" wherein Caroline had put her hands over her ears and had hummed softly to herself until they'd arrived home.

Now he sat in the drawing room of Hadleigh House taking tea and visiting with Brand and wondered how Caroline fared. Had she calmed abovestairs, found something that might soothe distress? He'd witnessed a bit of the same from her the night of the rout; it seemed she didn't know how to act in a crowd or with loud noises.

The situation was none of his concern, but he remained worried. Soon, he and Brand would both depart for Ipswich, and while that made him extremely happy, part of him rebelled, for that would mean leaving Caroline behind, with no one to advocate for her. She'd return to hiding—as she'd said in her own words—and he couldn't help but know sadness for that. The woman had so much potential; she merely needed the freedom and space to explore all she could be, and she needed someone to support her.

When a biscuit flew across the low table and glanced off his cheek, John yanked himself from his thoughts. He glared at Brand. "What the devil is wrong with you?"

"Me? You're the one here but not here." Concern creased the captain's brow. "What ails you?"

"I'm thinking."

"Always a dangerous prospect." One of Brand's eyebrows arched. "About?"

"Your cousin Caroline, if you must know." There was no embarrassment involved, simply a sense of duty and protectiveness.

"Why?"

"I feel she's being repressed here beneath the earl's care." It was a bold statement to be sure, but he couldn't help it.

Brand glanced over his shoulder at the open door. No doubt he feared his brother would come sailing into the room at any moment. "You should count yourself fortunate Drew is busy with his duties to Parliament right now. He'd have your head for speaking such things against him."

"Then he should take care of Caroline better." Would she come down for tea? Had she even been informed he and Brand were in residence? Perhaps they should have taken tea at Major Storme's house—Brand had chosen to stay with that brother while in London—and that had been the plan, but Brand had to bring a parcel to the earl's home, so here they were.

"I don't know that you should be mucking about in his personal affairs." He stuffed a whole seed cake into his mouth and chewed furiously, washing it down with a hearty swig of tea. "Besides, what should he do about Caroline anyway? She's not right in the head."

Hot annoyance stabbed through John's chest. "I rather think that's not true. She's as well as anyone else in this connection, but her mind works a tad differently than other people's. Why label her as insane when she's anything but?" He loved his best friend, truly, but the man's attitude regarding his cousin rankled.

"Why do you care?" Brand's eye narrowed. "You know nothing about her."

"Apparently, neither do you, or any of the Stormes, really." The more he talked on the subject, the more he realized Caroline didn't deserve the life she'd been handed. "Regardless, I want to come to understand her, perhaps help her reach her dreams."

"Again, why? As near as I can tell, she's content."

John snorted. "Then you haven't looked deep enough."

"Oh, and you have?" The captain's fingers tightened on his teacup.

"I'm beginning to, yes." He rubbed a hand along his jaw. It was time to share his idea. "Since my father is in London, his Surrey property is empty. I would like permission to take Caroline on a short holiday there, where she can enjoy the quiet and the fresh air. Perhaps with a bit of freedom, she'll be more apt to discover who she truly is away from the Storme fold. Once she does that, perhaps we can come up with a plan to move her forward so she won't feel like such a prisoner."

Brand's lower jaw dropped. He returned the teacup to its saucer with enough force that John feared the china might crack. "You want to take my cousin away." It wasn't a question.

"Yes." Slowly, he nodded. "It would do her good."

"You are invested that much in her future and well-being?"

"Of course. It's slightly offensive that her own family is not." Why was Caroline always forgotten or bundled up and kept on the sidelines when she had so much to contribute? Just because her viewpoint was different didn't mean it was wrong.

"I'll be damned. Dressed down by my best friend in the nicest possible way." Brand grunted. Finally, he shrugged. "I don't mind, but we will need to apply to Drew. You cannot just kidnap a woman, and my brother's the type to prosecute."

"At least you've agreed. You're the only Storme whose opinion I value." John chuckled. One obstacle down. "Perhaps I can talk to both Caroline and the earl about it tonight since I've been invited to dinner."

"Please promise me that you don't have an ulterior motive. I won't have my cousin compromised or molested, even for you." Warning rang clear in the tone.

"You have my word as a gentleman. That's the last thing I wish to do." He shrugged. "If you still have concerns, come with us. You and I can fish or laze about before we return to Ipswich."

"That idea holds merit, for London life is beginning to chafe, no matter how good it was to see my family again."

⇶⇷

"A MOMENT OF your time, Hadleigh," John asked later that night when the Storme family had gathered in the drawing room once dinner had concluded. Inspector Storme as well as Doctor Marsden—er, rather, the Earl of Worchester—were also in attendance. Before they'd all arrived, he'd pulled Caroline aside and asked if she'd be of a mind for a short holiday away from London.

Her eyes had sparkled, and the tiny smile of excitement she'd given had warmed him from the inside.

Yes, this was the right decision. Now he merely needed to convince her cousin.

When the earl turned away from speaking with Finn, he nodded. "What's bothering you, Mr. Butler? I can see it in your expression."

"Uh…" Would his courage hold? A few days in the country

would do Caroline so much good. There was nothing for it except to get to the meat of the matter. "I would like to take your cousin Caroline to my father's estate in Surrey for a few days."

Shock lined the earl's face. "Whyever for?" He looked at his wife, who frowned as she gently patted the baby's back.

"If you've had cause to notice, Caroline is miserable in London. It's too much stimulation on all fronts, and she's quite sensitive to such things." Again, he glanced at her. She stared back with round eyes and her sketch pad resting on her lap. "I believe that giving her a change of scenery and perspective would do worlds of good."

The earl's frown deepened. "Why Surrey?"

"Why not?" John shrugged. "No one is there this time of year and it's close enough to London to make the trip in one day." The hairs on his nape prickled. Both Finn and Brand stared, but he refused to turn around. He didn't want more opposition.

For long moments, Hadleigh regarded him with slightly narrowed eyes. He took a sip of brandy and finally shook his head. "I'm afraid I cannot allow that. If you were betrothed, perhaps, but as it is, it's simply too scandalous."

Cold disappointment snaked through John's gut. "Her creativity is stunted here, as is her inspiration." He threw a glance to Caroline, who sat riveted as she watched the proceedings. "She has so much talent with painting and drawing, that she needs greater scope for her subjects. Once she builds up a professional collection, perhaps we could see about selling them to private collectors."

"Oh!" Her whole body brightened as if someone had lit her from within.

"Indeed." He didn't know why but everything he was screamed at him to keep fighting. This would give Caroline so much joy, and she'd had precious little of that already. If he could give her that then potentially angering her family was worth it. Someone needed to champion for her.

"I'm sorry, Mr. Butler. My answer is still no." When the earl made to maneuver around him, John stepped into his path, staying his movement.

That was unacceptable. "Then let me have Caroline's hand."

Hadleigh gawked. The men behind him gasped. The countess stared while Caroline slowly rose to her feet. Her siblings outright protested. "You wish to *marry* my cousin."

Did he? Perhaps he did, for it didn't change the motivation behind getting her to Surrey. "If it gains me the permission I seek, then yes."

The earl scoffed. "You have no idea what's best for my cousin."

"No?" His pulse pounded loud in his ears. Every person in the room stared at him. Caroline looked as if he'd hung the moon, and a wave of heat went through him. Sweat plastered his lawn shirt to his back. John cleared his throat and straightened his spine. Perhaps what she needed in this moment was a hero like she adored reading about, and he didn't mind playing the part. "Frankly, Lord Hadleigh, I don't have the confidence that any of *you* know what's best for her, but at least I'd like to try and discover those answers for myself. For her."

Finn rolled over to their location. His eyes were full of skepticism. "Surely you can't possibly mean what you've just said. Caroline requires special handling."

"No, she needs understanding." Why couldn't these stubborn Stormes recognize that she wasn't as incapable or deficient as they assumed? "And I certainly can't do any worse than you have as a collective since Christmastide." Silence met his statement, but he warmed to his subject. "Consider this. Last December, Hadleigh had Caroline released from the asylum where she'd resided for over twenty years. But what strides has she been allowed to make since that time?" He met the gazes of each person present. "Little to none. You all coddle her, wrap her in your insecurities and fears regarding her instead of learning to know her for the woman she is."

A red flush stained the earl's cheeks. "You've only just met her."

"Not quite. I've become *reacquainted* with her, for I met her in Derbyshire." When he looked her way, she clutched her sketchbook to her chest with a faint smile curving her lips. Backlit by a candle, the light cast her in gold, made her eyes twinkle, sent faint caramel highlights into her dark hair. What secrets were behind those eyes? Where would she go if given the chance?

"Now see here—"

"Hold, Drew." Brand quickly inserted himself between the earl and John. "Perhaps John's concerns are valid."

"How so?" The earl set down his glass and then crossed his arms at his chest.

"If you object to Surrey, why not give them the use of Hadleigh Hall? I shall travel to Derbyshire a week after them once the last of my business has concluded in London." Brand met John's gaze and nodded. "In that way, I can keep an eye on them, but I rather doubt mischief will occur."

What the hell did that mean? Did he assume his cousin wasn't attractive or that either of them would ever think of the other with desire? An image of Caroline in that moonbeam gown from the night of the rout danced into his head. She'd been attractive in a wholesome way, and he really was coming to adore the way a tiny dimple appeared in her left cheek when she smiled.

Hadleigh remained unconvinced. "I'm not certain that's what my cousin needs or even if she can comprehend the complexities of what you're offering." His eyes narrowed. "You don't love her. She might not understand."

For the love of all that's holy!

"There is only one way to find out." Low-grade anger buzzed at the base of John's spine as he pushed through the ring of annoyed Stormes. Taking her away for a holiday would open doors to her she didn't have access to currently. Hell, if marriage was what it took to gain Caroline's freedom, he'd gladly do it. He strode across the room and once in front of Caroline, dropped down onto one knee. "Caroline, you've heard what we are talking about."

She nodded, her eyes round and twin spots of color blazing on her cheeks.

He captured one of her hands in his. "We hardly know each other, but I feel in my heart that removing you from London is what will help you grow and find yourself."

"But it's not forever," she said as her eyebrows drew together.

"What, the move or our engagement?" Slight panic took hold of his chest. What if she didn't go along with the plan? What would happen to her then, for there was no way Hadleigh would ever let him see her again.

"First, the move." Her lips curved into a smile. "London is noisy and big and dirty."

"That it is." The trust in her face humbled him, and since he had no answer to either of her questions, he plowed ahead. "If your priggish cousin won't let you escape London, I shall do it myself and vow to take care of you in the best way that I can."

The earl sputtered, but they both ignored him.

John searched her eyes but found nothing except curiosity and excitement there. "I suspect no one in your life has given you the freedom to explore and accept the woman you are, so I intend to do just that. Will you agree to a betrothal between us?"

Another round of gasps circulated about the room.

Caroline's hand shook in his, but there was an impish light in her eyes. "Convenience, an engagement?"

"If you'd like." He nodded with enthusiasm. "You can break it at any time if you find the arrangement unbearable. I merely wish to give you a chance where no one else will."

"Why?"

"Why what?"

She smiled. "Why would you do this? I am..." Her gaze jogged off to one side as she searched for words. "...No one special."

"You're wrong." He tightened his grip on her hand. "Everyone is valuable in this world. Some of us just need the right encouragement to find that realization." Yet did she understand that this wasn't a permanent arrangement and that it would never lead to a real marriage? For he certainly didn't wish for a wife out of fear he would follow in his father's footsteps.

For long moments she stared at him as if she might study a painting. Finally, she nodded. "Do you promise not to send me back to the asylum, if you cannot understand me?"

"Absolutely I won't." That she would think he might tightened his chest. "Locking you away due to the fact that your mind doesn't work like other people's is ridiculous."

"Or beat me," she added with a flicker of fear in those blue-gray depths.

That gave him pause while a few of the Stormes protested. What happened to her during her tenure in that asylum? "Perish the thought."

"You will read to me?"

"As much as you'd like." For whatever reason, he looked forward to such a domestic situation.

"Let me paint you?"

He pulled a face. "If it will make you happy."

"Then, I agree."

"Thank you." As John rose to his feet, he released her hand. Then, he sought out the earl while excited chatter broke out amidst the family. "I am now engaged to your cousin. According to your own words, I can take her to the countryside for a short holiday."

"I believe I said *if*." Hadleigh's expression was this side of shrewd, and John didn't much care for it. "As this exaggerated tableau has played out, I've had cause to think more on it." He nodded. "And as such, I've come to my *final* decision."

"What is it?" One of John's hands curled into a fist. What now? He didn't trust the earl by half.

"I won't let you take Caroline to Hadleigh Hall or anywhere else without you marrying her first. In all seriousness, this was a bit of Drury Lane acting you performed for us moments ago. If you've gone to the trouble of proposing, I want you to wed her instead of changing your mind down the line when the novelty of an engagement might wear off."

"Well, damn," Brand breathed from somewhere behind him.

"God, you never disappoint in being an arse, do you, Drew?" Finn asked softly.

Disbelief ricocheted through John's chest. Hadleigh had him by the balls and they both knew it. He looked at Caroline, and the expression on her face nearly broke him. It was as if she'd been given the best gift, but had it yanked immediately away. He refused to disappoint her where everyone else had. Slowly, he nodded. "Fine. If that's what it will take to remove her from the Stormes, then she and I will marry." The urge to curse rose in his throat, but he tamped it. What the hell would he do with a wife? Fear trickled down his spine, not for the act itself but for what might become of it.

Then he reminded himself of one glaring fact. *I am not my father*. And he would renew his efforts to follow that dictate.

"Excellent." The earl's smile held smugness. John wanted to land him a facer merely on principle, for he'd been manipulated, plain and simple. "Give me a couple of days to draw up a contract."

"I am *free*." A giggle from Caroline brought all eyes to her. "He has settled my future."

The implications of wedding her were staggering. He'd never been a rogue like Brand, nor had he frequented prostitutes regularly, but that didn't mean he'd been a monk either. In allowing Caroline the space she needed to heal, he'd sealed his own future as well as hers. They would both go into this union of convenience without the assumption of romance or even physical affection, which made for a very long life indeed.

And he would not betray those marriage bonds. Once he pledged his loyalty to her, he would mean every word.

Still, it was well worth it. No one gave a hang about her, but he did, and he hoped someone would do the same for him if the occasion demanded.

While annoyance crawled down his spine from the earl's highhandedness, his words came out on a faint growl. "Don't drag this out, Hadleigh. I wish to be certain Caroline is well away from the naysayers in her life as soon as possible."

Bloody hell. What was he to do now? He had not a steady income yet from the shipping business. Neither could he bring a viscount's daughter home to the rooms he rented at one of the premier hotels in Ipswich.

"If you think to order me about, let me disabuse you of that notion, Mr. Butler." Oddly enough, there was a certain amusement in Hadleigh's voice. "However, if you hurt my cousin…"

"I won't, but you must realize that *your* actions thus far *have*. I aim to reverse that."

"Argh!" With a hard glance, the earl swept from the room. "William! We need to talk immediately!" His roar echoed in the corridor beyond.

Both the inspector and his sister Isobel, raced from the room with murmured excuses. Stunned, and with a fussing baby, Sarah followed.

Silence roiled through the room like a heavy fog. The Earl of Worchester drew Caroline to the opposite side of the room. No doubt he would attempt to counsel her about the decision, but knowing the doctor, he wanted her out of the line of fire when her cousins dressed John down. Marsden was a good man.

As confusion racked his brain, John turned to face both Brand and Finn, who stared at him with expressions ranging from shock to amazement. "Well, that didn't exactly go as I'd thought."

"Seems to me you didn't *think* about any of this at all," Brand hissed. He shoved a hand through his hair. "You would willingly go into parson's mousetrap for the sake of my cousin's well-being?" Incredulity rang in his low tones.

"Aye." Though it meant the complete upending of his life, if he could help Caroline find herself, it was more than worth that sacrifice. There was a connection between them, a friendship, that he wished to nurture if only to show her that not every person she met thought her incapable. "Everyone deserves a chance in life, and London won't give that to her. Neither will the *ton*. Or, apparently, will the Stormes."

Finn cleared his throat. He didn't appear as flabbergasted as his brothers. "You realize marriage is permanent."

"Oh, yes, but only if she wills it."

Brand scoffed. "She said she'd marry you. No doubt she wants that stability, but are you that? Our friendship aside, we both know what your life has been up until this point."

"I will do the best that I can." If it meant becoming a better version of himself for her, then that's what he'd do. "If marrying Caroline gives me the right to oversee her care and healing, I absolutely will. It's up to her exactly how and what sort of marriage we shall have, and I will abide by that decision."

Both brothers exchanged glances. Finn shrugged.

"It's his prerogative and hers, Brand. They are both well past majority age, and it does appear Caroline favors him more than any of us." He rested his gaze on John. "But Drew was correct. If you hurt her, you won't be able to withstand the collective Stormes in retribution."

"You have my word and my promise. She'll be treated as a queen." He glanced at her while she talked—or rather, listened—to the doctor. "Everything I do from here on out will be with her in mind." Of that he was serious.

"I believe you." Finn nodded. "I can't see what you hope to gain or why, but I believe you'll be good for Caroline. Perhaps we can all learn from your courage." He then wheeled himself across the room toward the sideboard.

Brand dropped a hand on John's shoulder. His grin was genuine, and that brought John a modicum of relief. "I knew you were better than a brother. You'll show the Storme connection what it is to be a good man."

"I appreciate your support."

"I don't call you an honorary Storme lightly." The captain squeezed his shoulder. "I have a feeling you'll do more for my cousin in a month than anyone has in years."

"That is my hope." But was he strong enough—good enough—for that?

"We all deserve the shame of that when it's proven correct. We've wronged her and should grovel at her feet."

"I rather doubt she'd allow that." But he chuckled just the same. "It will be a huge change for both of us." Was he up to that challenge? When he glanced at her and their gazes met, she offered him that same sweet smile and her dimple flashed. He couldn't help a grin. A blush raged in her cheeks and shortly after that, she fled the room. His heart skipped a beat. "Caroline only needs someone to believe in her. I'll merely be along to see what happens."

Brand harrumphed. "You're not in love with her."

"No." He looked at his best friend and shrugged. "Neither were you when you sought out Elizabeth. That turned out rather well, don't you think?" Is that what he wanted, then? A real marriage down the line with Caroline?

He didn't know at this time.

"Sometimes a man knows where his future lies." A flush rose above Brand's collar. "What of your father?"

"What of him? He has no hold on my life or what I do with him. However, I'll try and see him before Caroline and I leave London." For the first time, doubts assailed him. Would he live up to her unspoken expectations? "Before that happens, I'll need to shop for a ring, perhaps other jewelry, apply for a license, as well as secure a clergyman." The magnitude of what he'd done crashed into him, and it must have shown on his face, for Brand laughed.

"I think first you need a drink." The captain propelled him over the floor. "And have a chat with the doctor. He can give you insight into what you might expect from a woman of Caroline's affliction."

"Right." In a handful of days, he'd wed a woman he barely knew but held immense respect for.

Please let me have wisdom enough to help her and the strength to survive her if she takes exception to this new shift in her life. The Storme family was well-named, and he'd already glimpsed rage at the backs of Caroline's eyes.

Sooner or later, she would snap. He didn't want to meet that storm head on without having laid down a strong foundation.

CHAPTER FIVE

September 7, 1818

EVEN THOUGH THE closed carriage had rolled to a stop in front of his father's home a handful of minutes ago, John made no move to exit the vehicle. He'd been forced to borrow the conveyance from the Earl of Hadleigh due to rain, and that man's expression of smugness had irked him. There was no doubt in his mind that the earl assumed he'd fail miserably at his upcoming marriage for he had little to recommend him let alone experience with women who required more attention than most.

I'll be damned before I let Hadleigh see he was right.

"We are here."

The sound of Caroline's dulcet tones swept away some of the aggravation from his soul. He gave himself a shake and glanced at her. "Yes, unfortunately." If only he could wed Caroline and immediately remove to Ipswich, but he'd already promised a countryside holiday, and that's what he would deliver.

I refuse to begin our lives together with a broken commitment.

"Is your father noisy like Cousin Andrew?" One of her dark brown eyebrows lifted with the question.

"No, but he's as obstinate."

She waved a hand. In the thin ivory kid, her fingers and palm appeared delicate. "Many people make up the world. You said that." When she turned her attention to gaze out the window, he studied her profile.

The tilt of her chin indicated her determination to have others see her perspective. High cheekbones gave way to a longish nose and a high brow. Aristocratic features to be sure, but those stormy blue gray eyes were always lit with the emotions she felt at any given time, and when she looked at him in a certain way, she had the power to mesmerize. Today, her hair was properly contained in a low chignon; atop it was a smart little bonnet trimmed with navy ribbons. A few tendrils curled at her temples and drifted over her nape, which only served to highlight her slender neck, as elegant as a swan's.

"This is true."

"You don't like your father." It wasn't a question.

"I'm not fond of him." Right now, she didn't need to know the details or hear an explanation as to why. "He makes everything more… difficult, let's say."

"I understand."

Perhaps she did. How much difficulty had she already experienced in her life? He supposed they had a lifetime to discover everything about each other. "Everyone has someone like that in their family." The longer he tarried here at the curb, the longer this unsavory business would loom over him when that time could be spent in more pleasant pursuits. "Caroline, would you mind an outing with me after we talk to my father? I'll take you wherever you wish to go."

She turned her head and met his gaze. Hers was inscrutable, which was odd. Her fingers restlessly pleated a section of her ivory and navy striped dress. A navy spencer done in military lines hid her bodice, which was just as well. He didn't like the idea of his father ogling her décolletage. Then she nodded. "Would that I like." Frustration lined her face. "I would like that."

"So would I. Perhaps we could take tea at one of the cafes unless you prefer coffee."

A fleeting smile tugged at the corners of her lips. "Have never tasted coffee."

"Ah. I'd like to say you're in for a treat, but it's a bitter brew indeed and requires many tastings in order to acclimate to it."

Her eyes twinkled with amusement. "I have never tasted brandy either."

Heat crept up his neck when he thought about being the one to initiate her into other things that might stem from drinking brandy. "Uh, perhaps we should start with coffee."

"Very well." Caroline nodded. "Shall we go?"

"Yes." This was a bold move for her, this voluntarily going out into society, and he couldn't be prouder. The fact she'd wished to accompany him, that it had been her own idea, took some of the irritation from the upcoming visit, and gave him a shot of confidence.

After he swung the door open and jumped down, the driver lowered the steps. John offered a hand to his fiancée and assisted her to the street. "We shouldn't be more than twenty minutes," he told the driver. Never in the history of visits with his father had he stayed long, for if he did, the conversation might come to blows.

"I'll be right here, Mr. Butler."

The rain drummed on his top hat. Water beaded on the brim by the time they'd gained the green-painted door. A lengthy pause followed John's knock, but eventually the panel opened, and his father's butler stood aside to let them in.

"Is the baron in residence?" It was too early in the day for him to have gone to the House of Lords.

"He is, Mr. Butler. In his study. Shall I announce you?"

"No, thank you, Ames. This visit might as well remain a surprise." Tucking Caroline's hand through the crook of his arm, he escorted her along the corridor until they came to his father's study. She encouraged him with a nod and curiosity in her eyes. The door was open, but he knocked on the frame anyway.

"Come."

As soon as he heard his father's voice, dread and loathing

twisted down John's spine. Caroline squeezed her fingers on his arm, and he pulled her into the room with him. "Father, I want you to meet Miss Caroline Storme. She is my fiancée." Damn, saying it aloud made it all too real, and it was the first time he'd referred to her in that context.

But it made him proud, also.

"You're engaged?" The baron glanced up from the ledgers he worked. "How the devil did that happen? I saw you a handful of days ago. You were adamant you would never marry."

"Yes, well, circumstances have changed. Life offered this opportunity, and I took it." His father didn't deserve to know anything more than surface facts regarding Caroline. That protection welled again when it came to her.

"I see." His father bounced his gaze between them. "Please, won't you sit?"

That meant an extended stay, but when Caroline perched on the edge of the nearest chair that faced the large mahogany desk, he stifled a sigh. "Thank you." He dropped into the matching chair beside Caroline's. "We'll wed in a few days. I'm merely waiting on a signature for the license."

A grunt came from his father. "I had hoped you'd marry an heiress, or at least a woman with connections throughout the *ton.*"

"We don't always get what we wish for," John said quietly. "Besides, I am happy with my choice in brides. It matters not to me how large or small her dowry is. That is not the purpose of the union." He glanced at Caroline, who stared at his father with a look of distrust. God, she was wonderful. "I believe she and I will rub along well."

"Only time will tell." The baron narrowed his eyes on her. When she looked back, he scoffed and flicked his gaze to John. "Is she a mute? Has some sort of deficiency?" He shook his head in apparent disgust. "You couldn't even choose a decent woman to take to wife. What a disappointment you've proven, even in this."

John bristled. "There is nothing wrong with her." He curled

on hand into a fist. "Miss Storme is everything kind in this world. She deserves to be given the same."

"Bah." His father waved a hand. "A mousy woman will not influence anyone. You'll need connections and alliances if you want to survive once you take the title."

"If that is true, it's your fault, and I don't want the damned title!" His roar echoed off the walls. No one sent his dander up like his father and his thirst for coin and power.

Caroline peered at him with round eyes full of surprise. Then she returned her attention to the baron. "A person's mental state is not determined by whether one speaks or not." The words were slow and precise, but they weren't jumbled. "However, it does say much about one who speaks without purpose or the intent to learn."

Dear God, she is amazing! She'd dressed him down in dulcet tones without resorting to an angry diatribe. Yes, marrying her and giving her the ability to be herself was the right thing to do. John's chest swelled with pride. He flashed her a grin. "Miss Storme is a creative genius. Connections aren't needed. She'll make a sensation in the *ton* merely with her talents."

"Hmph." His father tapped a finger to his chin. "Miss Storme, are you related to the Earl of Hadleigh?" There was a gleam in his eye John didn't quite trust.

Caroline nodded. "He is my cushion."

"What?" The baron frowned.

"Cousin," she corrected with a blush staining her cheeks.

"I see." His father summarily dismissed her as he landed his gaze on John. "What's her dowry? Enough to sink into my properties?"

As if his father would receive a farthing. "I haven't seen the contract."

"Ah." For a long moment they stared at each other. "Will you live in London?"

"I haven't discussed any of that with my betrothed." Did that mean their union was already doomed? The fact bothered him more than it should, but a glance from Caroline reminded him that there was plenty of time for learning.

And nothing mattered except setting her free.

CAROLINE FROWNED AT the man who sat behind the desk as he blathered on, lecturing really. This was John's father, but she didn't care for him. His eyes held secrets and he never smiled. There was no happiness in his tone when he spoke to John.

My fiancé.

The man she was to marry. That tiny little word held so much promise that she let it roll over and over inside her head. He intended to wed her, like one of the heroes in the books she adored. A life with a happily ever after and rides into the sunset. Which would prove a problem, for she didn't much care for horses. But she did like John. She trusted him, and he shouldn't be here with the man who was his father.

"I will live wherever John goes," she told the room at large. Caroline met his gaze. "I feel safe with you." Even as he sat in the chair beside hers, his big presence brought comfort and the sensation of being protected, and nothing or no one would ever again lock her away.

When he grinned, her heart fluttered. "I appreciate that."

"Bah. You'll both prove an embarrassment to me." He waved a hand. "I have tasks to accomplish yet this day. Keep me informed regarding your marriage."

John scowled. She didn't like it when he did that, for it marred the lines of his handsome face and put shadows in his eyes. "Will you not come to the ceremony? It will be held in the Earl of Hadleigh's drawing room two days hence."

"I'd rather not." The baron ran his gaze up and down Caroline's person, and she shuddered from the attention. No, he wasn't a good man. "I have much to do this week."

"You're a damned fool, Father." John launched to his feet.

"I'm not surprised you wouldn't even do this for me."

"Yes, well, I had so much hope when you'd become a Navy man, and now this. Can't even manage a decent union."

"Fuck off. I am happy with my choice." When he held out a hand to her, she slipped her fingers into his palm while gaping at him from his use of vulgarity. Such an interesting word. As he closed his fingers around hers, he brought her into a standing position. "We have a full schedule this afternoon. Please excuse us."

His hold on her hand brought a modicum of peace, but he shook, either from anger or something else, she couldn't say. She wanted to soothe him as he did her, but how? "Have us let tea," she murmured. A blush warmed her cheeks, for yet again her mouth jumbled the words her brain had given.

"Indeed." He looked at his father with narrowed eyes. "Miss Storme and I will have our wedding trip in Derbyshire, at Hadleigh Hall, should you wish an explanation for our absence from Town." Ice mingled in his tone for the first time since she'd met him.

I don't like the man who upset him.

But the baron had nothing further to say, apparently.

With a huff, John renewed his grip on her hand and quickly led her from the study. He kept silent on the way out of the house with its modest furnishings and décor. Some of the rugs were worn in places and the wallpaper faded in others. Only when they'd gained the privacy of the carriage did he speak.

"My father will never be proud of me or what I've managed to accomplish in my life. He cannot even appreciate you." He slammed the vehicle's door shut as if to emphasize the point. He rubbed his gloved hands over his face. "He's maddening."

The raw emotion in his voice tugged at her chest. Caroline frowned. She leaned forward and rested a hand on his knee. "You are not him, John."

"What?" Confusion roiled in his golden-brown eyes.

"Never will he see good, you are now." *Well, drat.* Concentrating, she tried again. "I see you, the man you are." She patted his knee. "Strong, good, honorable. Your father will never be that, and you will never be him. There is happiness in that."

"Yes." Delight crossed his face. He grinned and her cheeks heated. "That's the sweetest thing anyone has ever said to me." Fondness danced in his eyes. "Thank you for that."

She nodded. "With you I am wanted. I hope same to you do." He never made her feel less than when she stumbled over her words, never suggested she stay in her rooms because she couldn't abide loud noises or crowded places.

"Caroline Storme, I believe we'll be quite content as friends in this marriage." His grin widened as he rapped on the ceiling of the carriage. "Hyde Park, if you please, Ames."

"Of course, Mr. Butler," the driver replied. Seconds later, the vehicle lurched into motion.

"I don't have many friends," she admitted in a small voice. "Or any." Her mind revisited her life while in the asylum. While she'd come to know various members of the staff there, none of them availed themselves to secrets or shared confidences. Some cared nothing at all for the patients there, and oftentimes took out their frustrations on the weaker ones with fists or kicking with boots. There wasn't an opportunity to know any of the other inmates more than passing acquaintances, for she had been confined to her room. Caroline sighed and came back to the present with a tiny start. "Until you found me on that snowy lane, I'd never felt comfortable talking to anyone."

Thank goodness the words came out in the proper order. It was easier with him than even the members of her own family.

John sat back against the plush squabs of his bench. "That was quite a day, but I'm glad I came back into your life." He remained silent for a few seconds. "For fear of inciting your wrath, I think you need me more now than you did at Christmastide."

"The anger that is always with me here," she touched a hand to her heart, "is never for you." For long moments, she held his gaze. "You are rescuing me by marrying me."

"Perhaps." He shrugged, his big shoulders elegant, and she liked how the fabric of his green jacket pulled along the breadth of them. "I rather think it's opening the door to your cage and encouraging you to hop out. Given enough of a chance, you can rescue yourself."

Her easy smile wavered. "You aren't a hero?"

"I never claimed that I was." John leaned forward, rested his forearms on his knees so that his big hands dangled between his legs. "However, if you need to see me as such, I'm keen on being whatever your imagination demands. I am doing this for you because I believe you deserve the power of choice."

"No one cared ever about that."

"I do." An impish grin curved his lips while an answering light twinkled in his eyes. "Oh, before I forget, I want to give you something." Before she knew what he was about, John shoved off his bench and knelt on the floorboards in front of her even though the narrow aisle could hardly accommodate his large frame. "When I saw this, it immediately reminded me of you."

Excitement tingled down her spine as he drew out a ring from his waistcoat pocket. "Why?" Despite the rain and gloom outside the windows, the stone gleamed with a light of its own.

"This opal is dainty and delicate but holds an internal fire that brings out its true colors." While he spoke, John tugged the kid glove from her left hand. "That's what you are, and like the opal, you are strong, Caroline. Never forget that." Once the glove fell to her lap, he slipped the ring onto the fourth finger of her left hand. The silver was cool and smooth against her skin. "Don't listen to anything others might say."

"Beautiful," she breathed. Tiny round diamonds winked, two on each side of the oval-shaped opal. "Like in a fairy story."

"Exactly." He smiled, held her gaze with his. "Never lose that sense of wonder, no matter what has happened in your life. No one has the right to tell you how to act or to think. You are your own person." He brought her hand to his lips and first kissed the ring then her middle knuckle. "Thank you for agreeing to marry me. I'll pray every day I'll remain worthy of you."

Tears unexpectedly welled in her eyes. His kindness and caring overwhelmed her. Flutters danced through her lower belly, for John was by far the most gallant man she'd ever known. She concentrated on her next words. "May I wear my tiara when we wed?" What would it feel like if he held her in his arms for more than merely steadying her after a fall or rescuing her from a snowbank?

"If it makes you happy and comfortable, wear what you want." He enfolded her hand between his two big ones. "Wear a beautiful gown that makes you feel like a princess. Carry your wand or whatever magical frippery that reminds you of better times if you wish. I want our wedding day to be memorable for you and I want it to be the moment you've always dreamed about."

"Oh." One of the tears slipped to her cheek. She quickly dashed it away with her free hand. "That is lovely." Was he aware of how romantic he was, or was it merely a trap?

But the earnestness in his expression and the compassion in his eyes sent that thought away. "Our marriage can remain one of convenience or in name only unless you will it otherwise. The union is merely the key to your freedom, and on that I will not budge."

Never had she met a man—any person—like him. "Thank you."

"I look forward to where this will lead the both of us." When he returned to his bench, he took a bit of warmth with him.

"As do I."

"Honestly, I'm glad I'll no longer be alone. There is something comforting about having a friend by my side."

"Yes." Caroline nodded. She admired the ring and then slid her glance to him. What would happen after they were wed? Did she want him as a woman should a real husband? Never had she cause to think of romance as a reality.

Did he?

Perhaps it didn't matter. He was here and so was she. For the first time in her life since going into the asylum, she had a future.

It was a heady prospect indeed.

CHAPTER SIX

September 9, 1818

CAROLINE TREMBLED AS she gazed at herself in the cheval glass. She'd chosen a gown of pale pink. The overskirt of extremely sheer white tulle shimmered with her every movement due to the tiny clear glass beads and bits of silver spangles sewn into it. The same beadwork lined the bodice that showed too much of her bosom, but her sister Isobel assured her the cut was the height of fashion these days. Even Sarah had proclaimed it elegant and quite the thing for a wedding. The twinkle of small diamonds in the tiara nestled into her upswept dark hair kept pulling her attention, for the countess had given her the piece as a wedding gift.

"It's part of the Storme family jewels, so it's only right that it should be yours, dear," Sarah whispered as she fussed with the tulle puffs over her shoulders. "I thought you might appreciate it more than the tarnished silver one you had at Christmastide."

"So pretty." Caroline touched it with a fingertip. "I'm princess storybook like a." For once she didn't care that her words were twisted, for today she would leave this house and start an adventure with John. She would be able to do what she wanted, go where she wished, and no one would tell her nay.

Isobel snorted. "A princess who will need to toil for the rest of her life. Mr. Butler isn't exactly the wealthy type."

"Isobel!" The reprimand in Sarah's voice was all too clear. "Just because you married a man who happens to be a doctor as well as the Earl of Worchester doesn't mean that sort of life is appropriate for everyone." The countess adjusted the fall of a sheer veil that had been attached to the tiara. Fine lacework lined the edges of the tulle, for Caroline had insisted she have one. It sounded so romantic and dreamy, and she liked how it flowed down her back. "Caroline has an affinity for and a friendship with Mr. Butler. Perhaps that's all they'll need."

"Life doesn't work that way, and you know it." Obviously, her sister wasn't convinced. She peered into Caroline's face. "However, as poor as the man is, he's easy on the eyes, and is quite impressive in his form. I'd say you're a fortunate woman when it comes to the wedding night."

"For the love of God, Isobel, do hush!" This time the countess was quite scandalized. "That is a private matter between Caroline and Mr. Butler."

Warmth invaded her cheeks. She stopped touching the filmy gauze veil in order to concentrate on her next words. "Why fortunate?"

Isobel's grin was this side of naughty. "They say the bigger the man, the larger his, ah, appendage is, and *that* promises good things for you."

"I don't know what that means." Why was her sister talking about that?

"Well, *I* do, and I'm a bit envious." Isobel grinned. "But I'm happy with Royce, and I hope you'll be pleasantly surprised with John."

"Enough of such talk." Sarah took Caroline's left hand in hers. "He gave you a pretty ring, so I'd say he is not quite with pockets to let as we fear."

Caroline frowned. Did they not think him good enough to wed her? "John is…" How exactly did she feel about him? "He is a friend, and he *listens* to me." She glanced at her reflection again.

Her eyes sparkled. Was that... happiness there? "He makes me feel safe." They didn't need to know that when he grinned at her in a certain way, her insides felt tingly and hot, and she refused to share how much she adored when he laughed, for that made her wish to laugh too. Those were *her* memories, and like treasures.

"I wish you good luck if that's all you have to go on." Isobel shook her head. "And with how your mind is, you'll probably never know what you're missing. You will have the better deal than he." She shrugged. "After all, you spent the bulk of your life in that asylum. You know nothing of life, men, flirting, or anything else that makes one's existence deliciously fun or wicked. I can't imagine Mr. Butler has enough patience for that."

"Enough, Isobel." Annoyance rang in Sarah's voice.

"But it's the truth!"

"I don't care." Sarah took her by the arm and escorted her to the door. Her eyes behind her spectacle lenses held exasperation and a touch of concern. "Why don't you go downstairs and make sure the rest of the family has assembled? It's almost time."

But the damage had been done. Caroline turned away from the cheval glass. Some of the joy that the dress and veil had given her had vanished. Finally, she understood what her sister had meant. John was fine for her, but she wasn't good enough for him. She was too damaged to be of value and with the fractures in her mind, she'd hold him back, perhaps disappoint him.

Why is he marrying me, making such a sacrifice, when he can do so much better?

"Don't pay attention to her." Sarah returned and linked her arm through Caroline's. "Isobel has always been a wild one, according to Andrew. I'd hoped her marriage would have settled her a bit, but I think Royce encourages her behavior." She smiled at her. "You are doing just fine."

"I don't know." Perhaps marrying John was a horrible idea after all.

"Nonsense. You and John will have a marvelous life together." She led Caroline toward the door. "There might be small obstacles you'll need to overcome, but in the end, everything will work out as it should."

"What if it doesn't?" The future she'd looked forward to since John had told her of his plan suddenly dimmed.

"Then you'll need to decide what you most want for your life." She glanced at Caroline. Pity lingered in her expression. "It's the only thing any of us can do."

There wasn't time for anything else, for they'd reached the drawing room. A quick glance about the space didn't reveal John. Panic twisted up her spine. Had he changed his mind? Cousin Andrew spoke quietly with two men dressed in black—presumably from the church. Isobel sat on a low sofa with her head close to her husband's. Finn and Brand both watched her as she came further into the room.

"I'll just go and tell Andrew you're ready." Sarah patted her hand. "I wouldn't worry about things before they happen. Enjoy each moment as it comes."

Then she was alone, standing in the middle of the room while her family stared with varying degrees of speculation. She wanted to run and keep running until she found a safe place to hide. Beyond that, the urge to scream at the heavens and relieve some of the anger that always simmered below the surface grew strong. Did no one believe that she could do all the things any woman could do? Why couldn't they understand there was nothing wrong with her except for the fact her mind worked differently than theirs? It didn't mean she was insane or an imbecile.

As a ball of tears rose in her throat, her cousins approached.

Brand was the first to speak. "You are lovely today, Caroline." Genuine appreciation shone in his eye. He took her hand. "John is my closest friend and I consider him like a brother. He'll treat you well."

"He is a good man." Though she nodded, doubts chased about her mind, twisting the truth, and laughing at her insecurities.

Finn rolled closer. He was quite striking in his formal clothes decorated with cat hair, and with his hair sticking up at all angles, he had the air of a ne'er-do-well rogue. "Cousin Caroline, might I ask you a personal question?"

She nodded.

"Do you fully *understand* what marriage entails?"

Annoyance speared through her chest. "Never care you before of me. Why now?"

The men exchanged glances. Finn cleared his throat. "Brand was only a little boy when you were sent away. But the rest of us should have protested your parents' decision." He took her other hand and tugged her closer so that she was bending down toward him. "Please forgive us for our silence. We didn't know what had happened, and now, I—we—wish to make up for that oversight."

Was it possible all the members of the Storme family hadn't been of one accord during those dark days? Caroline slipped her hand from his. "Where were you all the years I was trapped in that asylum, Finn? I used could have an ally and friend." Oh, mercy, the words weren't overly jumbled for once.

He blew out a breath. A red flush crept over his collar. "The military took up much of my time when I became of age. After the war, my own mind wasn't as it should be, and I fell victim to my own demons." He shrugged. "It's not meaningful but it *is* an excuse."

"I was alone!" She struggled to keep her voice level, but all the old feelings sat heavy on her chest and rushed up into her throat. "There was no one for me. Just my thoughts." And her anger and confusion. The only thing that tempered all of that had been her drawing and painting.

Brand put an arm around her shoulders. "Much like Finn, the Navy took my time, but I have no excuse after that, for I'd made it a point to play the rake without remorse." A hint of embarrassment tinged his face. "I'll admit, I'd forgotten about you over the years." When she shook with anger, he rushed to explain. "But in my defense, my family never spoke of you, and up until Christmastide last year, I hadn't seen my cousins or other family."

She squirmed away from him too. "Don't pretend you car-buncle!"

They both stared at her in confusion.

The heat of mortification slapped at her cheeks. "I mean care. You were gone, living life, while I was locked away." No one could deny that, and nothing would ever make that better.

"Touché." Brand frowned. "But if you'll let me, I can be here for you *now*." He gestured at Finn. "We both can. Which is why we're concerned about your sudden nuptials. *Do* you understand what this will entail, Caroline?"

"It will be whatever I want it to be. John promised." For the time being, she didn't wish to forgive her cousins. That anger and hopelessness she'd felt all those years by herself wouldn't merely dissolve with a dozen pretty words. "I believe him. I do *not* believe you." They needed to show that they were truly sorry.

Then he was there, her soon-to-be husband. He paused at the door of the drawing room as he surveyed the room, and when his gaze landed on her, Caroline's breath stalled. He was magnificent in his dark formal clothing—tailcoat included. The waistcoat of bottle green satin embroidered with golden leaves drew her attention to his flat abdomen, but it was the awe and pride contained in his golden-brown gaze that sent a tremor of excitement down her spine.

"John." The whispered word had barely cleared her tight throat when he approached her. "You're here."

"Of course I am." His grin set some of her doubts at ease. He nodded at Brand and Finn. "If you boys will allow me to steal your cousin?"

Finn nodded. He briefly touched her hand. "We're here if you should need us." Then he wheeled himself toward Isobel and the doctor.

Brand clapped a hand to John's shoulder. "Take care of her, my friend. I shall arrive in Derbyshire a week after you."

"I'll do my level best." Once Brand stepped away, he looked at her and took one of her hands. "You are the most beautiful woman I've ever seen." The truth of that lay reflected in his eyes.

"Thank you." She brushed a bit a piece of lint on his sleeve. "You are… wonderful too." Oh, and he smelled good too. Those scents of salt, sea, and sunshine threatened to intoxicate her. "Still you wish marry me?" Why now did her tongue and brain choose to stop working?

"When I make a promise—especially to a lady—I always keep it." He put his lips to the shell of her ear. "The only thing you require is a bouquet of flowers. How remiss of me not to have brought you some."

Her pulse quickened, for his teasing sent flutters through her belly. "You can pick some for me in the country."

"Good idea." Then he tucked her hand into the crook of his elbow. "Shall we begin?"

"Yes." Tingles of anticipation played her spine. She walked beside him as he led her to the clergyman, who quickly introduced himself to the pair of them.

"Is everyone here?" He scanned the room from over the tops of his half-moon spectacles.

"I believe so." John's deep voice sent gooseflesh sailing over her skin. "Everyone who matters is already in attendance."

A wave of sadness crested over her, for her parents were both gone. What would they have thought on this day of her marriage?

"Very well. We shall start." The clergyman took a well-used book from his clerk and opened to a page he wanted. No doubt he knew the words by heart, much as she did with her favorite stories. Behind them, the Storme family settled into chairs and sofas. "Dearly beloved, we are gathered together here in the sight of God, and in the face of this gathering, to join together this Man and this Woman in holy Matrimony; which is an honorable estate, instituted of God in the time of man's innocency, signifying unto us the mystical union that is betwixt Christ and his Church…"

She didn't quite care for the cadence or sound of the man's

voice or the prickling feeling on her neck from everyone staring at her, so Caroline allowed her mind to drift. Soon, she would be John's wife. He would take her away from everything, away from the judgment and the whispers, away from the shame of being in that asylum, to somewhere that she could do whatever she wished.

But what would happen between them in the meantime? Did he wish for a real marriage in every sense of the word? If so, how could she agree when she couldn't stand being in the company of anyone, let alone having someone touch her so intimately as what would be required of her in that case?

He's made a terrible choice. This is a mistake!

"Caroline." John softly cleared his throat. He touched a hand to hers, and that tiny connection scattered her frantic thoughts. "You might wish to pay attention." Amusement threaded through the barely audible whisper.

The clergyman centered his gaze on John. "Wilt thou have this Woman to be thy wedded Wife, to live together after God's ordinance in the holy estate of Matrimony? Wilt thou love her, comfort her, honor, and keep her in sickness and in health; and, forsaking all others, keep thee only unto her, so long as ye both shall live?"

Oh, such romantic words! Like a poem. Caroline trembled, her breath held in anticipation. Would he truly go through with the ceremony?

In a clear voice, John answered, "I will."

A shiver of relief edged down her spine, but there was no time to wonder, for the clergyman addressed her.

"Wilt thou have this Man to be thy wedded Husband, to live together after God's ordinance in the holy estate of Matrimony? Wilt thou obey him, and serve him, love, honor, and keep him in sickness and in health; and, forsaking all others, keep thee only unto him, so long as ye both shall live?"

She squeezed her fingers upon John's arm. "Yes. Absolutely." Her answer came out breathless and in a whisper, for tears crowded in her throat. Life was rapidly changing, and oh how she hoped it would change for the better.

Then John was instructed to take her right hand in his right one, and hers shook so badly that he gently squeezed her fingers. Tendrils of calm emanated upward from the point of contact. When her breath came in tiny pants, he leaned into her, put his lips to her ear and whispered, "I promise this will not be yet another prison."

Her heart trembled. She grinned lest he think she looked upon the ceremony with dread. "I'm so happy," she whispered back.

The clergyman gave them a look of indulgence. He cleared his throat and continued. "Mr. Butler, repeat after me…" He intoned words that Caroline scarcely heard until he said them to her, his brown eyes locked with hers.

"I, John Terrance Butler, take thee Caroline Agnes Storme to be my wedded Wife, to have and to hold from this day forward, for better for worse, for richer for poorer, in sickness and in health, to love and to cherish, 'till death us do part." His grin awakened butterflies in her belly. "According to God's holy ordinance; and thereto I plight thee my troth."

They were directed to release hands, and Caroline was told to then hold John's right hand with her right one. The clergyman addressed her. "Miss Storme, repeat after me." He gave her the words, and she prayed she would say them all in the proper order.

Please, God, let me say them in order. "I, Caroline Agnes Storme, take thee John Terrance Butler to be my wedded Husband." She paused to swallow and clutch at his fingers. As well as to concentrate on this next bit. "To have and to hold from this day forward, for better for worse, for richer for poorer, in sickness and in health, to love, cherish, and to obey, 'till death us do part, according to God's holy ordinance." Her voice dropped to a whisper. "And thereto I give thee my troth." How wonderful and slightly terrifying such a thing was, but the words hadn't been jumbled. For that she rejoiced.

Please let me show him—and me—this isn't a mistake.

They were instructed to again release their hands. John proffered a plain silver band to the clergyman, who then laid it upon his open *Book of Common Prayer* along with what she assumed was a form of payment to the clergyman and his clerk. Then the older man returned the ring to John, who slipped it onto the fourth finger of her left hand, where it nestled snugly against the opal ring he'd already gifted her with.

The clergyman directed him to repeat another set of words.

"With this Ring I thee wed, with my Body I thee worship, and with all my worldly Goods I thee endow." The dear man's voice broke, but he gave her the grin that made her feel as if she could fly.

"In the Name of the Father, and of the Son, and of the Holy Ghost. Amen."

Slightly stunned, Caroline kneeled when John did, and she clung to his hand as if he'd suddenly vanish while the minister invited all in attendance to pray.

At the conclusion of the prayer, she and John stood. The clergyman intoned, "I now pronounce thee husband and wife."

I'm married!

And then it was over. No longer was she overlooked and ignored. Now she was someone's wife, a woman John had chosen because he saw something worthy in her. She glanced at him, and a tremulous smile curved her lips. "Thank you."

"No, thank *you*." He brought her hand to his lips and kissed the back. Warmth skated over her skin, for she hadn't remembered to wear her gloves. "You are one step closer to freedom, Mrs. Butler. I'll endeavor all of my days to give you the life you've always dreamed about. I hope it's all you need."

Tears gathered in her eyes. He'd found her first in the snow and then again in the rain. Both times he'd treated her as a queen. What would happen when they met in fair weather? Would that they had such in Derbyshire on their wedding trip.

The clergyman cleared his throat. "If you could both come and sign the registry, we can make everything official."

Caroline nodded. "Official." She belonged to John now. For the first time, she actually felt as if she were truly wanted... for herself.

CHAPTER SEVEN

September 10, 1818
Somewhere between London and Derbyshire

THEY'D BEEN MARRIED for four and twenty hours. John still couldn't wrap his head around that fact. He had a wife. For better or for worse, he was responsible for another person for the rest of his life.

What the devil do I do now?

Their wedding night had been spent at a posting inn, for he and Caroline had left for Derbyshire shortly after the wedding luncheon to make use of the light. He'd given her the bed in the room, while he'd bunked on the floor with a pallet of blankets. It hadn't been the most comfortable of nests or how he'd thought he'd spend that particular night if he'd ever given any thought to it during the course of his life, but she'd been panicked and nervous. He'd not mentioned any expectations, nor had he hinted at what usually happened between married couples. It had been her choice and would remain that.

Their union had never been based on physical need, and besides, he was a patient man. Once they knew each other better, perhaps their relationship would move into other aspects. It was enough that he'd gained the boon of removing her from the Storme influence, at least for a little while.

He didn't take that lightly.

Now, once more in the Earl of Hadleigh's traveling coach, he was still as stunned as he'd been the day before. Yes, with their nuptials, he'd intended to set her free so she could discover who she truly was once away from everyone coddling her, conversely ignoring her, or protecting her out of their own fears. But what of everything else life would hand them? Every union went through trials and tribulations. Would they have enough between them to weather those?

His attempt to stifle a sigh failed, and it sounded overly loud inside the coach. Caroline ceased her contemplation of the passing countryside to rest her curious gaze upon him. She was rather fetching in her traveling dress of moss green and ivory striped muslin. There was a matching bonnet, but she'd categorically refused to wear it, so it sat on his bench, for he'd picked it up from where she'd flung it on the way out to the coach earlier. That stubborn spirit was adorable; would that she'd always have it. He grinned in the hopes of further gaining her trust but to also set her at ease. "How do you like traveling thus far?"

"I enjoy seeing the countryside." She trained her attention on the window once more. "Peaceful. Want to paint it." Her fingers glided over the sketchbook that sat on the bench next to her. "So pretty and full of life. Colorful."

"You'll have plenty of time for that once we arrive." As much as he would have liked departing directly from Hadleigh Hall to Ipswich to begin their married life, it hadn't been feasible to delay due to packing her belongings. The time alone together was vital if this union was to survive in whatever form it would take. Once their wedding trip concluded, and after Brand paid his promised visit, they would all return to London together, and from there, go to Ipswich on Brand's schooner. Would Caroline enjoy being on the water? It would certainly expand her horizons and give her other views to contemplate.

"Will there be sheep?"

He frowned. "I beg your pardon?"

Again, she looked at him. "Are there sheep? I want to see them." Her words were slow and deliberate in an effort to make them release in proper order.

While he appreciated that, John wished she were comfortable enough to be herself. He didn't mind that her speech was sometimes jumbled. It was a part of who she was and a reason he'd wished to help her embrace that aspect. "I don't remember, truth to tell. The last time I was at Hadleigh Hall, it was winter." During that house party, he'd spent much of his days with Caroline or the doctor—now earl—for Brand had been newly married and couldn't bear to be away from his wife for too long.

Poor devil was missing his wife fiercely at the moment, though.

She nodded. "I think I would rather sheep like."

"I suppose they are quite congenial. More than goats, perhaps." No, this wasn't a conversation he'd ever thought he'd have with the woman he took to wife, but there was nothing for it. From everything he'd managed to glean from various Stormes, Caroline's life had not only been sheltered while she'd been locked away, but she rarely interacted with other people. To say nothing of the hint of violence she'd already let slip. His heart ached for the lonely life she must have led, far from anything of beauty, no doubt craving any sort of touch or kindness.

That ends now. I'll do whatever is in my power to see her life bloom. He couldn't explain the curious pull between them; he only knew she needed so much more than she'd been given. That coupled with the solitude, the disappointment, the abuse his own childhood had seen, he felt a bond with her that perhaps no one else of her acquaintance would. *We can help each other, if she's willing.*

That tentative smile curved her lips, and John dropped his gaze to her mouth. What would those two pieces of rosy flesh feel like if he stole a kiss? Were they as soft and plush as they looked? Would doing so frighten her too badly or open her world to other possibilities? He didn't know but he wouldn't do anything to rush his fences.

"Will you teach me to ride?"

The words startled him. He snapped his attention back to her gaze. "Ride a goat?"

"No." She shook her head and lifted one of her hands to wrap her fingers around a white enamel crescent moon pendant on a silver chain. "A horse. One never have ridden. Is it frightening?"

"That depends on the temperament of the horse and the attitude of the rider." Again, his chest tightened with empathy, for the woman across from him had missed out on so much women of her status should have done.

Caroline nodded. "I remember horses. From childhood. My father forbade me from riding." Her eyes narrowed. Annoyance threaded through her tone. "Mother said I wasn't capable. Isobel could. Got everything."

"While you were sent to your room," he finished softly for her. There was unresolved anger deep down within her. Of that he had no doubts.

"Yes." She traced the moon with a fingertip. The edge of the enamel was worn as if she'd done that for many years. "Nothing to look forward to."

"Those days are behind you, and now the world is at your feet." As much as he could provide those opportunities. It helped that the Earl of Hadleigh had given him five hundred pounds for her dowry. His father would not see a farthing of that money, for he intended to purchase a house and in that way care for his wife as she deserved. It was a good start in the event the new shipping outfit suffered pockets of slow commerce. When she met John's gaze, the relief there was so obvious that his heart squeezed, but he didn't want to be seen as her savior, her rescuer. He wished them to have a friendship, perhaps more later, based on mutual likes and things in common. "Tell me about your pendant. I'll wager it holds great meaning for you."

"This?" Caroline held up the moon so he could better see it. When he leaned forward, a bit of a face with features was visible, worn like the edges. "Mother this me gave birthday for my tenth." She shrugged and let the pendant fall back where it settled between her collar bones. "Only thing not taken from me at the asylum."

Ah, God. John swallowed down the rising emotion in his throat. "Does it hold special meaning for you?"

"The moon is a friend." Such sadness surfaced in her stormy-blue eyes that he wanted to bundle her in his arms and protect her from the world. "I watched it from my window at the asylum." Her words were slow, precise. "It was always there for me when no one else was. Constant. Unfailing. Many nights I sketched it."

"I understand that. While onboard ship in my navy days, I often contemplated the moon, marveled at it, really. That same moon is seen by every living thing the world over. It boggles the mind to think of how many thoughts and dreams it has collected since its creation."

"Yes." Her eyes lit and she smiled again. This time the delicate skin at the corners of her eyes crinkled. The gesture brightened her face, made her beautiful in a way many women couldn't achieve, and quite frankly, he gawked at her. "We looked at the same moon."

"Quite possibly." The knowledge she'd spent her formative years shut away from everyone, to say nothing of the years where she could have been courted, known romance, possibly had a family of her own, left him low. Anger against the people who'd been in control of her life curled through his gut. How could someone do that to another person merely due to differences? How could they not have tried to understand her or how she saw the world? Needing to connect with her, he dug into the pocket of his waistcoat and brought forth a battered brass pocket watch. "I carry this with me always."

"Why?" She leaned forward to trace a fingertip along its surface when he handed it to her. The dents and dings in it gave it character; the etchings of a world map on the front faded over the years.

John blew out a breath. Outside of Brand, no one knew this story. "It once belonged to the man who tried to kill me years ago during a fight at a tavern when we put into port in Jamacia." He wasn't proud of those days, but without them, he would never have met Brand, his best friend and the man who'd helped turn his life around. "I was hot-headed as a young man, given to anger, and when that fight blew up, I knew it would end in either my death or the Frenchman's."

Her eyes rounded as she gave him back the watch. "Did you kill him?"

"No." He shook his head. "I walked away after landing him a facer that put him out cold." A ghost of a grin tugged at the corners of his mouth. "Though I *did* take this watch." As he tucked it back into his pocket, he continued. "It now serves as a reminder to never lose my temper or my humanity, my compassion and understanding for others, no matter how angry I am or how trying life gets."

"That is a good story." She held his gaze for the space of a few heartbeats. "Sometimes, I sense anger you still have. Why? You don't look like it."

Heat crept up the back of his neck. She was quite observant. "I either shove down those feelings or find an outlet to release them." When she quirked an eyebrow in confusion, he grinned. "When I was in the navy, I'd often indulge in fisticuffs with Brand and some of the others. Now, I like to walk whenever I can. And sailing is good physical activity."

Would she consider him a risk? With everything else, would he not be a good influence?

Instead of shying away, she offered him a smile. "You and I are the same." Caroline touched her chest with a hand. "In having rage here, burning all the time."

"Perhaps." That might prove a perfect storm later in their relationship, but it was too late now. "I've seen said emotion in your eyes." But he wanted to know why.

"Why you are angry?"

He blew out a breath, for it was difficult to explain and he wasn't in the habit of talking about himself, but she was his wife, and they were together through thick and thin. "Due to my father, mostly. You met him."

"I do not like that man."

"Aye, neither do I, though I try to understand why he is how he is." John chuckled. "He's a drunk, usually. Has been for years. Used to beat my brother and me with his fists or whatever was handy." Those were not good memories. Long ago he'd made peace with that, which had helped him move past them. "We prayed that he would die of a pickled liver as his father did."

"He didn't." Caroline shook her head.

"No, he did not." The hot wave of anger rose in his chest, but he tamped it. "The horrid ones never do. They stick around and make life difficult for everyone." A muscle in his cheek twitched from the force of his control. "He's impossible to talk to or reason with."

"Your anger simmers. A part of you."

"Yes." She was adorable in her single-minded determination to discover his secrets. "It *is* a part of me, unfortunately, no matter how I wish it otherwise. No matter that I've forgiven my father for what he did, forgiven the violence and disappointment." John shrugged. "During this trip to London, I wanted to confront my father about his declining health, but he won't hear advice, refuses to change his ways. Once he dies, my whole damn life will become upended, and I want no part of that."

There would be time enough to reveal all of that to Caroline once she'd come to know him better.

"Because you love him?" Confusion had surfaced once more in her eyes.

"No." He bit off the word. "He killed any love I had for him years ago, and his actions now will ensure it will never return."

"Anger is a prison." A swath of silence fell between them. "It is mine as well. There is no escape. Always there. Waiting."

"Ah, Caroline." He rubbed a hand along the side of his face. "We must both make a conscious effort to not let that anger eat away at us else it will destroy us. There has to be a moment of letting go, of knowing we can only do so much, but others need to be accountable too." How could he help her do just that when he was like the pot calling the kettle black?

"I like the countryside, yet I also wish to visit the seashore." The change in subject matter made his mind reel. Perhaps the natural break made sense to her. In her mind, if she was finished with a subject, she might assume others were as well.

John's eyebrows rose in surprise. "Truly?"

"Yes." She nodded with a new grin. "With you, safe I am. We are angry together." Caroline caught up her sketchbook, flipped to a page, and then showed him. Two whirling vortices were side by side on the page, shaded in charcoal. The background was somewhere in Hyde Park. Had she felt that emotion from him when they'd met in the rain? With a forefinger, she pointed. "You. Me. Storms."

"Surely that can't be a good way to begin a marriage."

Her laughter was a light and airy affair, bouncing through the interior of the coach and lifting his spirits. "I don't know. Saw Isobel married last month." She closed the notebook and returned it to the bench.

Good heavens, she was opening up to him, and that trust humbled the hell out of him. Though he wished to learn more, he refused to push her. "How did that make you feel?"

For long moments she stared at him before answering. "Annoyed? Sad? More angry?" A sigh escaped her. "Isobel is happy but frightened."

"That's understandable." He didn't know much of the new countess' story aside from the fact she'd never wished to marry a man with a title, but when the doctor became an earl, her life had been upended. And there'd been some scandalbroth regarding a horse race. He disliked gossip so hadn't paid attention.

Caroline huffed. "She is increasing."

"Oh?" Now that *was* interesting. "Do you wish for babies of your own?" It was a valid question, and one he hoped didn't send her back to withdrawing into herself.

She shrugged. "I don't know."

"Fair enough." Perhaps she'd long given up the hope of such dreams after the lonely life she'd led. "Do you, ah, like me as a man?" It was daring, those words, yet part of him had to know there might be hope for more in his future.

"Yes. You make me have feelings here." She laid a hand over her belly. The frown that pulled the corners of her lips down shot fear into his veins. Had he angered her? Frightened her by merely introducing the subject? "Is that wrong?"

"No, of course not." He needed to tread carefully with her. "There is no wrong way to feel. You are unique, so it stands to reason how you think and feel is unique as well, but it is good we have a connection." How *did* her mind process things? Had she ever seen a doctor regarding her affliction? Despite his wish to remain confident, doubts crept in. Would he ever know a close, joyful marriage like Brand enjoyed?

"I like the tingles. They are special." Caroline tucked an escaped tendril of hair behind her ear. "Do *you* wish for children, John?"

How he adored hearing her say his name. It was as if she caressed the word with her lips before releasing it into the air like the most fleeting of kisses. "Perhaps later, once things are settled." He hated to be deliberately vague, but he refused to scare her so early in the relationship.

Confusion and curiosity warred for dominance in her expression. "Do you want to do the things men do to have children?" When a trace of fear flashed through her eyes, John's budding hopes were dashed.

At least for the moment.

In all probability, with her spending the bulk of her life in that asylum, there had been no opportunity for her to talk with other ladies—family included—about the things women expected from life, let alone relationships between men and women. It was a large responsibility that rested on his shoulders, but for her, he would do anything. They would find their way with understanding.

But she expected an answer. "Possibly… only if *you* are comfortable with moving forward into such things." He offered her a grin he hoped would bring comfort. "I won't rush you. This union is as much yours as it is mine. It's special to me. As are you."

For long moments, Caroline watched him. What she searched for, he had no idea, but he hoped to bloody hell she found it. Finally, she nodded, her expression solemn. "Is there kissing in a marriage?"

Her naiveté was endearing, and he appreciated her all the more for it. At least the asylum hadn't broken her curiosity completely. Interest flared in his chest as anticipation buzzed at the base of his spine. "Do you want there to be?"

She tilted her head slightly as she continued to regard him. "What feels like does it?"

Slowly, he was coming to know that when she was possessed of high emotion, her words had a greater tendency of being jumbled. It was a piece of the puzzle he could work with going forward. "Well, that is difficult to explain. Most people enjoy kissing. It makes them feel good… happy I guess you could say." His wife was a riddle, a puzzle, a challenge that hadn't revealed its full potential yet, and he looked forward to understanding her all the more. "Do you, ah, wish to try kissing, so you can see what it's like for yourself?" She was intelligent, and perhaps she learned best by doing.

A faint blush stained her cheeks. "Yes. Cousin Andrew kisses Sarah all the time."

"As a man should when he's married." Longing coiled within his chest, for he'd spent enough time in her company to know he carried attraction for her. No, Caroline wasn't deficient in the mind; she merely needed instruction in a different manner than others. "We shall practice kissing once we are settled at Hadleigh Hall."

"There is kissing in storybooks." Her frown returned. "Why not now?"

Because I'm apparently a nodcock. And he hadn't expected her to acquiesce so quickly. "Here?"

"Yes." She shrugged. Nothing but honesty reflected on her face. "Here are our mouths."

That tugged a grin from him. He rather liked her wit. "Fair point." As he shoved a hand through his hair, it shook. Why the hell was he suddenly so nervous? He'd kissed and bedded women before, but never a wife—*his* wife—and never a woman as unique and fragile as Caroline.

"Will you?" Obviously, she wanted his answer posthaste.

"Yes." Before she could change her mind, John moved to her bench, sitting between her and the sketchbook. The faint fragrance of violets teased his nose. Why had he never noticed that before? He grinned as she watched him with a certain wariness. "I won't hurt you, Caroline."

"I know." But she didn't relax either.

That worried him. What if she didn't enjoy physical contact? "We will only move forward if you wish it. On all fronts."

"All right." And still she watched him.

Damn, but he wanted to land facers to every single person who'd harmed her—both physically and mentally—during her lifetime, for each one of them had left scars behind that now she had to do battle with. But he was no stranger to defending the people he cared about, and so he would here. Slowly, so he wouldn't spook her, John slipped a hand up to cup her cheek. Her trembles transferred to him, and he was all too cognizant of the responsibility he carried. Equally as slowly, he leaned forward and brushed his lips against hers.

And she watched him the whole time. What was she thinking?

Pulling slightly away, he asked, "All right?"

Surprise clouded her eyes. "Yes."

"Do you want me to continue?"

"Yes. Please."

The properness of her request went straight to his shaft, tightening it. In his mind's eye, he could easily envision her begging him for other things in the bedroom, but that was an eventuality he'd need to wait for, and he would, gladly, for she was worth it. Shoving the thought away, he edged his fingers around to frame the back of her head, furrowing them through her hair. Then he pressed his lips to her again. This time, he kissed her with a touch more intensity, exploring both soft pieces of flesh with his, giving her a different sort of introduction, welcoming her into a new world.

And God he hoped he didn't muck it up.

"Oh." A sigh shuddered from her. She laid a palm on his chest and leaned into to him, pressing her lips to his while her eyelids fluttered closed.

He quietly rejoiced but continued to gently treat her to chaste kisses that held little heat or insistence. There would be time enough to introduce her to that. As it was, shock roiled through his chest while warmth enveloped him. She was soft and interested, and her fingers curled into his cravat the longer their kisses continued.

Perhaps there was a chance for them after all.

Eventually, he pulled away for fear he might go too quickly or demand too much. "That was quite nice."

Caroline trembled as if she'd been plunged into sudden cold. Shock and surprise pooled in her eyes. "It was… it was… I know didn't… too much!" She shook her head as her upset deepened and her words failed. She waved him away, shoved at his shoulder.

Well, damn. John returned to his bench. Failure sat heavy on his chest. "I apologize if I frightened you."

Caroline shook her head. Her eyes were round, and she kept touching her lips with her fingers.

It was difficult to ascertain what that meant. "Did you enjoy the kiss?" Perhaps she didn't know *how* to react to the new feelings being introduced. That made sense.

She nodded, but she still didn't speak.

"Good." He breathed a tiny sigh of relief. "We can work with that." While she snatched up her sketchbook and worked furiously on a drawing, he leaned back against the squabs and turned his attention to the window.

Kissing her, even chastely, had affected him more than he'd anticipated. John tamped his reaction and willed his awakening shaft to settle. It would be a long honeymoon period—hell, an even longer first year of marriage—if there were no carnal pleasures or even further kissing.

But then, he'd long ago learned patience, and he would wait for her because she deserved to experience everything the world could offer at her own pace.

Even if it was just him for the time being.

CHAPTER EIGHT

September 12, 1818
Hadleigh Hall
Derbyshire, England

IT WAS THE first full day at Hadleigh Hall, and Caroline was just beginning to realize that marrying John had meant forever. He was her husband, and he would always be with her.

During conversations while in the traveling coach, she'd come to know him a bit better, but he kept secrets deep down where no one could access—the same as she did. Was he fearful that if he shared, she would think less of him? It was certainly something that she thought about. According to her family, wasn't her mind fractured? Wasn't she touched by insanity and therefore unable to live her own life?

Yet John had married her anyway. He believed in her. That alone set him apart from everyone else.

As much as she detested having a maid, she submitted to the young woman's assistance, for the stays were beyond her comprehension. In the asylum, she didn't need to worry about such things. She'd rarely had visitors, and most of the patients within didn't have servants with them. Clothing had been manipulated by herself, but once she'd come into Cousin Andrew's household, she'd been given a maid. And more complicated clothing.

"How would you like your hair dressed this morning, Mrs. Butler?"

Tingles fell down her spine at the title. While traveling, John had taken care of most of the conversation with various innkeepers or the coach driver. This was one of the first times she'd heard her new state of address. "Matter, does it?" Even while talking with a young maid, she couldn't manage to put words into the correct order.

However, in John's company, she needn't worry about that. He either did most of the talking, or when she'd wished to share, if her words were jumbled, he never made her feel like a dunce. There was never judgment with him. It relieved her much.

"I would imagine you'd like to appear as lovely as you can for your new husband." The maid brushed out the long length of Caroline's hair. "You have such nice curls. Perhaps we'll leave it down with a ribbon to hold it back. Besides, the day will prove nice, and this softens your face."

Caroline frowned into the mirror at her vanity table. Though she was a married woman now, she'd chosen to sleep in the room she used to occupy in her childhood when the Storme family had gathered at Hadleigh Hall. None of the furniture had been updated, and that brought a small measure of comfort. At least that hadn't changed. "Why does my face need to be softened?" Concentrating on the words brought them out in the correct order, but the effort made her tired.

The maid—her name escaped Caroline—huffed. "Well, you have striking features, and you frown all the time." She slipped a yellow ribbon beneath the hair in question and then made a pretty bow that rested just over her left ear. "Don't you wish to entice your husband into your bed?"

Warmth invaded her cheeks. Though she and John had been married for four days now, he slept in a room different from hers, and aside from that kiss he'd given her in the coach, he hadn't initiated any other overtures of a carnal nature.

Because he had told her that the union would be whatever she wished it to be, and frankly, that sort of thing made her confused whenever she thought about it.

She didn't know what she wanted from her marriage just yet.

"I... I don't know." That kiss had left her both panicked, worried, and a tad excited. When he'd touched his lips to hers, cupped her cheek and head, it had made her feel both alive and chaotic, as if her brain and her body didn't know what to make of this new part of life. Those feelings were overwhelming, and they swamped her as she stared at her reflection in the looking glass. Yes, that was a good word, but in a nice way. Would that make sense if she spoke it aloud?

I can't focus on that.

John was big and intense, and his presence filled the spaces when they were alone together. Caroline couldn't help but pay attention to him, yet when he was near, he brought both calm and a certain anticipatory excitement she didn't understand. Yes, it was that, but there was also nervous curiosity. She was broken, wasn't she? How could he want her for a lifetime or for a real marriage? Oh, she'd seen those questions in the depths of his eyes when he thought she wasn't looking, and each time they sent more of a jumbled quagmire into her chest.

Which left her reeling. What exactly *did* she want her marriage to be like? And she certainly didn't want to disappoint him.

"You're an odd one, Mrs. Butler," the maid said, scattering Caroline's thoughts. "That man of yours is handsome in a plain sort of way. I imagine he knows his way around the bedroom."

"I should hope so, since he has been sleeping in one all his life." Her husband wasn't an animal, after all. And he wasn't plain either. When the sunlight hit his hair just right, illuminated the planes of his face and shaded others with shadow, he was breathtaking. To say nothing of how the sound of his voice was pleasing to her ears and made her feel tingly inside. Shivery almost.

The maid eyed her as if she were insane. Finally, she shook

her head. "You're good enough for the day. The yellow suits you, though Lord knows you'll ruin this dress with spatters of paint and grass stains. Ring when you're ready to dress for dinner."

"Thank you."

This was why she didn't enjoy talking to others. Not many people understood her. Grass stains meant she'd sat in the meadow and watched the day go by, communed with whatever animals happened her way, in the fresh air. Paint spatters said she'd committed something beautiful to her canvas to look upon years into the future and remember what had captured her eye and attention. And wasn't clothing a pedestrian concern? She wouldn't hassle with it if it weren't the height of scandal to go about clad in a nightdress all day long.

Putting the maid and her words from her mind, Caroline gathered her painting and drawing supplies, for she intended to spend the morning in the sunshine near one of the duck ponds she used to adore as a child… before everything changed, and she was taught to consider herself as less than.

Or broken.

Two hours later, John joined her like a ray of sun in the midst of clouds. "I missed you at breakfast."

Drat. That was something else she'd forgotten. So many rules! Why did she need to remember any of them? Hadn't John said she could do whatever she wanted with this marriage, that she was free? A niggle of doubt sank through her consciousness. Shoving it away as best she could, Caroline glanced up at him. He carried a basket in one hand and a raggedy blanket in the other. "I forgot about eating."

"So I figured, which is why Cook packed up a basket, filled with food for six people instead of two." He set the willow basket down near the medium-sized boulder she'd perched upon as a seat. Then he proceeded to spread the faded green blanket over the grass at the bank of the pond. "She didn't know your preferences, so I asked that she put in a sampling. There is also a jug of tea. I can't speak of its temperature, but you can have lemonade if you'd rather."

Her stomach let out a loud rumble that made him chuckle. Oh, how she adored that sound! What should she do to ensure that she continued to hear such a thing? Caroline lowered her brush and finally set it on the grooved ledge at the bottom of the easel. "I *am* hungry but didn't wish to lose the light."

"If this was my property, I'd set aside a room of your choosing to use for a studio." He swung open the lid of the basket. "Scone or bread and cold cuts?"

"A scone. And some tea. Care not hot if it is."

"I understand completely. Perhaps it's the act of drinking tea and not its temperature."

While he busied himself with pouring out a cup from a bottle, she took in his face and form with an artist's eye. The brown superfine jacket he wore set off his golden-brown eyes to perfection. A woman could lose herself in those warm depths if she weren't careful. The brown tweed waistcoat put her in mind of working-class men she'd spied once on an outing with the countess near some warehouses, and his buff-hued breeches showed his long, muscled legs to full advantage.

Yes, later she would paint him again. Would he agree to pose?

"I hope my lady enjoys her breakfast." John presented her the scone on a linen napkin with a flourish and then handed her the cup of tea.

She grinned. How could she not? He was good company. "Thank you." When he came closer to peer at her sketchbook that lay on the grass at her feet, she sucked in a breath. What would he think of that drawing?

"I know what the subject of this sketch is." Without apparent care to the grass, he sat upon it, and she rather liked his proximity, for the late summer breeze carried his scent to her nose. "Obviously, this twisting storm represents you." He flashed her a glance and she nodded. "And this," he tapped the image of a man, roughly drawn and running from the storm. "I fear this is supposed to represent me, and for some reason, I'm running from you, as if I'm afraid." A frown tugged at the corners of his sensuous mouth. "Why? Have I given you some indication that I find you abhorrent?"

"Uh…" Caroline took refuge in sipping her lukewarm tea. "I sometimes think you will truth discover me about." She sighed. "The truth about me and you won't like it."

Or me.

"You will run away."

For long moments, John studied the sketch. Then he laid the book back in the grass. "I *chose* you, Caroline. That particular fear will never come true. For the rest of my life, I will face the storm and embrace the chaos if you let me." He touched her elbow, and warmth emanated up her arm from the point of contact. "I want nothing more right now than to understand you, learn how your mind works, discover everything that makes you… you."

Shock rolled through her chest. "No one has ever wanted that."

"It's a new day." When he grinned in that special way he had, her heart fluttered like mad. "Right now, I'm trying to decide on where we'll live and what you want from our future."

Too many questions! She couldn't put her hands over her ears since both were full of the food stuffs John had offered. So she looked at him as panic bounced through her insides. "I… don't know. Never had cause to think about such things before while at the asylum."

There, she had no future. It wasn't an efficient use of her time to have dreams or hope things would change. Now that they had, she supposed she should probably pull those things from the trunks in her mind and dust them off. Caroline transferred her gaze to the pond, watched a pair of geese float stately over the surface. "I want to live somewhere I can paint."

"Of course. I would never ask that you discontinue that."

She nodded and nibbled on the cream scone. That she remembered from childhood, of how she and Isobel used to sneak into the kitchens and bedevil the cook for some though it might spoil their dinner. "I want a pianoforte. Cannot survive without painting and music." While she'd been consigned to the asylum, she used to pretend she had a pianoforte, which was in reality merely a windowsill. She'd practiced to continue her skills while imagined music had filled her head. In her mind, words might become troublesome, but music was always beautiful and could say everything that she couldn't. It never failed.

"I shall endeavor to bring that to you, though I might need Hadleigh's assistance."

"Why? Andrew doesn't play."

John chuckled, and that in itself was music. "I meant in securing such an instrument. At the moment, I only rent rooms, so we shall need to find a permanent residence before bringing a pianoforte with us."

"A house. For us." The concept boggled her mind. She, who'd for so long only occupied one room by herself would now have a home filled with beautiful, happy things.

"Or a cottage. Ipswich has pretty cottages. Some even feature a view of the sea." He found and held her gaze. "Wherever we go, I will support you, but I would like to reside in Ipswich. I wish you to see the beauty, experience the languid peace, the unhurried pace of the area. Brand lives there, so you won't be without family should you wish that. You can also meet my friends, and I can take you sailing. Our shipping outfit has a sloop and a schooner. Both are marvelous on the sea."

There was such fondness and enthusiasm in his tones that it pulled her along with him. "You'd let me go with you?"

Amusement danced in his eyes. "Sweeting, you are my wife now. I want you to do whatever makes you happy, whatever feeds your creativity."

"Oh." His words combined with the endearment sent warmth hurtling through her body that had nothing to do with the late summer sunshine. This man was much like a well-loved stuffed bear she had as a child, before it was left behind. It had brought comfort and strength and given her confidence, much like her husband did now. "You want to not be in London."

"Not particularly." He leaned close, broke off a piece of her scone, and popped the morsel into his mouth. "Besides, my livelihood is in Ipswich."

What would he look like on a sailing vessel? Suddenly, she wished to know right at that moment, but there were other things to discuss. "Will we come back here?"

"To Derbyshire or London?"

"Either?" She shrugged.

"Only if you will it."

Caroline gave him a smile. "I do not." She drained her teacup. "Tell me of snails." When he frowned and confusion passed over his face, she giggled. "Sails. Of sailing."

"It's a feeling of freedom as I've never known anywhere else on this earth."

Freedom. He'd told her marriage would bring her the same, and thus far, it had.

As he talked, Caroline couldn't tear her gaze from his mouth. What would another kiss from him feel like? Would it plunge her into panicked confusion again? Letting her cup fall to the grass, she grabbed her sketchbook, turned to a clean page, and quickly did a preliminary drawing of him, shirtless, as he lounged nearby. Is that what he looked like beneath his garments? Did she wish to know?

"Caroline?"

"Hmm?"

He touched her knee and she nearly jumped from her skin. "You haven't heard a word I said, have you?" There was no censure in his voice, only amusement.

"No, but you can say it again. Listening like to you I do."

That grin awakened butterflies in her lower belly. Why? No one had ever said being with a man could make her feel so... delightful. "May I hang my paintings in our cottage?"

"Of course. What is your favorite subject? I suspect once you catch sight of the sea, that will take priority."

Heat swept through her cheeks. "You." She showed him her sketchbook, had him look upon her recent drawing and then peer at others she'd done over the last month or so.

"What? Why?" He took the book from her, flipping through the pages as a red flush grew over his collar.

She concentrated on her next words. "You bring me calm. So, I sketch you. Sometimes paint those sketches. Cousin Andrew doesn't like it."

"Frankly, the earl doesn't matter right now." John scrambled to his feet. He stood a bit behind her and leaned near, intently studying her portrayal of the meadow's landscape. "You do remarkable work, whether the subject is of me or not."

A thrill went down her spine from his praise. All her life she'd wished her talent was acknowledged. "Thank you." But his words, all too close to her ear, had shivers chasing through her body.

"Why do I feature into your work so often? We hadn't seen each other since last Christmastide."

Caroline shrugged. That was an easy question to answer. "My mind said to. Doing so makes me..." She tilted slightly to one side. "...less angry."

"I understand." He rested a big hand on her shoulder. "It's why I enjoy riding or mucking out stables on occasion. Where your cousin might not wish to dirty his hands in hard labor, I find it helps to clear my mind and keep my emotions in check, so they don't consume me."

Yes, those feelings *were* consuming. "Like a storm," she whispered. "Swirling constantly around me until I become it. And not me any longer."

"It's a delicate balance, surely. However, sooner or later we shall both need to look what ails us straight in the eyes and confront it. That's the only way to release it, make room for better things." A hint of annoyance wove through his tones. "Today is not that day, though."

"No." If she let the anger and other emotions have at her, would she come out alive on the other side? They'd had years to fester and grow. Who was she apart from them? Not having the answers, she sat for long moments while she finished the scone and stared unseeing at the water of the pond. John stood with her, kneading the knots from her shoulders, and his touch both threatened to drive her mad and alternately send her into a relaxed state. Finally, she sighed. "It is a hot day."

"Indeed." He moved, turned her about on the boulder until their eyes met and her skirting twisted beneath her. Wicked intent played in his expression. "Would you like to swim?"

Tendrils of panic fractured through her chest. "I haven't done that since a child."

One of his bushy eyebrows lifted. "You can now."

"Don't like water."

"Why?"

"Forced my face at asylum into it. Happened just to see what would."

"Oh, God." Again, his hand was on her shoulder, comforting, stabilizing. "I'm so sorry. You needn't go in if you can't manage it. If it frightens you."

"It does." She glanced from the blue-green water where the sunlight twinkled on the rippled waves and then back to him but somehow she knew it wouldn't as long as he stayed with her. "Will you be there?"

"Yes." With mischief in his grin, he backed away, gaining the shore of the pond in short order. Then he toed off his boots, and as he winked, he stripped off his clothing until he stood clad only in his breeches.

Oh, merciful heavens! He was even more beautiful than her mind could imagine in her artwork. Ridged muscles. A mat of heavy blond-brown hair that spread over his wide upper chest with a thin line that tapered down over his abdomen to disappear into his breeches. Flat dusky rose nipples. Tanned skin that spoke of his days toiling on the boats he talked about with such pride.

Her mouth watered, for the urge to explore that skin with her lips grew strong and she didn't know why. She wanted to trace that stunning form with her fingers. Caroline rose to her feet as if he'd lured her beneath his spell.

"Should I... Should I also do that?" Weakly, she waved a hand to his semi-nakedness. A long, jagged scar snaked down his left side. Where had he gained that?

"Unless you wish to ruin your dress." His smile had the power to weaken her knees. "But might I say you're beautiful in yellow. Like a piece of sunshine personified. I especially like that your hair is loose today."

Her husband was beyond charming. Confusion crept in. She didn't know how to act around men; she barely understood how to interact with her male cousins. Were they always so perplexing yet endearing? But she wanted to feel the water on her skin, to perhaps confront one of her fears and be with John at the same time, so she removed her dress with shaking hands, as well as the pretty petticoat embroidered with vines on the hem. Once in her shift and stays, she hopped on first one foot and then the other while removing stockings and slippers.

"There's something about seeing a woman in undress that's quite wicked, don't you think?" He closed the distance between them and took her hand.

"I'm... not sure." Oh, it was embarrassing to be with him like this yet tingles of anticipation raced over her skin.

"The water will be refreshing. Then we can lounge on the blanket while our clothes dry, and we can have a picnic." Gently, almost as if he were guiding a skittish colt, he tugged her into the pond, foot by foot. "It won't hurt you and neither will I."

With a nod, she kept her gaze on his. "Ah! It's cooler looks than it!" Inch by inch, the water seeped up her body, quickly drenching her shift and stays just past her waist.

"That's one reason why swimming is such fun."

She couldn't stop staring at him. He was beautiful. "I should go back. To sketch—"

"Not yet." When he caught her into the strong circle of his arms and went deeper into the pond, she squealed. "Make friends with the water, sweeting."

"John!" Her heartbeat quickened with fright, but as she clung to his shoulders and her body pressed against his, shivers of excitement went down her spine. Yet, with him there was no reason to fear. He was big and hard as his form moved with hers. Muscles played beneath her fingertips where she clutched at him. Being in this water wasn't a punishment. "Oh." With one hand, she explored his chest, rubbing her palm up and down over that golden skin, trailing her fingers through the coarse hair there. "Oh!" So different from her.

His eyes darkened to a tawny brown. "Explore as much as you'd like."

"Why?" Without the support of his arms, she'd sink into the water, for her feet were no longer touching the bottom. She clung to him all the more.

"I'm your husband, Caroline. It's expected, and I'm sure you're curious. I can see it in your face."

The soft words in his deep voice rumbled in her chest. That coupled with the coolness of the water hardened her nipples. Her breasts ached with a longing she didn't understand but somehow knew he might have the answer. She caressed her fingers along the side of his strong neck, danced them over his broad shoulders, finding other scars in the process. "You are gorgeous." She dared to push those fingers through the hair at his nape. Soft as a bird's feather. The feel of his arms around her was both comforting and stimulating.

He snorted with laughter. "I'm average. Nothing special, especially if you ask my father." The amusement quickly died in the face of bitterness. His mouth took on a hard line.

"Don't be angry." Caroline didn't like it when he was in pain. In an effort to soothe him, she traced her fingertips along his eyebrows, the sweep of his cheekbone, his chin. The bit of stubble that shaded his chin and jaw made her itch to sketch that.

Both hard and soft. "You are not him."

"Just as you are not the Stormes."

"Yes." She grinned, thrilled that he understood. "I'm different, but not insane." It was important he also recognize that fact.

"No, you aren't." He bussed her cheek. "Your mind is beautiful, Caroline. I'll wager it's a colorful, amazing place in there. *You* are beautiful. Never let anyone tell you otherwise."

"Oh, John." With him she was both protected and in danger, not from an outside threat, but from the way he made her feel, as if she'd burst from her skin unless he touched her, continued to hold her. In his company, she could so easily believe she *was* beautiful instead of broken. Trembles danced down her spine to lodge between her thighs, and that confused her. Could he explain it to her? But then that made her feel inadequate and stupid, so she took refuge in the familiar. "Do you enjoy fairy stools?" *No, that wasn't right!* She tried again. "Stories. Fairy stories."

His laughter rumbled around and through her to further tighten the ache in her breasts. "I've never had cause to think about them."

"I do." She smiled while she held his gaze. "I dream of being rescued." It was too much of a risk to speak with long sentences. "Being rescued by a noble knight. He will carry me away to his kingdom." With a nod, she continued. "We'll live happily ever after."

For the space of a few heartbeats, he grinned, held her a tad bit closer while the water lapped about them. "Keep believing, Mrs. Butler. There's no shame in dreaming. Eventually, some of them might come true."

Her silly heart skipped a beat. Did that mean he wanted to be that knight? Wanted the story book ending? With her? He had truly already carried her away. Gooseflesh raced over her skin. "John?"

"Hmm?" His gaze briefly dropped to her mouth.

A shiver wracked her shoulders. "Will you, ah, kiss again

me?"

Interest lit those marvelous eyes, that now had specks of green in the irises. "Are you certain?" He moved them both back toward the shallower water.

When her feet touched the slippery bottom, she nodded. "Yes." For whatever reason, she absolutely needed to feel his lips on hers, had to be closer to him.

"Then I shouldn't disappoint my wife." Not once did he relinquish his hold on her, and she remained snug in his arms. He bent his head, lowered his lips to hers in the most gentle of kisses.

An involuntary moan escaped her throat, for this kiss was as warm and encompassing as the first, but now she knew what to except. The fear and confusion of the last one had vanished. In its place came excitement and an unexplainable hunger that began deep within her chest. Caroline looped her arms about his shoulders, pressed her body closer to his. A certain hard portion of his anatomy twitched insistently at her belly, but before she could wonder about that, he deepened their embrace.

When he licked her bottom lip and then did the same to the upper one, Caroline gasped, for the wild sensations he invoked were all too new and interesting. She let her hand drift to his nape, encouraging him closer. As his tongue touched hers, coaxed hers, bossed it, she explored, and soon the sensuous glide of satin on silk became her world.

Why had no one told her how glorious kissing could be? Just when she was beginning to delight in it, he slipped a hand from her hip up her ribcage, and as he cupped her breast, a shudder of need careened down her spine. She gasped again, and this time broke the kiss. His hand was big and comforting on that part of her, and oh how she wanted him to do more! The longing in her breasts practically demanded it.

"John…"

He kissed her again, teasing the corners of her lips with nibbles and licks. As he did so, he brushed the pad of his thumb over her hardened, aching nipple, and she gasped again. Pleasure streaked through her breasts to zip into that place between her thighs. No one had made her feel like that. Except him.

John pulled away. His grin was by far too wicked for her peace of mind. "I don't wish to spook you, so we'll stop right here."

As much as she agreed and needed time to breathe and think over what his touch did to her, she also wished he hadn't stopped. "Kissing is like how music feels me." Of course the words were jumbled, but she didn't care.

"That's a good thing." He tugged on her hand, leading her out of the water. When her gaze dropped to the front of his breeches to linger on the large bulge behind the fabric, his grin widened. "I, uh, am going for a walk. Back soon. Don't wander off."

Caroline had no intention of going anywhere, not when her feet felt like they barely touched the grass. With a wave, she dropped onto the blanket and smiled. She rather liked him cheeky and interested.

CHAPTER NINE

September 15, 1818

JOHN WHISTLED AS he and Caroline strolled through the village. They'd taken the outing to get away from Hadleigh Hall and also so that he could pick up a few gifts for her while they peered into shop windows.

However, his wife was apparently in a fragile mood, and she'd been exceedingly quiet up to this point.

"I must tell you how proud I am to have you on my arm," he mentioned as they'd paused at a dressmaker's window. "You're quite lovely in that shade of blue." The dress she'd chosen to wear today was of robin's egg blue and brought out the blue in her stormy eyes.

Caroline frowned. She huffed. "It is merely a dress."

Obviously, she wasn't in any sort of mood for compliments. "Shall I tell you some of the more ribald jokes I learned while in the navy?" As curious as she was regarding life, they would no doubt make her blush and laugh.

"No, thank you." She didn't look at him. Instead, she scowled at the gown hanging in the shop window. The peridot satin of the frock wasn't glorious enough for her, but if she desired it, he would snap it up.

He tugged on her hand. "Come inside with me."

"Why?" Finally, she turned those blue-gray eyes on him. Anger fought with despair in those mysterious depths, but why?

"I wish to buy you a gown, for I know how much you adore fancy dresses and pretty things." The image in his mind's eye of her in that sparkling pale gown she'd worn shortly before they'd married shimmered. Indeed, she was a woman who made clothing look spectacular.

"No."

That was it. A no. She hadn't offered an explanation or further commentary. Something was definitely amiss. This was the first time he'd come into contact with her stubborn streak. How interesting and another piece of the puzzle regarding his wife. "Consider it a wedding gift. From me to you."

She yanked her hand from his. "I need one don't."

Ah, she was upset. Caroline's words were jumbled or out of order more often when she was battling emotions. "I want to do this. For you. Because you're my wife and you deserve to be given things with no expectations." Perhaps afterward, they could find a quiet spot in the village to talk.

A huff of annoyance came from her. The glint in her eye gave him pause, and when she spoke, it was deliberate, which meant she didn't want her speech out of order. "If you wish for a gown so badly, Mr. Butler, then you go in and find one."

Well, she certainly had a backbone. John bit back the urge to grin lest she think he made jest of her. This was also a breakthrough, for she was finally relaxed enough in his company that she felt comfortable to show every side of herself over and above the politeness. "I truly only wish to offer you a gift, for I know how much you adore pretty things."

She merely blinked at him.

"All right." His shoulders drooped. "Will you wait for me here?"

"Yes." Caroline held up her reticule. "I have my sketchbook."

What he really wished to do was bundle her into his arms, hold her close and tell her that everything would be all right, that he would try to vanquish every demon that threatened her, even if it resided in her mind. The challenges she faced were more than simply removing her from the smothering clutches of her family, but if he could, he'd find the help she needed.

His detour into the dressmaker's shop lasted perhaps all of a half-hour, but the result was glorious. He didn't know much about women's clothing; he only knew that he desperately wanted to see Caroline in the silver satin gown. The sheer overskirt featured tiny spangles that sparkled each time the fabric moved, and some of them were shaped like crescent moons. It would pair nicely with her enamel pendant and perhaps she would smile at him as she'd done the day he'd coaxed her into the duck pond.

The dressmaker had spent a few minutes observing Caroline through the window to gauge her measurements and then finally proclaimed that she had what she needed, promising to see the gown delivered to Hadleigh Hall in a few days.

Once John joined his wife outside once more, she'd finished the sketch she worked on. He peered over her shoulder and frowned. Caroline had depicted herself on the page with her hair down and flowing, but instead of curls, the tresses had been portrayed as dozens of spinning storms. As was the skirting of the formal gown she wore in the drawing, spinning, spiraling storms. A tiara rested atop her head, the crescent moon pendant at her collarbones, but the expression she'd sketched portrayed deep disappointment and grief.

Why? What had occurred between the day at the pond when they'd shared that heated kiss and she'd looked at him as if he'd stepped from the pages of a storybook to now?

Gently, he touched her arm, hoping not to startle her. "The gown I purchased will arrive at the hall in a few days."

"You shouldn't have done that." Caroline closed the book and then stuffed it and her pencil into the reticule. "I don't need another gown."

"Perhaps not, but the purpose of gift-giving is to make another person happy because they *didn't* need whatever is being offered." He glanced at her bulging bag. "Why are you drawing yourself wrapped up in storms?"

She shrugged. "It is how I feel."

Fair enough, but there was something new there, a certain hopeless despair that hadn't been part of her mindset before. Not knowing what else to do while she was in such a mood, John offered her his arm. A sigh of relief left his throat when she slipped her fingers into his crooked elbow. As he led her along the street toward the village square, he racked his brain for a new topic of conversation. "Uh, Brand should arrive at Hadleigh Hall tomorrow." And if his business ventures were successful, they would spell good things for the shipping outfit, which meant John had a chance for a greater income to keep Caroline in style.

"Not alone anymore."

"I'm afraid not, but we'll have a jolly time with your cousin."

She wrenched her hand from his arm and took a few steps away from him. Her expression had become a thundercloud faintly reminiscent of her cousin Andrew's countenance when he was in a snit. "Spying on me."

"Of course not."

"You don't alone want to be with me." Her voice rose with each word.

A few people passing by cast them looks of concern. John attempted to mitigate the situation by giving them encouraging grins before he turned his full attention back to his wife. "That's not it at all." He lowered his voice to soothing tones. "Brand merely wants to help, to make sure you are happy in your marriage, with your choice."

And perhaps he'd report back to the earl, but that was beyond John's ken or caring.

"None of you believe I my own lemon I can live!" A cry of rage-tipped annoyance escaped her. "Life. My own *life*. I can live it." Tears sprang to her eyes, and before John could answer her, she stormed away, headed back in the direction that would eventually lead to the road where Hadleigh Hall waited.

Well, damn.

It wasn't a secret he hadn't a wealth of experience with women, but his wife was upset, and she wouldn't tell him why. It tore at his heart that she wouldn't trust him with her secrets. Had he not shown her he'd do anything for her? Perhaps this was how her mind worked. Did whatever she suffered from twist her thoughts and perceptions like her words sometimes were?

That was entirely possible. If so, and she was held in the throes of misinformation, then he had one hell of a wall to scale in order to access the truth of who she was, but he would try. Setting his top hat more securely on his head, he hurried after her. She moved quickly when angry, and he finally caught her up near the opposite end of the village.

"Caroline." He put a hand on her shoulder, halting her forward movement. Though her whole body stiffened, he gently encouraged her to turn about and face him. "Please tell me what's bothering you so I can make it better."

She snorted. A few tears fell to her cheeks. "You can't help my mind."

Those drops squeezed at his heart. "I realize that, but I can stay with you, and if you talk to me about it, I can more fully understand you, help you when times like this bedevil you."

For long moments, she merely stared at him, her eyes searching his, for what he had no idea, but he hoped to God she saw it in him. "Brand will tell me I'm wrong. That my marriage is not true. Just like the rest of them."

The rest of whom? Surely the whole of her family didn't feel that way. Had they told her that? Anger rose in a hot wave through his chest. Why couldn't the Stormes give him—and even her—the benefit of the doubt and let them forge their own path? "I am not them." For more of an emphasis, John took her hands in his. "Not them."

"But, you haven't..." She shook her head, clearly not wishing to finish the thought.

He held her gaze, hoping she saw the truth in his. "I married you to take you away from them and their overprotective smothering that clipped your wings." While rubbing the pads of his thumbs over her kid-covered knuckles, he continued, not caring that they stood in front of the village tavern or that people on the street stared. "Brand is a good man; my best friend in this world. He is like a brother to me where my own walked away from England and never looked back." Speaking that truth aloud left pain ricocheting through his chest. "He means no harm."

Sadness gathered in eyes made luminous with tears. "I'm your friend."

Was she jealous of how he spent his time? "Yes, but you are also my wife, which means you are better than a friend." What should he say that would unlock her reticence? "I want to make you happy." His voice wavered, for he'd believed so much that marriage would have fixed some of her problems. "Obviously, I'm failing you, and I'm heartily sorry."

Had his decision been too rash and now they were both trapped within a union that wouldn't work after all?

"You don't understand." Her chin trembled as did her hands in his.

"Then tell me why you're upset and running. Help me learn about you so I can do better."

A pink blush stained her cheeks. "Am I not a whole woman you look at when me?"

"What?" He hadn't expected that question. "When I look at you, I only see the woman I married, the woman I would do anything for. The woman who is stronger than she realizes. Whether your mind is broken is not relevant, for we will fight that together."

Another couple of tears fell to her cheeks. "You don't kiss me." When she tried to pull her hands from his, he held on tighter.

"We've shared two kisses." Any more than that and his control would strain, but he'd meant what he'd said. They wouldn't go forward if she didn't wish for a physical relationship.

She tossed her head. "Overheard servants in the corridor this morning. Outside my rooms."

Oh, God. "And?" His heartbeat quickened, for they were finally at the meat of her distress.

"Remember I don't their names." Her chin trembled again.

"Tell me what they said to upset you." Though he had absolutely no authority regarding household or staff matters at Hadleigh Hall, he would put a bug in the earl's ear about loose tongues.

"They said our marriage isn't real."

Hot annoyance stabbed through him. "How so?"

A cry escaped her. "That pitied me you." She took a breath to presumably calm herself. Moisture spiked her eyelashes as she peered up at him. "That there is no blood on the sheets and I'm still innocent." Her swallow was audible. "Not a real union."

Ah, *now* he understood. "Oh, Caroline." John released one of her hands in order to cup her cheek. He caught at the tears with his gloved thumb. "You and I agreed when we wed that this would be a marriage of convenience. Until you wanted it to change." His pulse accelerated. "It will remain that until *you* decide otherwise, for I don't wish to frighten you or push you into something you might not wish for." For he refused to bed her merely to slake his own lust. She had to be ready; she needed to want him.

A frown tugged at the corners of her mouth. "But..." She sighed. "You make me feel like... drowning when you are close."

That was certainly a step in the right direction. When he would have answered her, she continued.

"Do you want me as a wife?" Her blush deepened. "As a woman?"

Desire shot down his spine to lodge in his stones. "Dearest, of course I do. Couldn't you tell the day at the duck pond?" When she giggled, the tautness in his shoulders relaxed. "As much as I'm happy to kiss you senseless," he lowered his voice, for truly, discussing such things in a public place was beyond the pale, "touch you, caress you, gaze upon your naked body, it will lead to other things that might frighten you."

"I want that."

Those three words had the power to see him undone. He wanted to throw himself onto his knees at her feet and weep with joy, for she trusted him enough to at least let him closer. "I'm glad to hear that." His throat tightened from an excess of emotion.

She squeezed his fingers. "I want to see you like at the duck pond and… naked." The last word came sailing out on a barely audible whisper, but the despair that had previously been in her eyes had vanished. In its place was honesty and curiosity.

"I'm sure we can arrange that." She'd made such strides to-day, opened up to him, talked about her feelings and what bothered her, hinted at expectations within their union. Over-joyed, John laughed. He scooped her into his arms and then spun her about, right there on the public street. The trills of her laughter washed over him, let some of his doubts free. When he set her on her feet, he said, "I realize everything in life is difficult for you, perhaps even frightening. You haven't been accustomed to talking to anyone, let alone doing other more personal endeavors, but I want to know about you and how the world is for you." He peered into her face, hoping that sincerity reflected in his eyes. "Do you trust me with letting me in?"

"Yes." She nodded then a frown stole away her previous mirth. The determined tilt of her chin signified she'd gotten stuck on a particular point. "May I see you naked even if we are not in love?"

His chest tightened. It wouldn't do to rush his fences. Perhaps that would come in time. "We are married. There is no scandal in it." Though she wished to see him *sans* clothing, she'd made no mention of doing anything past that.

Patience, John. Give her time while you learn about her, understand her.

Caroline nodded. Her eyes brightened. "Now?"

"Right here on the street?" he couldn't resist teasing.

She shrugged, and to Caroline, everything was either there or it wasn't. "Yes?"

Another wave of heat washed over him. "Uh, how about as soon as we are back at Hadleigh Hall?" And God help him to survive.

A slow grin curved her lips, and all he wanted to do right in that moment was to kiss her. "Will there be tea?"

How adorable was she? Only his wife would want to enjoy tea while he apparently removed his clothes for her pleasure or study. Which he would gladly do. "Of course." Oh, Brand would laugh if he ever found out.

Her smile could rival the sun. "Good."

TRUE TO HIS word, John ordered tea. The apartment he'd been given upon arrival had a small dressing room that also functioned as a sitting room, so he had the repast delivered there. After all, there was no shame since they were married. If the butler looked askance at him, he ignored it, for Caroline was there as well. She'd perched upon the low sofa, and the green brocade upholstery contrasted nicely with the pink of her dress. The door to the adjoining bedchamber stood open, waiting, just as he was.

As soon as the butler departed, Caroline removed her gloves. They tumbled indiscriminately to the floor. Really, it had been a wonder she'd even donned them for their outing. Most times, she left them behind as irrelevant. She poured out a cup of tea for herself. John made certain the door to the corridor was locked. Then he did the same for the one in the bedchamber. When he returned, she'd stood, cup of tea in one hand and her sketchpad in the other.

His nerves suddenly felt as if they were strung too tight.

Which was odd, for he wasn't a green boy with no experience. There was something to be said about a woman who liked the looks of a man's form so much that she wished to draw him. "Uh, shall we adjourn to the other room?"

"Yes."

He let her precede him into that room. Never had he been asked to disrobe for inspection, but Caroline was different than most people. It didn't mean she was odd; it merely meant her mind dwelled in a higher place than others. "Would you feel more comfortable in that chair?" He indicated a straight-backed wooden chair nearby. "Or do you wish to sit on the bed?"

The four-poster bed was dressed with counterpane and curtains in the same shades of green found in the other room. Suddenly, the piece of furniture loomed large in the room. What happened by the end of the afternoon was anyone's guess, but he'd do whatever she asked.

"I shall stand first." After another sip of tea, Caroline set her cup on the bureau top. "You may begin."

Hardly an auspicious beginning to any sort of romantic overtures, but they had to start somewhere. And she *had* been receptive that day at the duck pond.

At his leisure, John tugged off his boots. They fell to the Aubusson carpet with two dull thuds. Socks followed. While she watched him, he kept his gaze focused on her. What went through her mind right now? Did she understand enough to become aroused? That remained to be seen, and if he could, he'd usher her closer to that point. She'd certainly been slightly that at the duck pond. Once he'd removed his gloves, cuffs, collar, and cravat, all of that fell to the floor at his feet.

"I assume you still wish me to remove at least part of my clothes?"

"Oh, yes." She turned to a fresh page in her sketchbook, the charcoal pencil waiting in her fingers. "Please."

He nodded. The struggle out of his jacket wasn't exactly noteworthy, but finally his arms were free of the tight-fitting garment. John tossed it to the foot of the bed. His fingers trembled as he worked the ties at the back of his waistcoat. *What is wrong with me?* Perhaps this afternoon's expectations were too high. What if he made a mistake and spooked her? Would she retreat back into herself, and they'd lose all headway? Shoving the thoughts from his mind, he removed the waistcoat and tossed it to the floor. Then he grabbed the hem of his lawn shirt. A few tugs had the garment up and off his body. He threw it to the bed.

"What would you have me do?" It was a tad awkward standing before his wife in such a state of undress for the specific purpose of her studying his body as if he were a statue at the British Museum, yet it was somewhat flattering at the same time. If that's what it took to arouse her, then so be it.

The scratch of her pencil over the paper filled the silence. Had she not heard him? But as she glanced between him and her drawing, a slight grin curved her lips. Was she... enjoying this? The little minx. Perhaps it wouldn't be such a leap to go from this point to eventually coupling. "Turn toward me."

"All right." He did as requested. More scratching of her pencil followed, and his nerves felt strung too tight again. "Do you, uh, wish to touch me?"

"Yes."

His shaft awoke. *Where* she'd like to touch him remained a mystery. "Sweeting?"

She showed him the drawing. The quickness of the sketch was a true testament to her talent, for he stood on that page exactly as he appeared in real life. "Details later. Now I want to fine tune through touch."

"Would you like me to undress you?" He had no idea how any of this would work, for his wife had never been around many people let alone men. Would she cry off at the last minute?

"Not yet." Caroline rested her sketchpad and pencil next to her teacup. Then she closed the distance between them. "Gorgeous. Like art." She placed her palms to his chest, and he inhaled sharply, for the heat of that innocent touch branded him.

"Such definition." Her fingertips danced over his skin, caressing, seeking, learning. When she leaned closer and pressed her lips to his left pectoral, he gasped.

It might not be intercourse, but her tentative exploration was just as erotic. Perhaps even more so. He stood as still as he could, not wishing to rush, not wanting to scare her. "Do you like how I feel?"

"Oh, yes." She raked her fingers through the mat of chest hair, and he thought he might expire right there as need shuddered through his body. Then her gaze fell to the tattoo of the North Star on his right pectoral. "Beautiful." She traced the artwork, the shading, and he trembled. Never had a woman been as apparently fascinated with his form as his wife was. When she ducked behind him and eased her fingers over the various scars he'd accumulated during his stint in the navy, he was nearly breathless from desire. "So many snores here."

"What?"

She giggled. "Stories."

That broke the tension. He chuckled and turned about, catching her in his arms, holding her between him and the bed. "I'd be happy to tell you of them at some other time."

"I would like that." Her eyes darkened to the hue of a storm over the sea. "Want to learn about you too." Again, she slid her hands up his chest and this time looped her arms about his shoulders. "Kiss me." It wasn't a question, and neither was it an order, but he fell beneath her spell all the same.

"Gladly." Then he lowered his head and claimed her lips with a string of kisses meant to tell her exactly how much he wanted her.

And he began to fall down that slippery slope where Caroline's heart hopefully waited.

CHAPTER TEN

CAROLINE GAVE HERSELF over to John's care with a soft sigh. She adored it when he kissed her; there was something unexplainable about the mystery of it, that two mouths when met produced the most amazing sensations.

And oh, the way his chest and upper body had felt beneath her fingertips! There was so much banked power there, such muscle and she hadn't been nearly done exploring. She wanted time to examine the tattoo on his chest in order to copy the exact artwork into her own.

While he moved over her lips, licking, sucking, nibbling as if he wished to memorize their shape, she furrowed her fingers through the hair at his nape. It was one of her favorite parts of him, along with his mouth, his chest, his ridged abdomen, his shoulders…

Pulling slightly away, she stared into his face with a smile. "I feel… different when with you I am. Lighter. Like singing."

"Good." That special grin of his returned. "Come." John hopped onto the bed and then made himself comfortable propped against a bevy of pillows. "Sit here with me." He patted the mattress at his left side. "I think it's time I showed you how titillating and powerful a simple touch can be."

Hiking up her skirting, Caroline climbed onto the bed and then crawled over to his position. "What now?"

"This." He leaned forward, put his hands on either side of her waist, and hauled her to him so that she reclined back against his chest between his splayed legs.

"Oh, dear." Trembles ran up and down her spine.

"Relax. You trust me, correct?"

"Yes." It was much different from when she was in the water with him in the pond. Now she was pressed intimately against him, sitting between his legs while he rested his large hands on her belly. Very nonthreatening but her senses were on alert. Anticipation and wariness prickled her skin. "This is…" Odd yet comforting. She'd never been so close to a man before and had certainly never been in such a position. While at the asylum, male doctors had given perfunctory examinations, and she'd touched her cousins' hands on occasion, but none of those interactions had made her feel as if she were preparing to jump off a precipice into the unknown.

"Yes?" His voice rumbled in her ear, tickling it, and provoking another set of tingles.

"It is… interesting." She skated her fingers along one of his forearms. So strong—protective. "You won't hurt me?"

"Never." His lips glanced along the side of her neck. "Tell me what you're feeling. Let me help you be more comfortable with me."

"I'm feeling frightened." It was honest. She concentrated on her next words so they wouldn't come out jumbled. "I wish I was brave, John. Like you." If she was, she wouldn't want to launch off the bed merely due to his proximity.

His chuckle sent butterflies awaking in her belly. "I am not brave."

"You are. You sailed. You were in the navy. Were hurt." She'd seen the various scars on his body. "I can never be that."

"Does being near me make you feel afraid?" He splayed the fingers of one hand over her torso just beneath her breasts.

Her heartbeat quickened. "Yes. No." She shivered. "I don't know."

"Then you must practice being brave a few minutes each day. After that, you might still feel fear, but you'll have the knowledge to conquer it."

She reveled in the sound of his voice as well as the nautical scent of him. "How?" If she had her druthers, he would read to her for hours and she could lose herself in his tone. Thus far, they'd walked the acreage and toured the manor. At the end of the day, she'd given into exhaustion and slept.

John shrugged. "Do one thing that frightens you. Every day."

"Everything frightens me." Even sitting here more or less surrounded by his big presence. What if she came to rely on him too much and he left? What if he discovered he'd made a mistake by marrying her?

"Such gammon." He closed his lips on her earlobe and chuckled when she squeaked. "You have been doing brave things since we married. Hell, going through with the vows started that change." Slowly, he eased his hands up her arms leaving gooseflesh in his wake. "You went into the pond with me. You've let me kiss you. And lastly, you practically ordered me to strip down and touch you."

Caroline couldn't help her smile even if the feel of his hands on her shoulders made her slightly breathless. "You were brave too. Believed I was worth nose hairs."

"I beg your pardon?" He hooked his thumbs beneath her neckline near her collarbones.

Merciful heavens! "I meant notice." Drat, but it was difficult enough to concentrate without his particular brand of distraction.

"You are. Never doubt it." He pressed his lips to a spot beneath her jaw and when he nibbled on the skin there, she shivered with unexpected delight. Then, bit by bit, John tugged at the bodice of her dress. He slid the whole upper portion down, down, down, along her arms until her breasts were bared.

"John?" Confusion and fear were evident to her own ears in that one-word inquiry.

"If at any time you grow too uncomfortable, bid me nay and

I'll cease."

What did one do with one's hands at a time like this? Caroline trembled, as much from excitement as anything else. "All right."

"Good." Again, his lips glanced over the side of her neck. She turned her head and he kissed her, softly brushed those two wonderous pieces of flesh to hers. Just as the customary fuzziness seeped into her head as it always did when they kissed, he cupped those big hands to her breasts.

"Oh!" She bolted upright and smacked the top of her head on his chin. "Ow!"

"Shh! It's foreplay, not torture." But immediately, he removed his hands from her person. A chuckle followed that rippled over her skin. "Well, I suppose it *is* akin to torture. It just depends on the perspective."

Caroline rubbed the top of her head. She twisted around to look into his face. "You surprised me."

"I apologize. I assumed you knew what would inevitably occur when I lowered your bodice, for women don't go around with clothing agape." When she huffed, he laughed, and she reveled in the uplifting sound. "Shall we try again?"

"Yes." Once more, she settled her back to the hard wall of his chest. "Will it hurt?"

"Not that I'm aware." When he cupped her breasts again, Caroline flinched but she told herself to relax. He would never harm her, and she *had* asked him for more intimacy. Instead, she concentrated on what he did to her, how it made her feel.

"I knew you'd be just as gorgeous as your smile." The steady, comforting buzz of his whisper in her ear worked to set her at ease.

"I… I…" She didn't know what to say, so she didn't bother with talking. Perhaps it wasn't needed. "Oh!"

With baby fine caresses, John drew ever widening circles around each breast. His touch was as delicate as an angel's wing, yet it left her with longing and an ache she couldn't explain. Then he switched directions and made the circles smaller, moving toward her tightening nipples.

"Still with me?"

"Yes." How was it possible that his touch on that part of her could energize her so much? Then he brushed his fingertips over the tip of her nipples, and she gasped. Wild sensation streaked through her body. When he strummed those fingers on the sensitized buds, she couldn't help but gasp her approval. The feelings were like music—crashing, breaking, dancing over her, threatening to suck her under. "John, I… I…"

"Do you enjoy that?" Amusement wove through his voice.

She squirmed from his attentions, unable to summon words even if she'd tried. Not knowing what to expect, Caroline put a hand over one of his, guiding him to where she needed him to be, and when he continued to rub his fingers up and down over her nipples, a moan escaped her. Her back arched and she pressed his hands more firmly to her breasts.

Her husband took the hint, only this time he changed his approached slightly. When next he cupped her breasts, he caught both tips between his fingers and gave them a tender squeeze. Electric fire jumped from her bosoms to between her thighs. Then he eased off, soothing the puckered buds with sweet caresses before rolling them between his thumbs and forefingers.

Foreign pressure built low in her belly. What it meant, she didn't know, but John was the only one who had the key. "You make me feel like painting, like music, like magic."

"Then I'm doing it right." He shifted positions, and instead of her being between his legs, he settled her onto her back while he lay on his side pressed against her. Caroline's head rested on one of his arms. "Shall I explore further?"

"There's more?" What she wouldn't give to kiss his jawline where that shadow of stubble clung so heroically. Would it feel rough or thrilling against her lips?

"My dear girl, there is so much more." While he maintained eye contact with her, he slid his free hand down her torso, smoothing it over her belly and then gathered a handful of her skirting. "Do you want me to show you?"

The glide of her dress along her legs heightened the sensations he'd already given her. "Yes." Need propelled the word. What else could there possibly be? Never once had her mother or sister talked candidly about relations between men and women, and she was grossly inexperienced. Except when Isobel referred to him being large… somewhere.

"If it's too intense—"

"John." She huffed in exasperation. "Continue." The waft of cool air on her bared legs caught her off guard.

He kissed her, drank from her as if he couldn't have enough, and while he sent her senses reeling, he caressed her inner thigh. Warmth washed over her; the callouses on his hands brought a sharp poignancy to his work. All too soon, those talented fingers drifted through the curls between her thighs. Immediately, she clamped them closed, but the man chuckled and lifted his head. "I won't hurt you, Caroline. In fact, this will bring you pleasure."

More than he'd already given? Both curiosity and fright played her spine, but she slowly opened her legs. "What will you—"

He eased his fingers along her private flesh. A gasp left her throat, followed by a groan, for with each pass of those digits, moisture gathered on those folds. Did he find that off-putting? Why was it happening at all? Then her thoughts scattered for his fingers edged upward, found the hidden part of herself she wasn't aware existed. Hot sensation coursed through her body. Tiny fires lit in her blood. Once more her back arched but she didn't know why.

The need and longing he'd evoked when he'd played at her breasts intensified. She trembled, gasped, and as he bedeviled the tiny button, she would swear she was drowning, but not in the water. In him, from him. His presence surrounded her, crashed over her, caught her up in it like a swelling wave.

"John!" She pulled his hand away as fright crept through the cracks where pleasure didn't flow.

"What scares you?" he asked in a soft voice. "Your feelings or what I'm doing to you?"

"I know don't." Trembles racked her body.

"Shh. This is why we're going slow." He kissed her again, tenderly moving his mouth over hers as if she were as delicate as a porcelain figurine.

Slowly, she guided his hand back with a sigh. The second he strummed his fingers over her button, she moaned, for the feelings were so exquisite. Tears leaked from the corners of her eyes to wet her cheeks. Over and over and *over* again, he caressed that little nubbin, which left her gasping and bucking her hips into his hand. He was magical in what he did, and he evoked the same in her until she feared she wouldn't survive it.

"When you feel as if you can't bear the pressure any longer, that's when you'll fall over the edge," he whispered while he pulled and plucked, tweaked and rubbed.

Caroline didn't know what that meant. How could one fall over an edge when one was lying on a bed? Barely had she thought about his words when a wave of indiscernible bliss rushed through her body. It tingled along her skin, pushed through every nerve ending and prickled every point in between. Contractions rocked deep in her core, and she cried out, completely ignorant of what was happening. She only knew that the touch of his hand had sent her… flying.

She sagged in his hold, exhausted and limp. "What… what was that? What you did?"

His chuckle held a satisfied edge. "Sent you over the edge. It's called finding release or hitting orgasm, and when someone has been sufficiently aroused enough, those feelings break over them, making them feel a brief euphoria."

"I rather liked it," she admitted and turned onto her side toward him. "Amazing." Too overwhelmed by what happened, Caroline gave into the urge and let tears fall down her cheeks.

"Shh. It's all right, and that's a perfectly acceptable reaction." John gathered her close, wrapped his arms around her. He dropped a kiss to her forehead. "I'm glad I could make you feel something other than anger."

"Me too." For a few moments, she buried her face into the crook of his shoulder while she softly cried. Eventually, she came back to herself and kissed his shoulder. "Thank you."

"You're welcome." Strain wove through his voice. "There is so much more."

Another tremble went down her spine. "I can't survive more."

He eased away enough so he could meet her eyes. "Ever?" Concern creased his brow.

Oh, how was it possible he was becoming so dear? "No. Only today." She forced a swallow into her dry throat. "It's too much, too big. I need to think about it."

"I understand." Though he nodded, a flash of disappointment pooled in those golden-brown depths.

Would she ever be ready? She didn't know. "It was nice." Caroline shifted her position, and her knee went into the soft flesh between his legs.

John groaned. "Give me a few moments for things to settle. Then we'll finish tea."

That didn't sound fair somehow. For all the pleasure he'd given her today, she should return the favor. Caroline struggled into a sitting position. She tugged her bodice back into place while running her gaze over the bulge straining the front of his breeches. "Can I touch you?"

"Yes, but beware, love, I'm teetering on the edge."

She gasped. Did that mean she could send him over like he did her?

"Caroline." He took her hand, tugging her slightly toward him until she met his gaze. "I promise I won't bed you until you're ready."

"I know." When she reached for his front falls, he anticipated her and quickly freed the buttons from their holes. "Go gently else I'll explode. I only have so much control."

"It's… amazing." She'd never seen anything quite like his member. He was so large. A tentative touch to the appendage revealed it to be both soft and hard at the same time, and so hot! Glancing her fingers along the wrinkled skin of the shaft, she marveled. "It is alive." When she rubbed her fingers over the wide head, a bead of moisture seeped from the slit. "You're so… big." Eventually, he would try to put… *that* inside her. She felt her eyes widen. Surely it wouldn't fit. Something akin to panic welled in her chest, made her heart pound with fright. How would any of that work?

"Yes, well, some of us are." His voice was graveled, a true testament to the strain he was under while she explored, but at least the words scattered her thoughts. "Here." He took her hand, showed her how to wrap her fingers around his shaft and then how to stroke him. "This will bring me pleasure."

"How wonderous." He was hot in her palm, and silky soft. Each time she pumped her curled hand up and down his arousal, the tool grew slightly thicker, fatter, harder.

"Caroline…"

Even more surprising, when she did that to him and he responded with groans of approval, the longing for that elusive something returned to throb deep inside her own body.

"Oh, God!" With a strangled moan, John scrabbled over the counterpane. He grabbed up his discarded shirt and quickly clutched it over himself, but his expression reflected much the same bliss that she'd felt when he'd played at her button. For a few seconds, he was lost to her. When he came back to himself, a flush colored his neck and cheeks. "My apologies."

"For what?" She peeked at the shirt, but when she went to tug at the garment, he batted her hand away. "Did you find release?"

"Yes, and I'm like a university boy, coming in my shirt like that. In front of my wife."

She smiled. He was so funny. "Might I see?"

"Not right now. It's messy." While she watched, John wiped

at the ejaculation, and after he'd thrown the shirt to the floor, he quickly did up the buttons of his front falls. All too soon, his glorious member—now flagging—was hidden from view. "Would you like tea?"

"Yes, but might we lay together for a bit?" She'd rather enjoyed being that close to him. "I like your arms around me."

His grin released butterflies in her low belly and stirred the restless feeling that coiled like a hungry serpent. "We can certainly do that. He lay down, stretching out on his side, and when Caroline snuggled into him with her backside to his front, she sighed when he wrapped her in the protective circle of his arms.

This day had easily been the best one of her life.

CHAPTER ELEVEN

September 16, 1818

JOHN STARTED WHEN a decorative pillow came hurtling across the space and smacked into his chest. He'd forgotten Brand was in the drawing room with him, so deep into thought had he fallen. "What was that for?" Grabbing the pillow, he sent it back, but his friend dodged the projectile.

"You're woolgathering." Brand, with no regard or respect for furniture, had propped his booted feet on the low table between his sofa and the chair where John sat. "And I'm bored. I thought that when I arrived, you would have welcomed me with open arms."

"My apologies. There is much on my mind." His gaze jogged to the windows. "Caroline is outside in the garden painting. If you wish to speak with her, I can call her in." Truth be known, he was glad his wife was outside, for the more time she lingered in his company, the more desire grew for her. Especially after that intimate session they'd shared yesterday afternoon when she'd surprised the hell out of him with her innocent explorations and the simple joy she'd found when he'd send her flying.

"Leave her. We'll go fetch my cousin in a bit. Perhaps show her the Hadleigh hedge maze. She might find that interesting." He cast a speaking glance John's way. "Unless you've already taken her through."

"No. In fact, I haven't taken her at all."

Well, hell's bells. He hadn't meant to say that nor reveal quite so much about his personal life, even to Brand. Though the man was his best friend and closer than a brother, matters between him and Caroline should remain secret.

"What's this?" Brand slammed his feet to the floor, leaned forward, and then rested his forearms on his knees. His hands dangled between his legs. "I was under the impression that you and my cousin had a marriage of convenience."

Heat seeped up the back of John's neck. "We do. Still have, actually."

The captain's eye narrowed. "Then why do you look both satisfied with life and alternately frustrated?"

John rubbed his eyes with his fingers. "It's complicated."

"Not as complicated as my convoluted courtship was with Elizabeth, I'll wager." Brand leaned back and propped an ankle on a knee. "What's been happening since the wedding?"

"Caroline and I have spent copious amounts of time together. Talking. Well, mostly I talk. She does upon occasion." John allowed a small grin, for his wife was quite intelligent. "She paints nearly every day, especially when the days are fine."

Brand snorted. "Is that all? Sounds dull."

"On the contrary, I'm grateful for this reprieve from daily life. She's wonderfully talented. Little by little, she's coming to trust me more. Occasionally, she'll talk about herself, but not often and not much." He sighed. "One day we took a dip into a duck pond."

"Caroline willingly let you put her into the water?" Brand shook his head. "By all things holy on land and sea, I'm impressed you managed to draw her out of her room to do anything with you."

"The only reason she stuck close to her room with you Stormes was the fact that none of you took the time to truly understand her. The family never wished to connect with her in a way that her mind could make sense of." A wash of anger went through him, for Caroline could have been farther along in being comfortable with others had the Stormes not mucked it up. "However, she's still not told me anything personal about herself or her history beyond bits and pieces."

"I'll admit, I don't know much about her myself." Brand held up a hand when John would have inserted censure. "And yes, what you've said is true. We Stormes, as a collective, have been horrid toward Caroline. It started with her father, but we allowed it to continue long after his death." Remorse shadowed his face. "And when Drew stepped in, he did it with his usual grace of a bull rampaging through a glass shop. Once he had Caroline in his house, I'm not certain he knew what to do with her."

"She still carries much anger toward her family." When she wasn't looking, he'd spied it in her eyes. Hell, she'd even admitted as much.

"It's understandable, I suppose. If I had been locked away for near twenty years, removed from everything I'd ever known, I'd be livid too." Brand met his gaze. "I can't imagine how she survived, to be honest."

"Neither can I," John agreed in a soft voice. "The more I come to know her, the more amazing she is. She's resilient, strong, but isn't afraid to laugh if the occasion demands." He snorted. "And, by Jove, she's the most stubborn woman I've ever met."

"Well, she *is* a Storme."

"True." John shoved a hand through his hair. "In any event, she enjoyed being in the water after her initial fright faded. I'm hoping that during our stay at Hadleigh Hall, I can teach her to swim."

A wicked twinkle appeared in Brand's eye. "Is that the only thing you want to teach her?"

The flush returned, pushing the heat into his face. "It is not. However, we've shared a few kisses." His best friend didn't need to know that he'd caressed Caroline, had touched parts of her best left between husband and wife. The sounds she'd made when he'd introduced her to pleasure, the way she fought fear with bravery when he'd put his hand between her legs continued to tug at his heartstrings.

"Oh?" Brand's eyebrows rose with surprise. "Did she enjoy the kisses? In my experience, she doesn't like to be touched let alone get close enough to another person to allow kissing."

"At first she was wary." The remembrance of the kiss he'd given her in the traveling coach popped into his head. Awareness for her swept over his skin. "But they seem to be growing on her. In fact," he chuckled for he would never forget how she'd rounded on him in the village yesterday, "she's been rather vocal about me not kissing her enough. Since we're married, you see. Caroline is rather a stickler when it comes to everything in its place and the meaning of various things."

Brand gawked. "That's interesting." He shook his head with a smirk. "Have you bedded her yet?"

"That is hardly any of your business."

"Listen to you! In the past, every woman was fair game, regardless of whether she was with you or me. I told you everything that went on between Elizabeth and me."

"Did you though?" John narrowed his eyes on his best friend. "I rather think you kept the good parts—the special parts—to yourself."

It was Brand's turn to suffer a flush of embarrassment. "Of course you're right." But he wouldn't leave the topic alone. "Yet you haven't had relations with your wife."

"No. Not really." John heaved out a breath that seemed to come from his toes. "For the time being, we are learning about each other, and I'm discovering how to interact with her in a way she can understand. She's never been around men, never had a Season, never has had the freedom to explore who is she and where she fits in with the world, so I'm going slow. I don't want to shock her, send her retreating further into herself where her mind might play tricks with her."

"Damn, John, you're a good man. Better than me, I'll wager,

but then I've always thought that."

He shrugged. "Perhaps. Caroline is my wife. She's not someone I'll trifle with for a while and then leave. Our marriage is for a lifetime, and it's my hope we'll eventually share a deep and profound connection." The admission surprised him. Where had it come from? His future certainly wasn't settled, and he had no idea how to keep Caroline in the style to which she'd become accustomed but being with her in any capacity right now was enough. "However, that doesn't negate the fact the desire I have is without an outlet. Yes, it's a tad frustrating, and I can admit I've walked the acreage more than a few times with a raging cockstand, but that's better than frightening her back into her shell."

"Sometimes women vex the hell out of us." Brand snickered. "I appreciate that you offered for her. No other man would have been right for her, and I know you'll treat her well, regardless of where your union goes." Brand remained silent for long moments. "Damn, but I miss Elizabeth and the baby." Longing filled his expression. "I hated to leave them so soon after the birth, but it couldn't be helped. Potential investors into the shipping business mean so much to our fledgling enterprise."

"Will you return to Ipswich soon?"

"I would like to, after my stint here is finished. Business in London has concluded. We've secured enough backing to purchase another sloop. That alone will expand our reach and allow for more clients."

"That's wonderful news." John grinned. "It'll provide a steady income for us all."

"Indeed." Brand leaned forward again and met his gaze. "You were worried about providing a life for Caroline." It wasn't a question.

"Yes. A man can't be married while still renting bachelor rooms at an inn." A wave of homesickness smacked into his chest. "Damn but I miss Ipswich. I miss the sea, the harbor, fishing, the unhurried lifestyle. London isn't as welcoming to me."

"Then why haven't you made inroads into leaving?"

John blew out a breath. "My first priority is to Caroline. I don't want to move her until our marriage is a bit more stable, until she's sure."

"Of the union or you?"

"I don't know." It was a question he asked himself all the time. He'd thought with the intimacy they shared yesterday that he might see a marked improvement, but his wife had been reticent this morning over the breakfast table. Had she not enjoyed herself? Or conversely, had the excess of feelings turned her against anything further between them? "Caroline remains an enigma to me, a challenge I'm not certain I have the wherewithal to undertake." He pressed his lips together as he thought about his next words. "She won't let me past her defenses. Much of that is no doubt due to her time in the asylum, but I worry it's me."

"You've taken the initiative. Perhaps it's time to do more."

"Like?"

"Do the same first. Open up to her about *your* life. Caroline has lived a different existence from us. I can't imagine what she's still feeling." Brand shook his head. "Show her you need her."

The new way of looking at him sent a thrill of excitement down his spine. "I *do* need her." John launched to his feet as a bout of restlessness suddenly took hold. "I married her so that she could be free, but I have a feeling she's doing the same for me, little by little." Heat infused his face. "I look forward to seeing how we'll grow together."

"If I didn't know better, I'd say you've already started that fall, my friend."

"I don't know about that." Yet he couldn't deny he wished already to be wherever she was. "She's a brilliant painter. I'd like to give her the space for a studio if we can find a cottage we both like in Ipswich."

Brand beamed as he stood. "Perhaps she'll get on with Elizabeth."

"We won't know until we try." Though Caroline had a sister,

regretfully, she wasn't close with Isobel. Granted, Isobel was a hoyden that even her brother couldn't handle. Still, John would like his wife to have a friend. He glanced out the windows once more. "Let's collect Caroline and take her to the maze. I'll wager her mind is sharp enough to zero in on the heart without instruction."

"And I'll wager I can make it to the center before the two of you, even though I've not been there since childhood." With a mischievous light in his eye, Brand darted from the room by way of the terrace doors.

"Prepare for disappointment, Captain!" John ran out after him. "Caroline! Caroline, we're going to the maze!" He tore down the few steps, nearly on Brand's heels. When they crashed into the garden, his wife yanked her head up from contemplation of the canvas on the easel. "I've a wager with Brand that we'll make it to the heart first." Reckless in his enthusiasm, John tugged her hand and brought her to her feet.

"I've not been there. In years."

"All the more reason to go together."

"But—" She squealed when he scooped her up into his arms and dropped her paintbrush to the grass below. "What are you about?"

"Encouraging you to remember." Damn but she felt good—right—in his hold, and when she clutched his shoulders, he grinned. "We can't let your cocky cousin win."

Brand laughed at that. "I have the advantage over you."

"We shall see." Spurred onward by Caroline's giggles, John increased his pace.

Soon enough, they reached the entrance to the hedge maze, which could be seen from the portrait gallery on one of the upper floors of the hall.

"All right, Mrs. Butler, I've never been inside this maze, but you have."

"Not for years. I was a young giraffe."

He snorted with laughter. "A girl, then?"

"Yes." She sobered. "It was a long time ago."

"Perhaps, but knowing you, you've often thought of this maze, built it into a storybook fantasy with you waiting in the middle, waiting for rescue." That was a certainty, and it was an endearing trait about her. When her blush confirmed his suspicions, he grinned. "It's in your mind, somewhere beneath all the history and disappointments you knew at the asylum. Just let them come to the surface."

"Win what you do if find you the heart?"

"Bragging rights and the knowledge that I—we—will have beat a Storme at his own game."

"You wish, Butler." Brand pulled ahead of them slightly.

Caroline hugged John's neck. Her lips were nearly at his ear when she whispered, "First left, then left, and next right."

"Thank you." Easily, he jogged along the gravel strewn pathway.

Brand remained two steps in the lead. "Nice try." They kept pace at the next left turn. Then he crowed with victory when he shot ahead and went left again. "Good luck!"

John met Caroline's eyes with a grin. "We won't tell him he's going far afield." He took the right-hand pathway. The pungent scents of pine and growing things assailed his nostrils. "Where next?"

His wife closed her eyes. "Right, right, left."

He hefted her more comfortably into his arms but followed her instructions closely. It still didn't put them in the heart of the maze. "Do you remember anything else?"

"Yes. Never forget anything." Her grin was brilliant as she opened her eyes and peered into his face. "Two lefts. One more right. Then you'll find it."

"You, my girl, are amazing." And she was continually surprising him. He went left, skirted around a few fallen branches, took another left on the path, tripped over an exposed root in the ground, and finally went right... directly into the heart of the maze.

Rose bushes grew in a clustered riot within a circle. A few stone benches done in the Greek style were arranged about that central circle. A fountain rested nearby. Moss covered one side of it, and a few inches of water were contained in the weathered basin. An equally worn statue of the goddess Aphrodite rose from the fountain's bowl.

"We did it!" John released Caroline enough so her feet could touch the ground. "*You* did it!" He held her head between his hands and grinned. "The next time someone tells you that your mind is broken, remember this day, sweeting. There is nothing wrong with you; you merely think differently from the rest of us, and your capacity for memorization is astounding."

Her eyes rounded with wonder. "Truly?"

"Yes. Together, we will pull you out of the maze of your mind. I promise. If not to rescue you from it then to live with it in a way that makes you happy and proud." Then, because he could, John touched his lips to hers. When she uttered a shuddering sigh against his mouth, he took her into his arms and sought to give her a more proper kiss. She melted into him, snaking her arms about his shoulders, and for the first time, she tentatively kissed him back, mimicking what he did to her, until he was breathless with awe and his shaft was tight with desire.

The sound of branches snapping preceded the arrival of Brand, who crashed through the shrubbery seconds later. He brushed leaves and evergreen needles from his clothing and then came to a halt in front of them. "I must say, usually I don't enjoy spying on a couple's private moments, but it does my heart good to see this."

John held Caroline a bit away from him. He didn't care that his grin might look as goofy as it felt. "Well, she *is* my wife." And never had he been as delighted to say that as he was right now.

A pretty brush stained her cheeks. "We won, Cousin Brand."

"So you did." He closed the distance between them, tugged her away from John, and gave her a gentle hug. She stiffened at the outset but then relaxed enough to let him continue. "I'm proud of you."

John couldn't stop beaming. Perhaps healing didn't rely solely on him to unlock years of anger from Caroline's soul. It merely started with acceptance from her family. "So, then, I can assume that bragging to Hadleigh about Caroline's intelligence is in order?"

"I wouldn't mind that at all." Brand bussed her cheek before releasing her. "In the interim, let's return to the hall and order a lavish tea. I'm quite famished after this unexpected exercise."

Caroline nodded with enthusiasm. "With honey cakes!"

"Absolutely! All sorts of sweets." Brand linked his arm with hers, and dear God, she let him, didn't pull away. "Keep pace, Johnny boy, else my cousin and I shall leave you lost in the maze this time."

His chuckle and Caroline's laughter rang in John's ears. Yes, they were all progressing well. The kernel of hope in his chest broke open and bloomed with a few baby leaves. No matter the outcome of his marriage, his wife would no doubt find peace at the end.

And that was the most important development of all.

CHAPTER TWELVE

September 18, 1818

Caroline tilted her head back. Sunlight filtering through the leaves of the oak tree she sat beneath warmed her face. The slight breeze cooled her skin, and since she was only clad in her shift, the contrast in temperatures was glorious. For long years while stuck in the asylum, she'd yearned for such freedom as she had now, to go about in the fresh air and sunshine with nary a care in the world.

Today, John had decided to take her to a different pond. It was bigger than the duck pond from the other day, and he aimed to teach her how to swim. She didn't particularly want to, but he had a stubborn streak, and swimming was apparently something he adored doing.

For now, she was content enough to paint him within the landscape. The acreage surrounding Hadleigh Hall was nothing less than spectacular. Beauty peered back at her from all directions. From the rolling hills dotted with late season wildflowers to the bits of forested areas to the fields turning golden in anticipation of the coming harvest, everywhere she looked delighted her artistic soul. The blue green of the pond's water contrasted nicely with the flower-strewn meadow beyond.

And of course, her husband once more featured heavily in her rendition.

She smiled as he propelled himself through the water, as acclimated to it as if he'd been born a fish instead of a man. The more time she spent with him, the more that tingling awareness for him came over her. Their last kiss in the Hadleigh maze had surprised her, but it had also chipped away at some of the defenses she'd erected about her heart as protection from being hurt. To see him so exuberant that afternoon, so whimsical and funny as he'd raced through the maze against Brand with her in his arms had called her own sense of humor to the forefront.

That big bear of a man possessed such gentleness and earnestness that it sometimes brought tears to her eyes. Had she never met him last December, she would even now still be hiding in her room in London, languishing beneath her cousin's best intentions.

But he *was* here, and they were married besides. What was more surprising, she enjoyed sharing kisses with him, and though the more intimate touches frightened her with sensations too overwhelming to process, there was a certain craving inside of her for more of that. She wished to know what true relations between men and women consisted of, what it would feel like when John pressed his large form atop hers, when he would put his manhood inside her…

Heat seeped into her cheeks. Such thoughts were naughty, but they'd bedeviled her more frequently since that day in his rooms. Especially when he insisted on swimming if the day was hot. A splash in the water wrenched her from the musings, and instead of focusing on her canvas, she watched her husband as he came out of the water.

"Merciful heavens, he is quite a work of art." The rustling leaves overhead disbursed her whispered words, and she continued to stare. Again clad in breeches—brown today—and nothing else, the sun and shadows showed his form to perfection. Water plastered his blond hair to his head, and when he raked his fingers through it, slicking it backward out of his eyes, a tremble went down her spine. Rivulets of water, more evident as he came closer, followed each other along the muscled girth of his chest; some glittered as they clung fleetingly to the tattoo on his right pectoral. That lightly golden tanned skin beckoned, and her fingers itched to chase those water droplets. "Grow tired I'll never seeing you be." She didn't care that her words were out of order. He always understood.

"It's nice to have a lady admire me." John shook himself as if he were a dog. Water droplets flew everywhere. A few landed upon her canvas, smudging the paint. "You promised to come in the water with me."

"I will." Caroline dabbed at the drops with paint-stained fingertips. "I was…" Oh, what was that long, interesting word for lost in thought? "Ah, woolgathering. Thinking."

"About?"

"You." She had never been good at dissembling or playing coy. Those were things Isobel excelled at, but Caroline found no point or purpose in.

"That's always good to know." He took possession of one of her hands and brought it to his lips then kissed the back of her wrist where her pulse hammered wildly. "If you continue to paint me in various stages of undress, we'll soon be the talk of society. There are only so many places we can hang your paintings before folks wish to drop by to view the scandalous gallery."

Though the whisper-soft touch of his lips as he dragged them up the inside of her arm was highly distracting, she frowned. "Should I stop painting you?"

"Absolutely not." At the bend of her elbow, he drew the tip of his tongue over her skin. When she shivered, he chuckled. The sound sent need between her thighs with memories of his fingers on that part of her the afternoon he'd sent her flying. "If painting me makes you happy, by all means continue. We shall find room for the canvases."

"All right." She breathed a short sigh of relief when he released her arm in favor of picking up the sketchbook she'd dropped at her feet. Surging to her feet, she attempted to snatch the book from his hand. "Private."

"You always show me your drawings." He held the book out of reach while wrapping his other wet arm around her waist and pulling her against him. "What about this one don't you want me to see?"

His warmth and proximity temporarily distracted her, but she huffed. "It's me."

"Let's have a look and you can explain the reasoning behind it." John settled upon the tree stump she'd used as a seat then encouraged her to sit on his lap.

Caroline frowned. She tapped the sketch with a finger when all she wanted to do was draw her touch along the breadth of his shoulders, explore the tattoo on his chest, possibly lick at some of the clinging droplets of water. Did women do that to men? At the moment, it sounded like a fine idea. "This is me." She pointed to the drawing she'd done of herself last night when she couldn't sleep. "See? Blue gown."

"You are quite the portrait artist, even when doing yourself." The praise in his voice was unmistakable. The bulk of the paper had been given over to a large, twisting storm. "Why are you holding the tail of this storm in your hand?"

"Promise you won't make jest?"

"Of course I won't."

She nodded. "The storm represents…" What exactly did it mean now that she had to explain it aloud? "It means the chaos in my mind all the time."

"Why are you holding it?"

"When you are near me, when you are here," she waved a hand to represent the general world she lived in, "I feel I can contemplate that chaos." No, that wasn't right. She bit her bottom lip as she delved into her mind for the correct word. "I can *conquer* it. That what is inside my brain," she touched her forehead, "and my heart," she laid her fingers over that organ, "is not as frightening as it is when I am alone."

Would he think her too needy, too odd?

"I'm glad I can bring you some peace." He dropped the sketchbook to the grass and then pressed his lips to her temple. "However, you can make further sense of the storms inside you if you talk about those feelings that you see as chaos."

She turned more fully toward him, ran her fingers lightly through the mat of damp hair on his chest. "Don't like talking." Saying words aloud meant the chance to look a fool, to not be able to articulate what she felt, which inevitably led to more frustration.

"I understand." John wrapped his arms around her and cuddled her close to this chest with her hands resting against him. "Neither do I, but sometimes in life, talking is the only way others can truly understand. When we hear concerns out loud, see those emotions reflected in your eyes, we can help sort them, explain them, or perhaps merely commiserate with you."

Though it made sense, the need to share loomed like a frightening shadow. "If I talk to you, I'll grow angry."

"Possibly, or equally possible, those feelings of anger will bubble up to the surface so you can look at them, acknowledge them, and then toss them away to make room for other, more pleasant memories." His chuckle warmed her ear. "It sounds strange, I know, but I've seen enough of life to realize if we keep things deep down inside, it will eat us alive, turn us into beasts we don't like."

"Even you?" She couldn't imagine him as anything but the kind, gentle soul that he was.

"Even me, sweeting." The words were soft, a fleeting string of sound. "I have things that fester within my soul that pick at the edges, that concern me sometimes so much I can't sleep. And even though Brand is my best friend, since we quit the navy, there haven't been opportunities to talk in-depth to him. Especially now that he's sorted his own life."

"That's sad."

"It's how things go, I'm afraid."

Caroline pulled away enough so that she could peer into his eyes. Those dear golden-brown pools with green flecks that always seemed to beckon her into another world. "I'll listen."

"I appreciate that." He tangled a hand in her flowing hair, gently pulling to further tilt her head back. "I promise to share with you sometime soon."

"Could you do something for me?"

When his gaze dropped to her mouth, frissons of excitement played through her nerve endings. "Anything."

How was it possible to feel both terrified and excited at the same time, merely from being close to her husband? "Will you find me a peacock?"

He blinked. Confusion shadowed his face. "I beg your pardon?"

Drat her mind! Caroline shook her head. "I mean a pianoforte." She nodded in the event that he didn't understand. "I… I wish to play music. For you. To tell you in notes what I feel." It was easier that way, and in music, she never had to worry if they would come out jumbled or wrong. Music just… was. It flowed through her like water, set her free in a way that talking never could.

Would he be able to understand her through it?

"I shall endeavor to do my best. I'll even enlist Brand's help. He is more knowledgeable about the manor than I am."

Relief shuddered through her chest. "Thank you."

"You are more than welcome. In the meanwhile, you are coming swimming with me." A twinkle danced in his eyes that captivated her. "But first, I'm going to kiss you, because you are so bewitching right now, and I can only fight with my control for so long."

"Yes?" Oh, how she wanted him to do that!

"Ah, Caroline, you remain a bright spot in a cloudy day." Then he lowered his mouth to hers in a kiss that sent heat pinwheeling through her chest.

Like the kiss they shared at the heart of the maze, she mirrored everything he did to her. Finally, she didn't feel so much like a novice at this showing affection business. When she traced his bottom lip with her tongue and he uttered a soft moan, need curled through her lower belly. Those sounds went straight into her blood to light tiny fires there. She moved her hands up his chest, and wanting to be further connected to him, she held his head between her palms as she kissed him with growing abandon. The second he swept his tongue inside her mouth to fence with hers, heat infused her body.

Oh, she needed so much more from him but couldn't think of the words to tell him that.

It didn't matter, for he understood her as he always did. John shifted her slightly so he could deepen the kiss while he skated his hands up and down her back. Caroline's eyes fluttered closed as she moved over his mouth, nipped at its corners, delighted in the slight prickle of his stubble against her skin, for he only shaved if the notion took him.

And still she wanted him.

"John?"

"Mmm?" He dragged his lips along the column of her throat.

"I…" What? What was it exactly she felt? This tingling tension that slammed through her limbs as if her nerves were strung too tight. "I like… this. Us. Together." It wasn't what she wanted to say, but it was good enough for the moment.

When she looked at him, he grinned, but his eyes had darkened, appeared more green now than brown. The same need was reflected in those depths. "I do too." He kissed her once more. "And if my dratted best friend wasn't due to join us for swimming imminently, I would perhaps cajole you to join me in the meadow there to show you how much."

"Oh!" Did that mean he would finally let her see him naked? She traced his tattoo with a forefinger then dared to lean in and lick the skin there, collecting the last few droplets of water on her tongue. The earthy tastes of water and man came away on her palate. "Is he on his way?"

"I don't doubt it. When I left to come out here, he was finishing a couple of letters. And he adores swimming, especially when the day is as warm as today."

"Then later again will kiss me you?" She was beyond caring about her out-of-order words, for in his arms, they didn't matter.

"Of that you can be certain."

"Good." A thrill moved through her insides to lodge between her thighs. "You like swimming."

"I do." He resumed his quest to nibble his way down the column of her throat.

Caroline shivered. His touch and attention were slowly hardening her nipples. Her breasts ached with need, perhaps his mouth on them. "As much as kissing?" Did she sound like a simpleton asking all these questions on a subject she had no knowledge about?

"My girl, I will always enjoy kissing you better than anything life has to offer." And then he pressed his lips to hers in a series of feather-weighted kisses that made her think of faraway castles and knights in shining armor.

"John?"

"Yes?" His breath steamed the shell of her ear. That part of him which was so large and alive that afternoon he'd made her fly was hard against her hip.

"Pick me up in your arms."

"Why?" His perfect mouth curved downward in a frown.

"Makes me feel pretty, like a princess in a book." She swept her fingers over his tattoo then down his chest. "Protected." When she met his gaze, she tumbled into those depths with a sigh. "Safe." For the moment, the chaos inside her mind quieted to a dull roar. The tension in her chest eased. This man had changed everything when he'd come along.

Did he realize how much she appreciated that? How grateful she was for him?

"It would be my honor." He hooked one arm beneath her knees and wrapped the other about her back as he stood up from the tree stump. "Would my lady enjoy a toss into the pond?"

Tendrils of fear seeped into the thin cocoon she'd woven around herself while in his company. "Will you be there too?"

"You have my word that I'll never leave you." His expression sobered. "And for as long as you need me, I will always come to your rescue."

He was everything perfect in a world that oftentimes didn't make sense or seemed a difficult challenge. With tears in her eyes, she nodded and then buried her head against his shoulder so he wouldn't see her weakness. "Will I like it?"

"That remains to be seen." Humor wove through his voice, and he tightened his hold on her as he carried her toward the pond.

"Later, will we go to the sea?"

"Ipswich?" He nodded. "I would like that very much, but only when you're ready."

It sounded like an adventure. "Will we swim there?"

"If you wish it."

Caroline nodded. "With you." She glanced at the water with its concentric circular ripples from where a duck bobbed his head beneath the surface. "And perhaps Cousin Brand. He has been nice to me."

"He's trying, dear heart. Give your family time. Let Brand show them how."

Despite the glorious afternoon she'd already passed with John, the slow simmer of anger in the pit of her belly flared. "They don't care."

"Perhaps they can't find the words to express how they feel. Just like you." He paused at the edge of the pond. "But don't count them out yet. Before we leave for Ipswich, perhaps they can figure out how to build a bridge between you and them. But if that doesn't happen, remember you are a Storme, Caroline. You need the approval of no one in order to clear your own path."

"I am trying to figure out how to be me." The words were

slow and precise, yet her anger receded to a point. "Now I am not alone."

"You are not." His eyes shone with emotion she couldn't read let alone understand. "Ready to learn how to swim?"

"Yes."

"Here we go." The muscles in his arms tightened and then suddenly she was weightless, arcing into the air, flying briefly over the pond's surface before she hit the water and sank beneath with a half-terrified scream.

But she shouldn't have worried. John was there not a second behind. He wrapped her in his arms and pulled her upward into the sunlight, holding her dripping self to his chest as if she were the most fragile flower.

"Now that you've gotten your head and feet wet, let's begin to expand your horizons, hmm?"

Caroline lost a piece of her heart to him in that moment. Though she knew he would fight fiercely for her, he also wanted her to do that for herself as well. He didn't think her incapable; he merely encouraged her to do things her own way. There was no coddling or suffocating her, no doing things for her on the assumption she'd couldn't figure them out for herself. In that, there was an independence she'd never known before, and it threatened to render her drunk on it.

And oh, how she wanted to discover everything about him, to help him as he was her. Then perhaps he wouldn't feel so angry either.

CHAPTER THIRTEEN

September 20, 1818

JOHN COULDN'T SLEEP. No matter that he'd spent the past half hour listening to the steady patter of rain against the windows, slumber remained elusive, all because he couldn't stop thinking about his wife.

Two days ago, she'd taken to swimming as if she'd been born to it. They'd amused themselves with lessons until Brand had joined them, whereupon he and Brand had set out to tease her with good natured humor. Afterward, while they'd lounged in the sun, she'd redressed and resumed her sketches. No doubt her cousin featured into one of them, for that seemed to be one outlet she had for expressing her feelings without talking.

Yesterday, it had rained for the bulk of the day, so they'd attempted to teach her whist, but that had proved her Waterloo. However her brain worked, it didn't allow concentration on the cards. She'd become overwrought and embarrassed, fleeing upstairs to her room, and had refused to come out. Only with the promises of reading to her from some of her favorite books after dinner did he coax her downstairs. That's when she curled up on a sofa in the drawing room and picked at the tray of food the butler had brought to her.

And today had featured more of the same miserable weather.

Brand had slept most of the time, and when he wasn't, he'd gone in search of a pianoforte. Once secured, transferring the instrument to the drawing room had become a two-person affair, and it had needed tuning badly. John had gone to the village to see if he could find a craftsman for the job. Caroline had remained in her room, and he feared the progress they'd previously made had unraveled.

Which brought him back to the present, with the rain drumming on the window glass and the ache of missing her sitting heavy on his chest. Never would he have thought he'd marry so soon. Nor had he expected to become quite so enamored of Caroline as he was. She was easily one of his favorite people; she lit up a room when she walked in. At least she did for him. There was an otherworldly quality about her, sure, but the talent she possessed for painting couldn't be kept a secret. The London *ton* needed to know about her skill, and if that won her a career or commissions, he wanted her to pursue that.

If she wished it. As of yet, she hadn't really said what she wanted for her life over and above feeling safe while in his company.

Or enjoying the act of kissing. His wife had found a certain affinity for that. So much so that if he weren't careful, he'd end up spending in his pants due to a loss of control. She might not be ready for intercourse, but damn. All too often he was hard for her, and it would require an outlet.

Soon.

Why would it not stop raining?

Frustrated on many fronts, John turned over yet again. Not even punching his pillow could help him settle. If he helped Caroline to calm, she had energized him, made him feel more alive than he ever had before. So why the hell was he here instead of with her right now?

He swung his legs over the side of his bed. If he were to visit her in the middle of the night, would the invasion of privacy frighten her? It was worth the risk. They were married, after all.

No one could say it was scandalous. After pulling on a pair of breeches, John sneaked from his room, being sure to close the door behind him. Hoping to God Brand wasn't restless this night either, he crept along the corridor, past his best friend's room, past the three doors that separated that room from Caroline's. At her door, he knocked softly, pressed the latch, and gently pushed open the door. A shiver of relief went down his spine, for she hadn't locked it.

"Caroline?" The whisper sounded overly loud in the silence. Shadows played about the darkened room, but the rustling of the bedclothes betrayed the fact his wife wasn't tucked into dreamland. "Are you awake?"

"John?" She propped herself up on an elbow as he approached the bed. "What are you doing here? Are you unwell?"

"I couldn't sleep, but I'm fine." This was a dangerous prospect, being here in her room, with him randy as hell, and her probably warm and soft and tousled. "Do you mind if I lie next to you for a while?"

"All right." Sleep had rendered her voice smoky, and the sound went straight to his stones. She scooted over. "Do you not like the rain for sleeping?"

Oh, he enjoyed doing a host of things while it rained, but it remained to be seen what would transpire this night. "I'm too restless for slumber." Not daring to believe this boon, John slipped beneath the top sheet, and the moment his body came to rest next to hers, pressure bedeviled his length.

Bloody hell.

"Why?"

Why indeed? He tucked his hands behind his head to prevent idle wandering, but her pillows smelled like the fields full of daisies they had walked through since arriving at Hadleigh Hall, and each time the scent wafted to his nose, it drove him a little closer to madness. "I'm not sure," he finally answered as he watched the play of shadows and raindrops dance over the ceiling.

She snuggled into his side with a palm resting on his bare chest. Awareness of her plowed into him with all the force of a runaway pony cart. "I couldn't sleep either." When she blew out a breath, it tickled his skin. "My mind is too busy."

"I can't even imagine." John tamped hard on his control, for it would be all too easy to roll her over and begin the process of seducing her. "Perhaps I can tell you a bit about my life." At least in that way, he could focus on his stories instead of her and how the nightgown of silk and lace would hardly prove a barrier between them.

"I would like that." She moved her hand to his tattoo. "Start with this."

He grinned into the darkness. "This happened a few years before I met Brand." The abstract circles she drew on his skin both lulled him into a state of calm as well as enhanced the desire he had for her. "The ship I served on tarried in an American port. I'd been drunk at the time, and some of my friends wagered me that I wouldn't go through with it." When her hand drifted to the center of his chest, he laid one of his on top to prevent further exploration lest he shoot his wad right then. "In the end, the small, simple tattoo I wanted became this work of art."

"Does it have special meaning?"

"Aye." While rubbing the pad of his thumb over her knuckles, he encountered her rings, and a sense of pride filled him. This extraordinary woman was legally his and would remain by his side for the rest of his life. If he was fortunate. There was a certain comfort in that. "At least this is something decent in the way of artwork. It's the North Star. That point in the heavens has always been a guide for sailors the world over. It's one of the brightest stars in the sky, and is said that it will always lead a man home."

"Is that true?"

"Who can say? There are many ways to chart the stars and steer a ship." He heaved out a sigh. It was rather nice being in the same bed as her, talking in the dark. "As for me, I believe the best thing that steers a man home is what tugs at his heart. And a man can call anywhere home, not necessarily where family lies."

"Where does your heart lead?"

"Back then, there was no particular place. I loved the sea more than almost anything. It still whispers through my blood every so often." He draped his other arm about her hip. The warmth of her seeped through her thin night dress. "Then I met Brand, and we enjoyed a few more years in the navy. He became my best friend. Incidentally, I saved his life."

"What?" She pushed off his chest, but it was too dark in the room to read the emotions in her eyes. The living waterfall of her hair tumbled over her shoulder, fragrant, soft, tempting. "How?"

"The scar on my left side is a result of that fight." It had been a long time indeed since he'd talked about that day. "We'd been boarded by a French vessel during one of the lesser-known battles of the war. Hand to hand combat ensued. Brand lost his footing, for it was raining and the deck was slick. When he went down, his opponent came at him with a cutlass drawn." His chest tightened with the remembrance, and not only because her hand still pressed upon him. "I'd disposed of the man I fought. When I glanced up and saw Brand in peril, I didn't think. Just sprang into action, sprinted across the decking, and took the blow meant for him. It caught me in the side, and though I was injured, I'd prevented his death."

"Oh, John. That must have pained you."

"It did. Hurt like the devil for a few weeks, earned me a few stitches in places, but it was well worth it, for my best friend lives to this day. That's when he declared me closer than a brother." He frowned, for there was wetness on his chest, and it took a few moments to realize Caroline had been silently crying during his tale. "Sweeting, it's all right. I'm healed and your cousin is hale and hearty."

"He was away… for the years I'd been in the asylum." She sniffled. "He didn't know about me; I didn't know the danger he was in." Another sniff echoed in the silence. "We are the same." How odd it was that her words came easy and in the correct order as if she weren't upset or stressed. Did that mean she felt no attraction to him whatsoever?

John forcefully shoved that thought away. "Perhaps." He hadn't thought of it that way. Yet she was thinking beyond the small boundaries she'd previously set for herself. That was growth, and he hoarded it to his heart. "Now you are both living your lives to the best of your abilities."

"And we have you."

"I suppose." If he'd not met Brand, he would never have known that Caroline existed, and that would have been a tragedy.

"Cousin Brand is nice. He's funny."

"Indeed he is." John hoped the remainder of her family would make inroads into befriending her. "Do you wish to learn more about me?"

"Yes." She laid her head on his chest, her body nearly plastered against his. It was all he could do to draw a breath that wouldn't jostle his painfully tightening prick. "You fascinate me."

Yes, but in what way?

Perhaps it didn't matter. "My father was the reason I left home."

"He is not a nice man." Her whispered words tickled the hair on his chest. The muscles in his stomach clenched.

"No, he's not." There was no point in trying to say that he had been at one point, because he'd never been kind or nurturing. Hell, he'd never shown an interest in him or Mark unless it was to use them as an outlet for his bitterness, jealousy, or anger. "When I was a young man, I couldn't stand life at home any longer. I lied about my age and joined the navy. For years, I knocked about the world, saw more than a few battles. It was a good life."

"Were you lonely?" Her fingers drifted lazily along his abdomen, leaving acute need behind.

"Yes and no. I had my friends onboard the various ships I sailed upon, and when I wished for female company, it wasn't hard to find in the larger ports, but I hadn't anyone I trusted enough to talk with." He clenched his teeth against the sensations of exquisite torture she unknowingly inflicted on him. "Until the year I met Brand. He took me under his wing. We grew into the men we are together."

I miss those days.

"Why hate your father do you?"

Once more, he stilled her fingers on his person, for his shaft was hard enough to prove embarrassing if she explored further south. "He has run his title into the ground, has no regard for honorable living. So much debt has been piled atop the barony I rather doubt two generations can dig their way out."

A tiny intake of breath betrayed her understanding. "You will be a baron."

"Unfortunately, yes. I can't escape that fate." As much as it went against everything he believed in. "It will ruin my life." John blew out a frustrated breath. "I never wanted it, or anything do with the *ton*."

Yet the fact remained that he would be the next Baron of Westfield. Of course, he could simply refuse to take up the title or touch the money—if there was even any left by the time his father popped off. Yes, he would still be the title's holder, but if he were never confirmed before Parliament, he wouldn't have the full title and honors to ensure he was the correct heir.

And still, the anger his father as well as the situation fostered swept through his chest in an ever-present tide. *Why must I choose? Why can I not ignore it, renounce it, pass it to Mark and be done with it?* "Perhaps I won't claim the title or call myself baron." In that way, the title would remain in place and at his disposal should he ever change his mind, but right now, his heart and soul lay in Ipswich, in the fishing village he called home, where he'd begun to put together a simple life he could be proud of, far away from the aristocracy. "I don't even need to send in a writ of summons to the House of Lords." However, someone must care for the Surrey property as well as the London holdings. Long ago, he'd made general inquiries on what a man could do if he didn't wish to assume a title. "Should you and I have a male child, all of it can be held for him."

Damn, he hadn't meant to mention starting a family or introduce talk of the future tonight, but the words couldn't be recalled.

"You aren't happy in London."

"No, I am not."

"Your father makes you angry."

"He does. The man has failed in every way as a gentleman." Those long-ago beatings had taken a toll on John, and the wounds ran deep. How could he tell his wife that she needed to square with her past if he couldn't do the same? "Promise me that should we have children, if I grow angry with them, you will not let me beat them. I refuse to give them a life lived in fear and disrespect like I had."

Why did the subject keep surfacing? Is that where he saw his life going with Caroline? Did he want a house full of young ones, perhaps with her brilliant eyes and talents as well as her grin and hair? Then his next thought chilled his blood. Would whatever it was that affected her mind pass to their offspring? Is that why she was so reticent to discuss the future?

To say nothing of the fact that if he did claim the title, Caroline would be Lady Westfield. Was it fair to thrust her into the light of the *ton* where scrutiny would be upon her whenever they went out into society?

She means too much to me. I can't do it.

"You are *not* him, John." She turned her head and pressed her lips to his chest. "Never will you be the same as him. Your heart is good, not rotten."

Small comfort, that. The baron's blood flowed in his veins. "How is that even though I've forgiven him long ago for what he did, those times still haunt me? When every time I see that man, the old anger wells up and I want to land him a facer? He has learned nothing." He fairly spat out the word. "The man is a plague."

Caroline was silent, but he appreciated her presence.

"Every day that he lives, he's doing more damage to the title.

Hell, he doesn't care what Mark or I do in our lives. Never will we have his approval."

"Do actually need it you?" She must have grown upset on his behalf if her words were out of order.

John thought about that. With a sigh, he put his arms around her. "No. I don't." And he should always keep that in perspective. "I have friends, a life I adore in Ipswich. I have Brand and his friendship that has meant so much." He dropped a kiss to her forehead. "Now I have you." Some of the stuck anger eased beneath his breastbone. "If we want beautiful things around us, we must actively keep the horrid ones at bay."

"You are beautiful to me. Your soul shines out to mine." She entwined her hands about his neck. "When you make that decision, I will support you because I am your wife." Though the words were slow and deliberate, the meaning behind them was unmistakable.

"Aw, Caroline, whatever did I do right in my life to deserve you?" With unmistakable tears in his eyes, John urged her onto her back and then claimed her lips in a series of tender kisses. Every day that went by brought him a new understanding—a new appreciation—for this mysterious, troubled woman he'd taken to wife. The drama that was his family didn't seem as frightening when she was there, for in her he had the belief that everything would come out right in the end.

Eventually, she planted a palm on his chest and shoved at him until he'd levered off her. "Your presence consumes me." Her words were breathless. "I am drowning in you."

"Is that a good thing?" Hot damn, but if he couldn't couple with her soon, he'd go out of his mind with need. Did men die of unattended erections?

"Yes." When he dipped his head to kiss her again, she held him off. "I'm frightened of what comes now."

The admission was as effective as being struck in the face with a bucket of icy water, but he lost a piece of his heart to her in that moment. "There is no need to be. I'll go gentle, slow, give you time to acclimate."

She shook her head and prodded him fully off her body. "Need more time."

"I understand." Oh, he understood, but damn it was growing more difficult to let her come to him, trust him enough, and the responsibility of that staggered him, humbled him.

A sound suspiciously like a stifled sob issued from her. How much had it cost for her to deny a coupling? For that matter, what the devil were her thoughts telling her? Did her mind hold that much sway on her actions? "Stay here tonight, with me?"

"Of course." It was more than he'd had thus far, and he wasn't a complete nodcock to throw that away. "Would you like me to hold you until you fall asleep?" It would strain his already tenuous clamp on control, but what wouldn't he do for Caroline?

"Yes." The bedclothes rustled as she turned onto her side, presenting him with her back.

"Just remember, sweeting, you have nothing to fear from me. I will always be here protecting you, keeping out the demons." He resituated himself so that he spooned her, holding her safe in his arms while his shaft strained to the point of pain. "I'll wait for as long as you need."

Because, after all, he was becoming rather fond of his wife, and there was a lifetime ahead to continue that fall.

CHAPTER FOURTEEN

September 21, 1818

I T HAD BEEN a day and a half since John had crept into her bed and shared a little about his life. A day and a half since her heart had broken over the situation with his father and the title he didn't want. A day and a half since she'd known she wanted to be a real wife to him in every way a woman could, yet she couldn't move past the fear that held her captive.

Those feelings stemmed directly from her time at the asylum where, again and again, she'd set out hopes in her mind, let them build up, and when they didn't materialize, the disappointment was extremely crushing. Depression and anger would usually follow, rendering her "difficult" and "insane" to the staff at the asylum because she didn't understand how to voice her emotions or even live with them.

Eventually, she'd stopped dreaming, stopped hoping... until the day Cousin Andrew came and took her from that horrid place.

Until she met John on that snowy road, when he'd shown her the first real kindness she'd ever had, shown her what being a hero meant.

And now, due to all of that and being married, her mind was lost in a morass of confusion and emotions she didn't understand, a longing for something she had no idea how to ask for, feelings that stemmed for her husband and grew each time he was near.

"Caroline!"

John's call yanked her from her musings, and she looked up from the drawing she had just finished. It was of two people, both depicted as storms, one designed as a man and the other as a woman in a ballgown, and they were waltzing about an opulently decorated room. It was her intent to do a series of drawings showing how, over the course of the dance, in each other's arms, they became more like themselves instead of the storms inside them.

He burst into the morning room with that cheeky grin she adored so much. "There you are. I've been searching all over." With no less enthusiasm, he bounded over the floor and then scooped up her hand. She dropped the sketchbook as he tugged her into a standing position. "It's finally ready."

"What is?"

"Your pianoforte." John threaded their fingers together. "Brand and I wrestled it into the drawing room and then we had to wait for the fellow to come and tune it, but finally, it's ready for you." The excitement in his voice transferred to her.

A thrill shot down her spine. "I can play music?"

Oh, how she'd missed it!

"Absolutely, you can, and I can't wait to hear it. Brand says you used to be a musical prodigy when he was a little boy."

Warmth filled her cheeks. "Notes come easy to me." She only had to look at a piece of sheet music, play through it once, before it was imprinted upon her brain. Each time she played one, different emotions seeped into her renditions. No performance was the same.

"What you put into the world gives it depth, where many people only remain shallow." He pulled her along the corridors until they arrived at the drawing room. Brand stood near a pianoforte. His grin was as wide as John's. "Look. There it is. We even located some various sheet music in the attics. It might be outdated, but you probably don't mind that."

Caroline drifted closer to the instrument. For so long she'd been without a way to express herself through music that tears sprang to her eyes at this boon. She glanced first at John and then at Brand. "You did this. For me?"

"Yes." Brand nodded as if his head were on marionette strings. "Do you like it?"

She looked again at the pianoforte and then to John. "I feel… happy." Over the course of their association, everything he'd done had been to bring her to this point. Was she worth so much to him, then? It was staggering to ponder.

"Good!" He led her to the bench with the green brocade cushion. The colors had faded over time, and the stuffing was rather lumpy in spots, but she sat because he was so enthusiastic. "If you wish to play now, Brand and I will be your willing audience."

"Yes, I'll play." Caroline rested her fingers upon the keys. There was no dust on the keyboard, which meant it had been protected by a cover. The relative coolness of the ivory was reassuring.

"Marvelous!" John patted her shoulder. Then he and Brand moved a bit away to slip into matching chairs. Anticipation lined their faces.

With excitement riding up and down her spine, she shuffled through the yellowing sheet music. All the pieces she'd seen before, and as soon as she read the titles, the music popped into her head as if she'd never been away from the instrument before.

Seconds later, she struck the first notes of her selected piece, and the familiar light notes of the music filled the air. Caroline gasped with delight and pleasure; the sounds embraced her like long lost friends. The last time she'd played had been a few weeks before she'd been uprooted from her life and deposited in the asylum. More than ever, she was convinced she'd been born to produce lovely things that brought joy to others. At least in this she excelled.

Midway through the piece, something inside her broke and the sea of emotions she'd had no choice but to hold back all her life came rushing to the forefront. They were overwhelming enough to cause a sharp pain in her chest. Her fingers briefly stumbled over the keys, but she was helpless to stem the tide.

"When I was first sent to the asylum, I thought it a lark." She kept her eyes closed as she continued to play the music. It allowed her to concentrate more fully on her words, putting them into proper order. "Stupid, naïve I was. Didn't know it was forever."

"Caroline, you don't need to share if you don't wish it." John's deep voice rumbled through the room. Fabric rustling and the faint squeak of a spring betrayed that he'd stood up from his chair.

"Have to else these emotions will suffocate me." Her fingers flew over the keys as she built toward a crescendo. "My family abandoned me. Left me at a strange place, strange people." She pressed the keys with more force than strictly necessary. "Didn't love me anymore."

"I'm certain they still love you, deep down." John's voice sounded from behind her. When he lightly touched her shoulder, she flinched, and her eyes flew open.

"How is true that? They didn't come." And she'd remained there, trapped.

Brand sprang up from his chair. "We didn't know where you'd gone." He quickly crossed the floor and once at the pianoforte, he leaned against it. Concern lined his expression. "No one told us anything about your absence. When Drew asked, our father shouted us from the room."

"Tried harder you could have!" Oh, she hated when she got upset, for the words had more of a chance at tripping over themselves. "I was afraid, alone, confused."

"I didn't know!" Brand shoved a hand through his hair. "But as soon as I did, as soon as Drew brought you home, when I met you at that Christmastide house party, I've been racking my brain of how I can make it up to you."

Her heart trembled a tiny bit. "But that was long ago."

"I realize that, and I have no excuse. Life happened. The navy consumed me. I met Elizabeth. Started a shipping outfit, but all I can say is that I'm here now, and if John moves you to Ipswich, I fully intend to get to know you better." Nothing but earnestness reflected on his face. "So we can be the cousins we were cheated out of being by our parents."

"That sounds lovely." She nodded even as her fingers continued to press the right combination of keys. "What about Andrew?"

"What about him? He can go to the devil for all I care. I'm done towing the Storme line." He leaned over until he was back in her line of vision. "Forgive me?"

For a few seconds, she pounded away on the keys, building up into the next crescendo in the piece. Once she crested it and the melody slowed, Caroline nodded again. "Yes."

Brand exchanged a speaking glance with John, who gestured toward the door with his chin.

"Perhaps you should leave us alone for a bit," he asked of her cousin. "It's obvious Caroline is upset. I'd like to help her reach the turning point she's sorely needed for a while."

"Will I see you both at dinner?"

"Of course." John waved him off. "Go write your wife a letter." Finally, her cousin left the room, and her husband returned to stand near the pianoforte. "You seem to have more on your mind that you wish to speak into the air."

She nodded but continued to play. "Yes. I am very angry with my family. They left me." Tears stung the backs of her eyelids.

"But that's not what I'm going to do." When she didn't know how to answer him because the churning emotions in her chest roared loud, he went on. "It's sometimes helpful to understand your perception is nothing but pain from the past discoloring your view of your life now."

"How?" Caroline frowned.

"All those old feelings cloud your mind, make you pretend that you still see them."

"But I feel them *now*."

"I understand, for I fight with them too, but we can't let them win. The past is not your present nor your future. If I must remember that, so do you." He patted her shoulder, let his fingers drift along her nape. Tingles swept through in his wake. "Drop all those dead emotions that aren't doing anything for you. You're safe now. You aren't trapped and forgotten any longer. Those old stories you keep fighting with? Those chapters have closed. There is a whole new book to step into that's filled with light and amazing things."

Caroline shook her head. "My future, though settled, is still confusing."

"That's as to be expected."

"I am fearful." Her playing grew more and more frantic. No longer did the keys soothe or the music calm. All the emotions in her chest twisted with the notes to create a violent storm she couldn't outrun. "You want children; have talked of having them. What if they are as broken in the mind as me? How can we do that to them?"

"Sweeting, you are *not* broken. Neither are you insane. Don't put stock in anything people say. Pity is just as destructive as an ugly soul."

That made sense on some level, but it didn't help slide the puzzle pieces into place. Her mind reeled and whispered to her that no one loved her. It was all a joke. "After the asylum, after Cousin Andrew, I dreamed of being free."

"You are. Do you not feel that way? That was the purpose in marrying. So you could find out who you were away from the Stormes, away from all that brought you pain." Confusion reflected in his golden-brown eyes, and she wanted to cry, for it was her who made him feel that.

"I am here, with you," she said slowly, not wanting her words jumbled. "But I'm *waiting*. Any day I fear you will discover I am a fraud, a pretend woman and wife, that I am truly mad. That I can do nothing but paint and play music. I've trapped you." The reality of that tightened her chest. It had never been her intent to pull him down into her world.

"That isn't true at all." John's deep voice seemed to fill the space around her, and that only brought her closer to riding that angry wave. "You are *not* a fraud, Caroline, but I hope you'll change your way of thinking. This way no longer serves you."

Why couldn't he understand? "You will never love me! Don't you see? Joke already we are to servants who laugh. No one has ever loved me." She slammed her hands onto the keys, uncaring when a discordant noise echoed in the room.

"I am *not* your family." A touch of anger had entered his voice, but he breathed deeply and let it out. "Even now, I… I'm learning to see you for who you are and who you are becoming." His tone had modulated. "Already I'm quite fond of you." The warmth in his voice stood as a testament to that fact.

And it made her all the more confused. "But not as a man is to a woman, a husband to a wife. We are not real."

He shoved a hand through his hair. "You know this marriage is based on what you want it to be. When you're comfortable we can—"

"You never asked me what I wanted. No one does." She whirled around on the bench to face him. *Dear Lord*, he was a tall man, and all she ever wished for was to burrow into his arms and let him fight her demons. "Everyone assumes I am unfit to live my live. That's why you married me. To pluck me from it. To give me another that you dictate." Hot anger surged through her veins. The more she talked, the more she believed it. "I am tired of it."

"Caroline, listen to me. Your mind is playing tricks." A trace of panic clouded his eyes. "Your cousin Finn suffers from depression. It isn't outside the realm of possibility you would too. But I didn't marry you because I thought you incapable or in need of a nursemaid. I married you because I knew your potential was such that it only needed someone to believe and a touch a match to your flame in order to launch you into the life you've always dreamed of. Never once have I imposed restrictions upon you or given you orders on what you should do."

That was true. He had been nothing but kind and patient, had given her the freedom he claimed. "Oh, I..." It was too noisy inside her head that she pressed her hands over her ears for a few seconds. Perhaps she wasn't like what those insidious thoughts said. "I am like a storm, John, and you came in anyway despite the risk."

"You aren't that, and even if you were, I'd brave it. For you."

She couldn't listen anymore, didn't deserve his kindness, for if she let herself, she'd be swept away in his presence, and be quite happy to do so. A different kind of prison or the freedom he'd offered? "But you said you don't care for the rain, and I feel like a hurricane most times." With a poorly stifled cry, she ran from the room. "Too different we are."

Would he ever see her as a complete woman, a woman with a functioning mind who didn't need to be looked after all the time? Would he see her as his wife, fully capable of all that the position entailed? Oh, some of this confusion was of her own making. How to find her way out?

That she could love him and know what that meant? It had been her fault, her reticence, that kept him from her bed, but now? She needed him that way.

But...

A gasp left her, and each breath hurt to draw. *Did* she love him? It was so difficult to know what was real and what she'd made up in her head to escape from what life was. As she ran and ran and ran through the manor with no destination, she acknowledged that it had felt cathartic to get angry and start verbalizing that emotion to be rid of it.

Her husband finally tracked her to an unused parlor on the opposite side of the manor. Dust covers lay over most of the furniture, but it was cozy and quiet and felt safe.

"Caroline, may I come in?"

She wasn't ready to concede defeat and return to her normal routine of not talking or hiding in her room. At this point in her life, she had grown tired of being ignored by the bulk of the people she knew, of being overlooked, or cast aside, of having to make sense of things she didn't fully understand. In some ways, she was beginning to crave the presence of other people, or at least the ones she felt comfortable with. "I suppose."

Yet John wasn't like all the others. Why couldn't her mind recognize that truth?

When he entered and closed the door behind him, she shivered, for being alone with him made her feel as if magic were about to happen.

"When we married, I thought you knew our pacing was slow so it wouldn't frighten you." He approached cautiously, lightly, as if unsure of his reception.

"I did." Were her emotions as jumbled as her words? Why couldn't she ever make sense of anything without twisting it? "I want you to take me seriously. I want to explore everything I can in life without people pitying me."

"Then focus your energy on those of us who don't."

That was fair. "And I want you to see me as a woman you're proud of." Then because she couldn't hold back the oncoming tide of emotion, she burst into tears and threw herself into his waiting arms. "I want so much more out of life than I've been given, and I want... I want..." She huffed and beat her fists against his chest. "I want feel to happiness like what, the happiness I knew when you gave me the pianoforte."

His chuckle sent tingles down her spine. "There's no reason you can't. Embrace the good, sweeting."

For long moments, she sobbed out her concerns and fears. "I feel alone. Even with you. I am too messy in my head. My thoughts don't quiet. I am too much for you."

"Never." Though he made soothing noises, he didn't attempt to stem her ire. "Take out your frustrations on me if you must, love. After the storm abates, I'll help you pick up the pieces, assemble them into something beautiful."

She wiped her runny nose on his cravat. When he didn't berate her or show disgust or lecture, she lost a piece of her heart to him. "Already beautiful am I."

"Yes, you are." The dear man removed his collar in order to unknot his cravat and then unwind it from around his neck. "Use it how you will," he said as he handed it to her. When she did, he grinned, and flutters filled her belly. "I'm beginning to see just how beautiful you are, like a sunset over the sea, as the sky is painted with multiple colors, each greater and more glorious than the previous one."

The words sank through the cloud of confusion. They brought a new awareness of him to her, one that she gasped at from its depth and strength. Slowly, her tears stopped as she mopped her face with the length of fine linen that carried his scent. "I am a ninny." John had been her support since Christmastide. He'd truly given her the world and her freedom the day he'd proposed. When no one else would take a chance on her, John had stood in the gap with an outstretched hand, asking nothing of her except her trust.

He'd beat back the storm, fought it for the chance to be with her. Was fighting it now because she was the same. She owed it to them both to do the same.

To fight. To be brave.

"You are not."

"I am." She nodded. "Because you saw me, rescued me." There was awe in her voice that filtered to her ears. "It has always been you, but I refused to believe it. My mind, said it was false."

"I do my best." He shrugged, clearly wishing to downplay her statement.

Caroline rushed to continue. It was important she tell him everything that sat on her heart. "You chose me. No guarantee of the future you wanted." As if some of the chains binding her to her past fell away, she stared at him with a new respect and very different feelings than she'd previously battled. "I have been too afraid to see… you." Her swallow was audible. "To see you and me together, but now…"

"Yes?" Such hope rode in that one-word question and sat in his eyes that shivers of anticipation went down her spine. "But now…" The cravat slipped from her fingers. She held his head between her palms and stared into his eyes. "Now I am not going to hide behind fear. I am going to be brave, to do something that frightens me." She swallowed audibly. "You sacrificed your freedom for mine."

"No."

"Yes." She tugged his head down and brushed her lips over his. "You hero are my, John."

A red flush crept up his neck. "I only wanted to give you a chance to explore life on your terms."

Another round of tears fell but this time John kissed them away. "You have, and now I…"

"Yes?"

"I want you as my real husband. Know you servants like think should we already do." Of course, when it really mattered, her words were jumbled. She sighed. "I want to know you physically, as your wife." Her eyebrows rose. "Please?" What if after everything, he said no? What if she was indeed too much for him?

"Oh, sweeting. Of course." Pride twinkled in his eyes. "You don't know how long I've waited to hear those words, to know you're comfortable enough with me in that way."

Another few tears fell. "I'm here now."

"Yes, you certainly are."

Then she sighed, for John wrapped his arms around her and crushed his lips to hers.

Caroline's world spun out of control the longer she kissed her husband. The storm inside her abated and in its place came other sensations, more pleasurable ones that swept through her blood, leaving her heated and aching with the sweetest longing. A yearning that wouldn't cease until John touched her, claimed her, showed her what such feelings meant.

"Put your hands on me," she asked in a whisper as she peered into his face. "Make me fly. Like you did before."

Those gorgeous eyes of his had darkened. "You're certain?"

"Yes." She fumbled with the buttons on his jacket. There was nothing more that she wanted in this moment.

"Good." Then he strode to one of the sheet-draped sofas, whipped off the dust covers, and waggled his eyebrows. "I suppose this makes as good a bed as any."

Caroline giggled. "It doesn't look like one."

"I don't guess you'll critique the décor once we're underway, my dear." Slowly, he returned to her location. "Allow me to convey you." He scooped her up into his arms and grinned when she squealed. "Ah, Caroline, we're going to have such fun together."

"You will sleep in my bed now?" She'd liked it all too much the other night when he'd stayed with her, when she could reach out in the night when something woke her or she was afraid and touch him, feel his warmth, find comfort to know she wasn't alone.

"If that's what you want. You only need to say the word and I'll be there." He kissed her again, and her world tilted, and as he laid her down upon the low sofa, she murmured a protest when their connection was broken.

But she needn't have worried. He was right there, his big body coming over hers with a pleasant weight. The hard wall of his chest contrasted nicely with the soft cushions at her back, and he kissed her again with such gentleness, she wanted to always feel that contentment wrapping around her.

She ran her hands up and down his back. Daring much, Caroline put a hand to the tautness of his buttock as heat burned through her cheeks. Oh, he felt so good! So very different from her. The scents of the sun and sea infiltrated her nostrils. It made her feel giddy, drunk, even though she had no idea what that meant. Finally, she had the freedom to press her lips to the underside of his jaw where the stubble met smooth skin. Dear heavens, that disparity was extraordinary on her lips, her tongue! She tugged at his lapels in an effort to have him closer.

John chuckled. The sound reverberated deep in her chest, encouraging the butterflies in her belly to take flight. "I never knew you'd be so impatient."

How could she not be when every part of her cried out for every part of him? "I want you." There was simply nothing else to say.

That grin of his would drive her mad one day, for she adored it so much. "I want you too." He peppered the underside of her jaw with gossamer kisses then dragged his lips down the column of her throat. While her heartbeat quickened, he followed the bodice of her dress and slowly, oh so slowly, he pulled at the fabric until he'd bared her breasts.

The relatively cool air of the room wafted over her exposed skin, prompting a shiver, but then he was there taking one of her hardening nipples into the warm cavern of his mouth. As he sucked on the bud, he rolled the other. Wild sensations bounced through her body, zipping between her breasts to between her thighs. Caroline cried out, her body shifting, her back arching, which put her more firmly into his care.

All she could do was clutch his shoulders and ride each wave of feeling as it broke over her. Everything was new and different—colorful, as if she'd previously lived in a world of black and white; everything he did, everywhere he touched rendered her both hot and cold. And beyond that, something deep inside her awakened, pushed toward the light as if it refused to stay buried any longer.

When she moved, restless, and one of her legs bumped the hard bulge between his legs, John hissed with discomfort. "Sorry, I don't—"

"Shh. I know." He resituated himself so that his legs were between her splayed ones, and as he did so, he tugged up handfuls of her skirts, bunching them at her waist, and all too soon the rest of her body was visible. Though he'd touched her there, between her legs that one afternoon at the duck pond, having him gaze upon her most private of parts left heat burning in her cheeks. "So gorgeous." Awe lingered in his voice as well as showed in his expression. "And you're mine."

"Yours," she repeated with a grin of her own. She belonged to this man—her husband—and for the first time in her life, it felt as if she'd found her way home. "You are mine too."

An expression of wonder crossed his face. "That's the first time you've ever asserted any sort of possession about me." He leaned over her and brushed his lips over hers. "I rather like the sound of it."

That made her unaccountably happy, but she didn't know why, and couldn't discern that feeling from the heated desire being with him sent through her veins. She took one of his large hands and put it on her breast. "Please hurry. These feelings… so overwhelming…"

"I understand, but this will go all too quickly once we're underway and I—"

Caroline pressed the fingers of one hand to his lips. "Other will times there be." When he chuckled, she nodded. "Just want you."

For long moments, her husband looked at her as if he couldn't quite believe she was there, then he shook his head as if to clear his thoughts, yanked at the buttons on his front falls, and when his engorged, hardened length tumbled out, she gasped. He winked. "Do you wish to touch it?"

"No." She could hardly force the word out from a tight throat. "Later." A shiver of fear went down her spine as she gazed at that enormous shaft, and she attempted to scramble out from under him. Isobel's words from her wedding day rang in her ears. "Too big. It can't, I won't be…"

"Sweeting, it will be all right." John came over her once more with a hand between her thighs. "Our bodies will fit. I promise." His fingers at that sensitive flesh brought back memories of the day at the duck pond, and she relaxed by increments. "Some men are bigger than others, but if you find it uncomfortable, we can stop."

She nodded, squirming as the familiar waves of pleasure swept over her when he found that tiny bundle of nerves. Her back arched. A moan escaped her throat. Again, she was awash on a sea of sensation that stemmed from his touch but also pushed her ever closer to him, drowning in him.

The tumble over the edge this time came quickly. A strangled scream of surprise left her throat. She clutched at his shoulders while contractions fluttered through her core. It was so fast, so unexpected. Before she could catch her breath, John was there, or at least the wide head of his shaft was, bobbing at her entrance, and another shiver shot down her spine, but not of fear. Oh no. There had been too many nights she'd thought of feeling him move inside her, and she wanted to see if her imaginings were as good as reality.

"There will be discomfort initially." His whispered words skated across her cheek, but then he claimed her mouth in an urgent, intense kiss that shoved all thought from her head. At the same time, he flexed his hips, thrust into her body, and kept going until she was completely and irrevocably filled by him.

"Oh!" The sharp prick of pain that accompanied that joining had tears welling in her eyes. So much so that she hid her face in the crook of his shoulder. "Didn't realize… Too big!" He filled her so much, and they were truly joined as man and wife.

It was at once both marvelous and frightening.

"Do you want me to withdraw?" He rested his forehead against hers.

Did she? The experience was by far the most interesting and incomprehensible she'd ever experienced. But then she wriggled her hips, slowly acclimating to his intrusion. "We're together."

"Yes. Does it make you feel afraid?" Strain graveled his voice.

"No. Yes." She trembled in his hold. "No. But…"

"But?"

"It is not as good as your fingers there."

"Oh, my girl, we've yet to start." He kissed her and at the same time withdrew from her body. Before she could protest the loss, the heat of him, he stroked back in, and this time the previous pain faded. Unexplainable pleasure took its place.

Caroline had no idea what to expect let alone what to say. Perhaps there was no need to say anything. She met John's gaze, nodded when he lifted an eyebrow, and then sighed from the sheer pleasure of finally being a woman who was desired and wanted.

And finally, she knew the rest of the freedom he'd talked about when they'd wed.

Each time John moved, the sensations he invoked threatened to steal her sanity. Slowly, ever so slowly, he thrust in and out. She had no idea what to do, tried to move her body in some semblance of a rhythm but failed miserably.

"Don't worry about doing it correctly right now. Enjoy and let the feelings wash over you. We've a lifetime ahead to perfect the mechanics."

His words brought her comfort, but the unrelenting pressure circling through her insides stole it away. With each new push, every subsequent stroke, the need for something rose and grew. Of what she had no idea, but suspected that only John could give it to her. Oh, how she wished they were naked so she could marvel at the powerful form that moved over hers, feel the play of his muscles beneath her fingers, and then the pace changed.

Faster and faster, he moved. When he drew her legs up to settle about his waist, he went so deep that she feared she'd lose herself in him. The urgency of his thrusts increased; every time he pushed inside pressure increased but so did the pleasure brought on by friction and his shaft rubbing against every sensitive spot she had. And then he put a hand between them, touched that button and shivery pleasure washed over her.

It was all too much, too overwhelming… drowning, needing to breathe but only wanting him. "John, I…" Before she knew what was happening, a roaring vortex of bliss rushed up to engulf her. It spun her about, catching her up into its rings, and then flung her into a brilliant white light where the only thing that existed was pleasure and a great throbbing relief between her thighs where he continued to pump for all he was worth.

Seconds later, he gave a hoarse shout of her name. Warmth filled her core. He collapsed on top of her, and the pleasant weight of him anchored her back to reality.

Caroline's heartbeat hammered in her ears as she clutched him closer, and her inner walls convulsed around his member. Tears streamed down her face, for the all-consuming wonder he'd given her couldn't be explained or calculated. She only knew it was much like music or painting and was beautiful like the art she created.

Eventually, John stirred. He lifted off her enough to peer into her eyes. Concern clouded his. "I didn't hurt you, did I? It wasn't really well done of me not to finesse this, and it went by too quickly, for I haven't been with a woman in—"

"Hush." She smoothed a shock of hair from his forehead and gave him a tired sigh. "I have no words except... are amazing you."

"Ah, my girl, so are you." He dropped a kiss to her cheek, to the tip of her nose, her closed eyelids, and then finally her lips, and it was the sweetest kiss she'd ever been given. "I'm so grateful you are my wife."

"Oh!" Her heart squeezed, and no matter how illogical it seemed, she lost a piece of that organ to him. "You are my hero."

"For as long as you have need of me." He shifted, rolled onto his side and he took her with him. When she sighed, he gathered her into his arms and settled her against his chest. "Has the storm inside abated?"

She'd completely forgotten the anger. For the time being, she couldn't detect it. "Perhaps your sort of storm is stronger—the one we make together."

There was no need to say more, so she snuggled into his embrace and let her eyes close. Perhaps that was what she'd needed—a stronger storm or else a man who was large enough to withstand hers.

CHAPTER FIFTEEN

September 23, 1818

J OHN GLANCED ACROSS the drawing room at his wife with what felt like a foolish grin as she played a gentle sonnet from Beethoven at the pianoforte. Two days ago, they'd finally consummated their marriage, and beyond that, Caroline had opened up to him about some of the things from her past. He couldn't be any prouder of her. Yes, they still had miles to go—both of them—but this had been a good start.

In the intervening days, they'd walked the Hadleigh Hall property. She'd painted while he fished. Brand usually joined them for breakfast and dinner but let them have the rest of the time alone, especially after John had casually mentioned—in the briefest of terms—what had happened. And since they'd been left to their own devices, yesterday afternoon, they'd made use of the relative privacy in the heart of the Hadleigh maze by coupling in the soft, shady grass there.

And it had been no less wonderful than the first time.

Caroline had an affinity for such things, she was a quick learner, and she was enthusiastically interested in exploring his body as much as he was hers. With every subsequent coupling, they continued to find a rhythm that worked for them, and each time his wife cried tears of wonder when she fell over the edge into bliss. He found it adorable, and what was more, he'd lost pieces of his heart to her. They'd bonded deeply over the past two days as if their souls had connected, stuck together, and he was continually amazed at the boon he'd been given. She was such a warm person, full of life and love and verve—magic perhaps—that she'd only needed the chance to shine and fly; to have someone believe in her and her different way of learning.

I did that for her.

It humbled the hell out of him, as did the fact he'd been entrusted with growing old beside such a remarkable woman. And that only drove home the fact he needed to sort out his affairs. She deserved a life they could both be proud of, and that meant going home to Ipswich, and soon.

"Why do you stare at me so?" she asked without a pause in what her fingers were doing upon the keyboard.

Damn, but she was amazing. "Can't a man look at his wife and feel so fortunate that he might burst?"

A smile curved her highly kissable lips. "Yes?" The afternoon sunlight streaming into the room highlighted subtle caramel-colored strands in her dark hair, and in the dress of robin's egg blue, she was simply stunning. Her stormy eyes twinkled, healthy color bloomed in her cheeks; never had she seemed more alive or ready to take on the world.

"Good." The urge to pluck her off that padded bench and kiss her senseless took hold. Perhaps that would lead to other delicious offerings. What would she do when he introduced her to intercourse against a wall? She would no doubt giggle and laugh, look at him in that special way she had that turned his blood to fire, and they'd pass the remainder of the afternoon twisted in his sheets.

Let the servants talk about that!

But before he could act upon the urge, Brand strode into the room. Determination lined his face, as did a certain longing John knew all too well.

"Good afternoon, Captain. What is on your mind?" John

asked, but he *knew.* "You look like a man who has made a decision."

"That's because I have." He crossed the room to Caroline's location, bussed her cheek, and then joined John, dropping heavily into a chair. He and his cousin had made great inroads into forming a tentative friendship. So much so that it tugged at John's heart. "I miss Elizabeth and babe too much to linger in Derbyshire any longer."

Knots formed in John's belly. "I figured as much." He rested an ankle on a knee, but the negligent, relaxed pose was far from the truth. "You're going back to Ipswich." It wasn't a question.

"I am."

"When?" John shot a glance at Caroline. She'd stopped playing the pianoforte in order to watch both of them.

Brand shrugged. "As soon as I can." He rubbed a hand along the side of his face. "While it's been idyllic meandering about the old familial property as well as spending time with you and Cousin Caroline, I wish to resume being within the folds of *my* little family. As well as take up the reins of the shipping outfit again." He met John's gaze. "Do you wish to go with me?"

Did he? More than anything, but in his heart, he acknowledged that such a decision didn't include only him any longer. When he glanced at his wife, her gaze was on him. A hopeful expression crossed her face, and his pulse accelerated. "I do, of course, but I shall need to discuss it with Caroline. I hadn't anticipated leaving Derbyshire this soon."

"Understandable." Brand grinned. He waggled his eyebrows. "You're rather enjoying your honeymoon."

Heat crept up the back of John's neck, but he couldn't deny it. "I am." Then Caroline was there. She settled onto the low sofa next to him and immediately, the scent of daises and violets assailed him. The warmth of her called out to him, urging him to touch her. "This time with my wife has been... both surprising and fulfilling."

And he wished to keep the bubble surrounding them intact

for as long as he could before reality intruded.

She laid a hand on his arm. Need ricocheted down his spine to lodge in his stones. "We should go." In the event he didn't understand, she nodded. "Show me the sea and squirreling."

Both he and Brand chuckled.

A faint blush stained her cheeks. "Sailing." She squeezed her fingers upon his arm. "You miss the sea." The statement didn't require inquiry.

"I do." He wouldn't make any secrets about it. "Every day it calls to me." But recently, that call twisted with the desire to be wherever Caroline was, to seek her out for no other reason than to be near, attempt to draw her out further from her shell to discover the other facets of the woman she was finding. "And it's beautiful, much more so than the countryside here."

She smiled up into his face. "I want to go. To make you happy. You and Cousin Brand will trunks my pack?"

"Aye." He exchanged an amused glance with his friend. "You don't enjoy packing?"

Caroline huffed. She waved her free hand in dismissal. "There are other things I wish to do while here."

Both he and Brand laughed. Oh, she had an independent streak a mile wide, and every day that went by it strengthened, as did her confidence.

Brand winked at her. "You know, Cousin, I have thoroughly enjoyed my time with you, and I'm so glad you're coming to Ipswich. Somehow, I think you'll have a great affinity for the area."

"She'll no doubt turn the village on its head with her intelligence and talents." John couldn't stop beaming. Never had he been prouder of her. Even now, a couple of the unused bedrooms upstairs contained many of her paintings as they dried and cured. Where the devil they'd put all of them remained a mystery, and each one was more beautiful than the last.

If only she'd cease painting him nude. It would prove embarrassing soon.

Caroline beamed. "I *am* quite unique." The words were slow, but that only meant she was extremely focused on what she said in front of someone other than him.

"Indeed, you are, sweeting, and we adore that about you."

Slowly, Brand nodded. "There is no pressure in Ipswich, and very little *ton* society. I'll wager it's a hidden slice of heaven in England and hope it stays that way."

Before John could respond, the butler came into the room bearing an ivory envelope on a silver salver.

"A letter came today for you, Mr. Butler." He extended the tray, and when John snagged the envelope, the man straightened. "Shall I bring tea?"

Brand grinned. "That sounds like a good idea."

While his best friend and Caroline told the butler what they'd like to see on the tea tray in the way of edibles, John cracked the familiar green wax seal bearing his father's crest. With a sigh, he pulled the letter from the envelope, unfolded it, and scanned its contents.

> *John,*
>
> *If you could please return to London posthaste, I am throwing a ball in honor of your recent nuptials on the 27ᵗʰ of this month. I would appreciate your presence and the opportunity to know Caroline. I have already issued invitations to her family in London.*
>
> *Westfield*

The letter had been dated a week and a half ago, and the alleged event would occur in four days. At a normal pace, it would take three to arrive in London.

"Well, damn."

The butler eyed his askance. "Will there be a reply, Mr. Butler?"

"No, thank you, but do put the staff on notice. Caroline and I might be leaving for London immediately."

"Very well." Then the butler left the room, no doubt to ponder with the servants the contents of the letter.

"What is amiss?" Brand asked as soon as they were alone while Caroline looked on.

"I fear our removal to Ipswich will be delayed by a week." Without further comment, he passed the letter to his friend, who then read it aloud, no doubt for Caroline's benefit, for she'd told them days before she didn't enjoy reading. "Though, I really shouldn't indulge him. What has that man ever done to benefit anyone besides himself?" As he talked, a hot wave of anger rose in his chest. "And the bastard has already sent invitations. I can't very well let them go without showing up myself." The bugger had probably known that and used it as leverage.

"What do you think is his real intent?" With a narrowed eye, Brand gave the letter back to John.

"I'm sure I couldn't say, but I don't entirely trust him." He shoved the missive into the envelope and then tossed it onto the table. "Men don't change." *Especially not my father.* He hadn't cared one jot when John had told him about his engagement, and he hadn't attended the wedding either.

Why all of a sudden had he changed position?

Caroline patted his arm. She frowned. "Perhaps he wants to make amends."

He covered her hand with his. "I've known him too long to think that. He's a selfish man." Without a feather to fly with as well. Unless the man was on his deathbed, and even that confession would provoke doubts. "This delays our removal to Ipswich. That is, *if* we return to London." He glanced at Brand. "By all means, if you wish to continue on with your plans, I'll understand."

For long moments, his friend considered him. Then he bounced his gaze to Caroline and back to John. "As the saying goes, I do think there is something rotten in Denmark. I don't trust your father by half, and I've never met him." He rubbed a finger along his temple. "If you choose to go back to London, I'll accompany you. After your father's ball, we shall all go to Ipswich together." His grin was tight. "I refuse to leave you behind."

"Thank you for that." John caught his wife's gaze. "What say you, Caroline? One last trip to London before we take up the reins of our life?"

"Say goodbye to Cousin Andrew?" Her expression was unreadable.

"Only if you wish it."

She pulled a face which had Brand chuckling. "If he isn't noisy, but I wish to try and make friends." Again, her words were precise, slightly delayed as if she were attempting to set them in the correct order. "Like I am with Cousin Brand." When she caught John's gaze, the trace of sadness in hers made his chest tighten. "Need to move forward, out of the old and into the new."

"It's always a good idea. There is much to look forward to." John grinned, for he couldn't be happier with the direction they were both going. "However, I'll admit, Hadleigh is full of bluster usually. I'm certain you can handle him, and you can also say your goodbyes to the countess and their baby."

She shrugged. "My own might have babies soon too." The words, though jumbled, were said in such a matter-of-fact manner that he stared.

Regardless that Brand was in the room, John's whole being went taut. "You want young ones of your own?" When had she changed her mind? For that matter, he hadn't used a sheath or any other form of prevention, so it stood to reason such a thing could happen.

A pleased grin curved her lips, and he was hard-pressed not to keep staring at her mouth. "It is what comes next, John. Don't you know that?"

Brand's loud guffaws echoed through the room. With his eye streaming with tears, he scrambled up from his chair. "Ah, Cousin, you do a heart good. And by all means, yes, keep teasing my mate here. He'd prove a wonderful father. Our children can grow up together as best friends." The look he gave John was mischievous. "Now, if you'll excuse me, there are last minute plans to make before we depart tomorrow morning."

"But what about tea?"

He waved a hand at the door. "Enjoy! Besides, I rather think your wife wants you to herself just now. I recognize that look, you lucky bastard. That's another thing I miss about being away from Ipswich…"

Once he'd left the drawing room, John studied Caroline's face. She certainly was thinking hard about something, and when her focus kept jogging to his mouth, his neck, a wave of heat swept over him. Now that she'd had a taste of intercourse, it seemed she was bound and determined to enjoy the hell out of it.

And devour him along the way. Catch him up in that storm.

"Are you certain you wish to go back to London and see my father again?" For he wasn't. Not at all. The more he thought upon the idea, the more cold foreboding twisted up his spine. Something was in the wind. He'd wager his savings upon it.

"Yes." She nodded. When she threaded their fingers together, she traced his palm with her other hand. "There will be dancing, yes?"

"Of course." And knowing his father, it would be lavish celebration which would sink the title deeper into debt. "As long as you don't mind being out in society." They hadn't tested her endurance since being in Derbyshire. It was one thing to see her calm and comfortable when in his company or that of Brand's, but quite another to thrust her into a situation she wasn't ready for. Would that undo the progress they'd already made?

She shrugged. "I will ignore people."

Oh, if only he had the luxury of doing the same.

While the butler returned with the tea service, Caroline continued. "I can wear a pretty dress and tiara." Her eyes lit and sparkled. Had she always been such a beauty? "You will put on fancy clothes too. Then will we dance. Like the storybooks."

John nodded his thanks. Once they were alone again in the

room, he sighed. "I suppose we can, and you do look smashing in ball gowns." That would afford him the exquisite opportunity of getting her *out* of said gown...

"You're handsome." Caroline patted his cheek. Again, her gaze drifted to his mouth, and he stifled a groan. "Dancing is romantic."

"It can be, of course." He brought her hand to his lips and kissed the back. Did he dare to kiss her into a state of passion that she might wish to copulate right here in the drawing room? Then another thought occurred that he hadn't considered. "Have you ever danced before?"

"No." She glanced to the tea tray. "I memorized all the different ones, though. Have watched others do them countless times." When she focused on him, her chin quivered. "Teach me?" There was such hope and expectation in those blue-gray depths that his heart squeezed.

"I can't think of anything else I'd like better." Oh, his wife was so endearing and vulnerable that he wanted to scoop her up and protect her from all of life's ills. Though he harbored huge reservations about putting her back into the lion's den of his father's presence, if she wished to do this, then it meant she wanted to conquer something she didn't like about herself. He'd learned that much about her, at least. "Do you want tea first or a dancing lesson?"

Again, she eyed the tea tray, but when her gaze met his again, her grin was brilliant. "Dance first. Then tea. Then *you*." The way her voice lingered over that last word lit tiny fires of need in his blood.

"Never let it be said that I kept you waiting." He gained his feet and brought her into a standing position with him, but the warmth of her, the trust mixed with need in her eyes, the floral scent of her distracted him from his purpose. "However, I think there's something we need before dancing lessons." Cupping her cheek, he slid his fingers into the silky mass of her hair and then gently lowered his mouth to hers.

She surrendered with a tiny sigh. As she looped her arms about his shoulders and stood on her toes to better kiss him back, John wrapped his arms around her, settled her more comfortably into his embrace. Never in his life had he known such perfect contentment or the sensation of coming home as contained within another person. Caroline had easily become his North Star in the short time they'd been together. Her light and determination to be seen as an individual guided his own path, made him want to be much more than he was merely because she already thought of him as her hero.

As he moved over her petal-soft lips, reacquainted himself with her mouth, learned even more how she enjoyed being kissed, an image appeared in his mind's eye of her standing at the door of a modest cottage with the sea in the background. At her side was a child of perhaps five—a boy—who had his blond hair but her storm-tossed eyes, while a girl child sat on her hip, all dark brown ringlets and brown eyes with a thumb in her mouth, no older than three. Caroline's belly was slightly swollen with another child on the way.

He wanted the vision more than he'd wanted anything in his life, yet how could either of them have such when declarations of love hadn't been uttered? It was one thing to lie with one's wife of convenience but quite another matter entirely to develop deep feelings for her.

Would that ever happen? Already, he was exceedingly fond of her, and there were moments when he'd felt a profound *something* that he couldn't name, didn't dare to lest it slip through his fingers. But what of her? Would she ever learn to love him back should he complete the fall down that slippery slope?

In the end, it didn't matter, for he had her in this moment, and it was as damned near perfect as it could be as they continued to kiss. Eventually, he set her at arm's length in order to catch his breath. With a grin and a shaking hand, he lifted one of hers to his lips and kissed the back. "Sweeting, if we don't stop, we'll never complete tea nor get to those dancing lessons."

Her slow smile and knowing glint in her eyes nearly had him spending in his breeches. "You make me feel like…"

"Yes?" Would she declare her feelings?

Caroline shrugged, and those kiss-swollen lips curved in a soft grin. "Magic. Like springtime. Like I have become music."

It wasn't exactly what he yearned to hear, but it was uniquely Caroline and it made him the happiest of men. "Ah, my girl, what the devil have I done right in my life to have been given you?" But he thanked the Creator that he was, for he suspected he rather liked her more than was good for him. "We're going to have such fun in Ipswich and the sea."

The only fly in the ointment was his father's ball. Would that everything would go smoothly, and they could all go their own ways without the typical Drury Lane drama.

CHAPTER SIXTEEN

September 27, 1818
London, England
Westfield House

IT WAS THE night of the celebration ball at Lord Westfield's townhouse—John's father. Since arriving, Caroline stood on the sidelines of the drawing room near a collection of potted plants, watching the crush of people and wondering how she would manage to not bolt from the room in terror.

Yet, in all honesty, those feelings didn't batter her insides as strongly as they'd once before. Why? Her brain searched for answers while she observed the party guests. Across the room, her Cousin Andrew and his wife Sarah chatted with two other couples. Jewels glittered around her neck and at her wrists, sparkling like fire in the candlelight. A ruby in the depths of Andrew's cravat did the same. It looked much like a drop of blood. Why did he choose to wear such a stone?

The soothing sounds from a string quartet reached her ears. In her mind, she followed the piece of music, for she'd played it often enough on the pianoforte. Now that they weren't at Hadleigh Hall, would John procure her a similar instrument? She hadn't inquired into his yearly income, for that wasn't important to her; she'd only wanted him and all he stood for.

Near the open terrace doors, her cousins Finn and Brand chatted in some animation, if the gestures of their hands and heads were any indication. Did they argue or merely discuss something with passion? She didn't know but seeing them tugged a faint smile from her as well as gave her a sense that everything wasn't as bad as she'd once thought. Already, she considered Brand a friend. Finn was more of a challenge, but he was so jolly and easy to talk with—and he wrote books that had happy endings which had elevated him in her opinion—that she hoped he soon would be.

As her gaze drifted, it encountered the baron, who stood at the door to the room with a snifter of brandy in his hand. He watched her with dark eyes and an assessing expression, but there was no mirth to be found about him. What was he thinking? The longer she stared at him, the less she decided she liked him. The muscles in her belly tightened. He was *not* a friend. As of yet, he hadn't made an effort to talk with her outside of greeting her upon arrival.

Finally, she looked away only to have her attention snared when she found John, who walked her way with purpose and intent in his long strides and a certain light in his golden-brown eyes that made her breath catch. Oh, it was glorious how handsome he was in full evening clothes! The tails on his black jacket gave him a distinguished air, and the peridot satin waistcoat drew her eye to that abdomen she enjoyed and had only three days prior explored with her tongue and lips. But what held her attention and had flutters of desire dancing through her lower belly was the grin of pleasure on his lips; he always looked at her thusly anymore.

"John." Even though she'd arrived at this location with her cousin as well as her husband and had already seen him in his finery, she couldn't stop staring. "I thought you wished to talk with your father."

"He can wait, for right now, I know a powerful urge to take my wife out for the waltz the musicians are preparing to play."

He held out a gloved hand to her. "Will you?"

At each posting inn they'd stayed at during the journey back to London, he'd made certain they practiced waltzing so she wouldn't feel self-conscious or afraid now. "Yes." The sensation of falling assailed her, and as soon as she slipped her gloved fingers into his palm, the slide accelerated, but with John there, she knew he would catch her at the end. He always did, was always there encouraging her.

"Besides, you are easily the most beautiful woman in attendance tonight," he said as he led her to an open spot in the makeshift dance floor. "That gown makes you look as if you've tumbled from the heavens merely to tempt me."

The low rumble of his voice reverberated in her chest. That tickle enhanced the other more pronounced trembles moving deep inside her core. How was it that this one man had managed to captivate her so much and so quickly? But then, she supposed they *had* known each other since last Christmastide... "You already said that. First at Cousin Andrew's home and then in the carriage."

"Can I help it if it's the truth?" He arched a bushy eyebrow. "And I like giving my wife compliments. I suspect you didn't have many in your life and now you should be showered with them."

She'd yet to become accustomed to them. For a few seconds, Caroline blinked away tears from her eyes. "It's a favorite gown." John had gifted it to her some days ago while still at Hadleigh Hall but she hadn't had cause to wear it. The pale blue silk was almost white in some lighting. An overskirt panel of sheer gauze sprinkled with tiny, embroidered silver stars and crescent moons winked each time she moved. It was attached to the front part of the gown by a silver ribbon that tied in the back with trailing tails. The enamel crescent moon pendant swung at her collarbones every time she moved, while the softest pale blue tulle lined the low bodice and capped sleeves.

"I knew it would look wonderful on you when I bought it." He winked, and when the first notes of the music lifted into the air, he led her over the floor.

"Silly man. Bought it you did in a temper when I was" Caroline blew out a breath. She couldn't concentrate on the steps of the dance and converse at the same time.

"Indeed, but I know how you adore fancy, ethereal gowns, and I wished to gift one to you. It was coincidence you had an occasion to wear it."

"Oh." Ever since she'd shared about the crescent moon pendant, he'd never forgotten. Her heart fluttered. Truly, her husband was the most kind-hearted man, but would he ever love her? Tell her that? "You are…" She searched her mind for the appropriate words. There were none. "Amazing."

And he was hers. That was perhaps the great miracle and one she couldn't quite stop marveling at. This man had plucked her from obscurity, from a miasma of fear and loneliness, merely to set her free with understanding and perhaps love, in time.

Each time the steps took her away from him, her stomach bottomed out and she feared she would stumble or forget all he'd taught her, but then he was there to collect her once more, twirl her over the floor in the midst of a handful of other couples, and the emotions in his eyes worked at stealing her breath. Not once did her feet fail her. Did he feel as fortunate as she? And ever since he'd introduced her to the joys of coupling, she couldn't have enough of him.

"If you continue to look at me like that, Mrs. Butler, the whole room will bear witness to me embarrassing myself."

That struck her as funny, so she laughed and realized she'd done more of that while being with him than she had all her life. She shrugged as the dance came to an end. "I like you."

"Oh, that's more than obvious." The rumble of his laugh enhanced her awareness of him.

"Shouldn't have to hide it." Why did everyone insist on making things so complicated? A thing was either there or it wasn't.

John chuckled. He escorted her to the side of the room where Cousin Andrew waited. "Agreed, but perhaps wait until we're alone." When he raised her hand to his lips and placed a fleeting kiss on her middle knuckle, heat went through her cheeks. "Thank you for the dance."

She nodded and caught her cousin's eye. "John is a marvelous dancer."

"So I saw. I had no idea you knew how to dance, let alone waltz."

"John taught me." Under his tutelage, her confidence had grown. No longer did she see individual people as twirling storms. Instead, faces had become evident as well as clothing, and the storms inside her didn't howl as much. The emotion was still there, but it was manageable. "Life with him is... lovely." And something she'd never known before. She craved that stability, that familiarity, the sunshine he brought to her life merely by existing.

"Ah." Andrew gave her a smile, but it died when he looked at John. "I'm sorry your honeymoon came to an end so soon, Mr. Butler. I wonder if you had enough time together with my cousin. Finding good footing is oftentimes delicate work between two people, let alone someone of Caroline's... temperament."

At his side, Sarah murmured a protest. "Andrew, stop. Can you not see how well they're already getting along?" The candlelight glanced off the wire rims of her spectacles.

"I've been with her nearly a month, Lord Hadleigh. Your cousin is a joy. I honestly don't know how I've existed without her up until this point." He gave her the grin that never failed to set her at sixes and sevens. "If you don't believe me, perhaps you should dance with her and ask her yourself. Who knows what you'll discover about Caroline that you haven't previously?"

"That's an excellent idea." The countess linked her arm with John's. "I'm going to take Mr. Butler to procure a glass of punch or two and engage him in what I hope will be a wonderful conversation."

"I'd be delighted, Your Ladyship." He looked at Caroline. "Will you be all right?"

"Yes." She'd wished to speak privately with her cousin anyway.

"I'll return shortly. Then we'll perhaps look for my father." Though he grinned, it wasn't the one she adored, neither did it crinkle the delicate skin at the corners of his eyes.

"Come, Cousin." Andrew offered her his arm, crooked at the elbow.

The next set was a country reel. It didn't provide much opportunity to converse, and Caroline needed the time to think about the steps. Changing partners and hopping about tried to confuse her, but she bit her bottom lip and pretended she was performing the dance with John instead of her cousin. By the time the set ended, she was slightly winded, but she hadn't stumbled more than a few times. A month ago, she would never have consented to dancing let alone would have joined the gathering, but John's belief in her had somehow changed that. He'd encouraged her to be herself regardless of what others thought or how they acted. There was no longer a need to hide.

It was another sort of freedom that she cherished, for she'd never been able to find that all the years in the asylum when she assumed there had been something wrong with her.

She waved to Brand when he glanced her way across the room. Would she ever feel comfortable in Andrew's presence like she did with Brand? When she looked at the man leading her back to the side, she sighed. "I am happy, Cousin Andrew." And now that she finally understood what that was, she never wished to be without it again.

"Are you certain?" Andrew frowned. Annoyance and confusion clouded his eyes that were so much like hers. She didn't remember much about his father—her uncle—but it didn't matter now. The future was hers, and it didn't contain the old hurts from the past.

"Yes." Caroline nodded. "Marriage interesting been has." She didn't care that her words were out of order. This was her real self. The people around her could adjust. "John makes me feel the same way that painting does, like there are so many colors in my mind, but are in my body instead."

His frown deepened as he stared at her. "I assume that is a good thing for you?"

"Yes." She patted his arm. There was nothing about the man that reminded her of him as a child. How had he changed so much? Wanting her words to be exact without question, she spoke them slowly. "John and I have a future. It is exciting." She grinned at her cousin, and the urge to giggle rose in her throat. "Having a husband is lovely."

"I see." Her cousin pulled her more closely toward the wall and out of the stream of traffic. "Caroline, I must ask you this. Do you love John? You married him in haste and for reasons only known to you, but you certainly were not in love with him. Hell, you barely even knew him as a friend before that."

It must be difficult to see the world as black and white like Andrew did. He simply would never discover how beautiful everything was if he always kept his perspective closed. Then she frowned as his words sank in. Didn't she struggle with the same? Confusion tightened her chest for a few seconds. What did that mean? "Is love what makes me want to fly? And fall and sing and despair?" The more she spoke, the faster she went. "I feel all of John those things with, and they are big, overwhelming." She smiled as she looked at her cousin. "I drown but have so much joy here." Caroline touched her chest. "He is there; everything good is with him."

To her astonishment, a grin tugged at the corners of his mouth. It completely transformed him from the unreachable earl to the boy she used to know before she went away. "Yes, Cousin. All of that is exactly what love feels like."

"Oh?" Caroline couldn't stop her own grin. "Then perhaps I *do* love him." As soon as the words were released into the air, her heart skipped a beat. More than anything she wanted to find John. "I should him tell."

"Indeed. Men like to hear those words." Andrew touched her

arm. "You're certain you are happy." It wasn't a question.

"Oh, yes." She craned her neck but didn't see her husband return to the drawing room. "John is…" He was what? It was difficult to pin down exactly what she'd found in him and with him. "… unexplainable."

Her cousin chuckled, but the sound didn't make her feel shivery inside like John's did. "That's about the size of it. Love is oftentimes unexplainable except to the people that are connected through it."

"Cousin Andrew?"

"Hmm?"

"What me happened to wasn't your frog." When his eyebrows furrowed together as he attempted to decipher her words, she sighed. "I mean, it wasn't your fault."

"But I didn't stop it."

"How could you know?" She squeezed her fingers on his sleeve. "You were a boy. Stormes don't always need to stay broken." With a grin, she released him. "I am not."

"The more I talk to you, see you, the more I'm coming to realize that. Forgive me for not seeing it sooner. It took John coming in and challenging me to make me know that." Confusion ran rampant through his expression. "And you're right. Ever since I met Sarah, I have felt compelled to repair relationships with all the Stormes—you included if you are of the same mind."

Never would she have thought he'd be the one to extend the proverbial olive branch. "I like that would." Giving into the impulse, she lifted onto her toes and hugged him. For the span of a few seconds, he froze, and then with a sigh, Andrew hugged her back before quickly releasing her. "Thank you."

Her cousin nodded. "But if John ever mistreats you or squelches that happiness you've found, please tell me. I will dress him down."

"We are moving. To Ipswich soon. Because it's not London."

Andrew's eyes widened. "He didn't talk to me about that."

"You are not married to him." The happiness bubbling

through her chest made her feet feel just as buoyant. "Need to visit the ladies' retiring room." And to find John. She wanted to tell him that she loved him, that there was nothing else she wished to do than be with him. "Oh, John says I should sell my paintings. I would like that." Then she moved toward the door, leaving her cousin behind. "I could joy to people bring."

I love John. Having a name for those feelings was quite exhilarating. It was certainly another sort of freedom. *I love him!* Now they were finally a real husband and wife… if he returned those sentiments.

And if he didn't?

She ignored the knots of worry pulling in her belly. That was a worry for another day. Nearly to the door of the ladies' retiring room, she was stopped by a woman she didn't know or recognize.

"Mrs. Butler?"

"Yes?" Being addressed by the title sent a tiny thrill down her spine.

"Someone said I should give this to you." The nondescript woman pressed a folded note into Caroline's hand.

"Thank you." With shaking hands, she unfolded the note.

Caroline,

Join me on the curb in front of this house. I wish for a stroll with you, for I have something wonderful to tell you.

John

"Oh!" Her heart shivered. Excitement buzzed at the base of her spine. Would John tell her he loved her tonight? As quickly as she could, she visited the ladies retiring room, did the necessary things to relieve herself, and then she returned to the corridor, searching up and down in the event John was nearby.

He wasn't, so Caroline continued down the corridor toward the front of the house. Her skirts whispered with each step. The further she went, the less noisy the sounds from the drawing room became. Would they dance again once the stroll concluded? She rather hoped they would. Dancing with him made her feel like a princess or a damsel in a storybook. With a nod to the footman at the front door, she made her way outside and down the few steps.

The night air slightly cooled her overheated skin. Stars twinkled in the deep navy heavens. If they were fortunate, there would be no rain to mar the remainder of the evening. "John? Where are you?" No matter how hard she peered into the shadows, she didn't see him.

A few more steps brought her to the wrought iron gate. She unlatched it, swung it open. The creak of the hinges echoed weirdly in the silence. Somewhere in the near distance, the sound of carriage wheels scraping against the pebbles in the street reached her ears. It was an odd juxtaposition, this life where there wasn't any.

"Ah, Caroline, right on time."

She whirled about at the baron's voice. With a frown, she looked him up and down. His cravat was already loose, his hair a bit wild as if he'd shoved his hands through it. "Where is John, Lord Westfield?"

"I imagine he's inside doing the pretty with all of those well-to-do people in there." He took her hand and tugged her nearer to the curb. There was a black hired hackney cab waiting; the driver pretended not to notice them.

"He sent me a note." Why would he do such a thing if he had no intention of meeting her?

The baron snorted. "You really aren't as clever as my son claims." His fingers slipped around her upper arm with a tight grip that bit into her skin. "I sent the note to lure you out here."

Caroline frowned. "Why?"

"Isn't it obvious?" He hustled her toward the cab. "I intend to hold you for ransom."

Her heartbeat slammed through her veins as alarm bells sounded in her head. "No." There was no reason for such a silly game. She wrenched her arm from his hold and retreated a few steps. "John sent this note." It was still clutched in her free hand. "He might love me."

The baron's laughter held no mirth. His dark brown eyes glittered dangerously in the moonlight. "I doubt that." He lunged for her, latched onto her upper arm once more. "You are a broken woman, daft surely if you don't even believe me when I tell the truth." He pulled her once more toward the waiting carriage. "My son feels sorry for you, and that's all."

As Caroline struggled to free herself from her hold, the note fluttered from her hand. "Lies." But the damage his words created had been done. Her heart felt ripped, torn, cracked in half. Was that why John hadn't revealed his feelings toward her? Had he married her from pity?

"Think about it. Has he actually said those words to you?"

"No, but—"

"Don't be more of an idiot than you already are." His fingers were like ice and iron on her arm. He dragged her another two steps, but she struggled the whole way, trying to peel his hand from her person. "John told me himself. Wanted to marry another, but felt sorry for you instead. Would have dumped you at my Surrey estate when he gained the title, lived in Town without you."

"Never John would that do." Each beat of her heart cried out to him. Would he know she was in trouble? "He is not like that." At least those words came out in the correct order. "Magic we are together." If he'd wanted another, those feelings wouldn't be present.

"Shut up!" The baron swung about. He caught her face in a backhanded slap. Pain exploded through her cheek and chin. "You know nothing about him and even less about the situation." This time when he hauled her toward the carriage, she stumbled after him, still dazed from the slap that brought back memories of the few times she had been declared difficult at the asylum and then subsequently manhandled. The fear of those times stunned her, shook her to her soul. "John left me. He refused to help me with the title. Wanted the sea more, and then he chose you over me. The longer I live, the worse the situation grows, and now I have no other recourse but to raise coin the only way I can."

Caroline tried to twist away, but he buried a hand in her hair, pulling tight. Pain crawled along her scalp. Tears welled in her eyes. "You are hurting me."

"Good. At least your reaction will lend truth to the scene." His breath stank of onions. "Get in the cab."

"No." If she did that, John would never know where she went.

"Now!" He balled his free hand into a fist. Then he hit her. Pain exploded through her temple. Darkness hovered on the fringes of her vision. She slumped as her knees buckled.

"John will come," she whispered, fought against him as he shoved her at the carriage and its dark open door.

"If you don't behave yourself, I'll make certain he won't find you alive." He lifted her bodily off the curb and then tossed her into the musty vehicle as if she were nothing more than a sack of potatoes.

Immediately, Caroline stilled. She curled into a tight ball on the floor, the same way she'd spent the first few weeks at the asylum. Memories of that time poured into her mind. They were always telling her to behave herself, to act like the other girls her age, to stop wanting attention. To cease being difficult. That if she didn't quiet, they would tie her to the iron frame of her bed. No amount of thinking of other things could banish those shadowy specters.

And she was reduced to that frightened, alone girl again.

She should have told John all of that but hadn't known it still held a grip on her until this moment. Silent tears tracked more heavily down her cheeks. He would hold her, rock her in his strong arms and tell her that nothing could hurt her ever again because he was there, because she was strong.

But he wasn't there. Not now. Because of his horrible father.

Through it all, she kept saying John's name like a mantra into the darkness, softly, whispered, hoping the connection they shared would make itself known. John would come. He *had* to. He promised to always rescue her whenever she needed him.

Tears fell to her cheeks as the baron sat heavily on the bench and slammed the door behind him. Even if her husband didn't love her, he would come.

He promised.

CHAPTER SEVENTEEN

JOHN ESCORTED THE countess back to Hadleigh's side, but then frowned when Caroline wasn't standing with her cousin. He'd procured a cup of punch for her, thinking she might be thirsty after two sets, yet she wasn't anywhere around.

"Where is my wife?" God, he would never tire of saying that. It was one of the most joyful things to have ever happened, something he'd never thought he would have.

The earl frowned. "After our dance, she indicated an interest in going to the ladies retiring room, but now that you mention it, she should have returned by now."

"I'll go check. Perhaps she's torn a hem." As the countess moved away, Brand and his brother joined their little circle.

"Never say you've already lost your wife, Mr. Butler," Finn joked. His eyes were alight with amusement. "Not a good thing and you so recently married."

"Indeed," Brand added, and gave him a mock punch to the arm that sloshed the punch in the cup John held. "Married for less than a month and can't find his wife."

"I'm sure she's about somewhere." Had the crush in the drawing room as well as the stresses of dancing and conversing caused her to hide? Concern circled through his gut. "I should go search for her."

Seconds later, the countess returned. Worry etched her forehead. "Caroline isn't in the retiring room. None of the ladies there have seen her." She looked at her husband with a silent appeal. "I went to the refreshments table, but she's not there either."

Brand frowned. "I'll check the terrace. It's possible she wished for some quiet and air." He darted away through the milling crowd before anyone could stop him. When he returned not two minutes later and shook his head, the earl cursed softly beneath his breath.

"I should never have allowed this." Of course Hadleigh would grouse.

John narrowed his eyes. "Allowed what, Your Lordship? My marriage or Caroline coming here to circulate within society on her own terms?"

"All of it."

His fingers tightened on the cup of punch. So much so that he feared the crystal might crack. Something inside him snapped. "You—and the Stormes collectively—have done Caroline a grave disservice. Not only this past year but the last twenty that she was sent away to that asylum." A wave of white-hot anger swelled inside his chest even as concern for her rattled around his head. This needed to be said. When Finn took the cup of punch from his hand, he nodded his thanks. "I've already talked about this with Brand, and he has since made inroads into befriending Caroline, but the rest of you *will* hear me out." His voice shook with the force of his ire and the effort at keeping his tone low.

The earl crossed his arms at his chest. Though his expression resembled a thundercloud, amusement danced in his eyes, which only annoyed John more. "Go on."

"My wife is a beautiful person, both inside and out." He shoved a hand through his hair, upsetting the easy style he'd worked on during his earlier toilette. "She doesn't think like everyone else, and yes, her mind operates on a different plain than perhaps ours does, but she's highly intelligent, creatively talented, and endearingly sweet."

Finn cleared his throat. "Perhaps you should arrive at your point of how we've failed her instead of waxing poetic about her."

The droll comment had the corners of John's lips twitching despite his upset. "She was left to her own devices in that asylum. Lonely, afraid, neglected. No one cared, and your familial visits twice a year did nothing to help her. I doubt she was even aware you were there, for she'd retreated into her mind. She developed trust issues and shied away from people. Do you know how much it would have helped her to have one of you believe in her and her abilities despite her difficulties?" Undeterred, he met each of the Storme family member's eyes. He hoped to God they wouldn't yank Caroline back into the fold after this. "She has bloomed since she married. I won't say that it's due to my influence, but it *is* from the freedom and encouragement she's been given."

The countess laid a hand on John's arm. "You could have knocked me over with a feather when I came into this drawing room and saw her dancing with you, as well as conversing as if she weren't aware of anyone else here." Her eyes were kind. "She rather adores you, Mr. Butler, and whether or not you want to claim the credit for letting her grow, none of us is denying that fact."

Heat crept up the back of his neck. "I merely believed in her, but what she needs now is for her family to do the same." He glanced about the crowded drawing room but didn't spy either Caroline or his father. The latter wasn't a surprise, for he'd probably slipped off with his cronies to drink or gamble away the rest of his coffer's contents. "Caroline has befriended Brand, and it's my hope she'll give the rest of you the same latitude."

Hadleigh cleared his throat. He leveled an assessing glance at John. "Why do you care, Mr. Butler? Is not your marriage one of convenience? An excuse to pull my cousin from my own household?"

The heat bled into his cheeks as four pairs of eyes landed on him. "It started out in that fashion, yes. I won't deny that, but over the course of the weeks I've spent with her, I've come to know her, understand her, appreciate her for what she is instead of wishing she was something she's not." For long moments, he held the earl's gaze. In this profound handful of seconds, the realization hit him that his feelings for Caroline had grown and changed.

Bloody hell. Why didn't I see it before?

"Is that all you would say?" The earl cocked an eyebrow in challenge.

"I..." Some of the anger slipped away in the face of these new emotions. "I rather think I've fallen in love with my wife," he admitted in a low voice. Though it shocked him down to his soul, a blanket of peace wrapped about him. While Brand and Finn stared at him, John nodded. Now that he'd spoken those words, he had no intentions of taking them back. "Yes, you heard me correctly, Your Lordship. I love Caroline more than life itself. I only just realized it, so if you think to take her away from me, you will have to fight me for that right."

Dear Lord, had he just issued a threat to an earl?

Remarkably, a chuckle emanated from Hadleigh. "It's not going to come to that, Mr. Butler—John." He unbent enough to drop a hand on his shoulder. "However, before you decide to get your dander up once more, you should know that Caroline and I have come to an understanding, have begun a tentative friendship this evening. She was the one who initiated it, and I will say the change in her is remarkable."

"Oh." Some of the wind had gone from John's sails. He looked at Brand—his best friend in the whole world—and gained comfort by the delight in his expression. "Well, I suppose it was only natural, but..." His words faltered. A sick feeling rose in his throat. "But Caroline is gone, apparently." The muscles in his stomach clenched and the urge to retch grew strong. Quickly, he swallowed as he met the earl's gaze. Damn, but he was the one now who needed comfort. "Has she run from me because she can't bear to stay married? That she realized tonight I'm not good enough for her?" Despair rushed through his chest to dampen everything else.

It was Brand who pushed his way forward to clap his hands on John's shoulders and gave him a hard shake. "Snap out of it, man! Never have I seen two people more suited for marriage to each other than you and Caroline."

The earl nodded. "I quite agree with my brother. After talking with Caroline tonight, I'm glad you married her. She certainly holds you in high esteem."

Then why hadn't she said anything? He remained unconvinced, for once tendrils of doubt took root, they went deep; too much rode upon the outcome. Had her mind once more played tricks on her? "I'm not all I could be, but I'm happy with who I am and how she sees me," he said as panic mixed with pain through his heart. "Where is she, Brand?" His wife was missing, and he'd lost the opportunity to tell her just how much she meant to him.

Was that why she'd run? Didn't women put much stock into hearing those cherished words of love?

Oh, God. I can't lose her.

"I don't know, but we *will* find her." Brand shifted his position until John had no choice but to meet his eye. "You believe that, right? We'll find her."

"Yes." John nodded. He felt like a man who had received a mortal blow but hasn't realized yet he needed to fall. "For the first time in a long while, I don't know what to do."

Finn maneuvered his Bath chair closer to John, nudging Brand out of the way. "First off, welcome to the Storme family. You finally understand why we're all a little mad and protective of our wives. When a Storme falls, he falls hard and there's no going back." He stuck out a hand, and when John clasped it, he shook it hard before releasing it. "Secondly, I don't think you can be a Storme—or an honorary one—without having some sort of doubts until you sit down and have a heart-to-heart conversation with your chosen lady."

Both the earl and Brand nodded, while the countess looked on with a slight blush on her cheeks.

"And lastly, because none of our relationships have ever started without some sort of drama worthy of a stage or a storybook—it's rather a Storme shortcoming—the fact my cousin is missing should indicate that something untoward has befallen her."

John's chest tightened. "The devil you say." Again, he glanced about the room, sifted through the crowds with narrowed eyes. He curled one hand into a fist. "We need to locate my father." Though he wanted to believe the best in people, he'd known his sire all of his life, and if something nefarious was afoot, he'd wager everything he owned that the baron was involved.

But why?

Hadleigh nodded. "Since Lord Westfield has been startingly absent this evening at his own event, I don't feel it's out of line to order the household staff to begin a search." His grin was grim, his eyes full of annoyance. "If my cousin has truly gone missing and the baron is found responsible, he will have my wrath to reckon with. It's time I started making up for lost time with Caroline."

"Andrew, behave," the countess warned in a low voice. "We are still in public."

"I am allowed my ire, dearest. She is a Storme." His tone of voice changed as he addressed his wife. "However, if we find Caroline and she's unharmed, that's all to the good."

Apparently, Brand didn't care, for he let loose a whoop into the air. "I'm up for a proper arse kicking if need be. One last hurrah before I return to Ipswich."

John couldn't help his grin. "Let's find Abrams. If anyone will know about the goings-on in this house, it's the butler." And so help him, if he discovered the butler was complicit in some sort of ill-fated plan, he'd land the servant a facer.

Twenty minutes later, despite the society event in progress, the Earl of Hadleigh plunged the household of Westfield House into chaos and uproar worthy of any good summer storm. Though it wasn't the approach John would have used, he appreciated the results that being an earl could bring about in a short time. Abrams was summoned to a quiet parlor away from the partygoers, and the Stormes plus John stood staring him down as the older man sat stiffly on a chair facing them.

"Mrs. Butler has gone missing, Abrams. Have you seen her or know of her whereabouts?" John asked in a state of odd calm even as anger and worry fought for dominance in his tight chest.

The man's face blanched. He shifted his gaze away, but when he encountered the earl's steely stare, he snapped his regard back to John. "Uh, one of the footmen told me that Mrs. Butler received a note that summoned her outside."

"What?" The exclamation was uttered by the earl, John, and Brand at the same time.

"Who sent it?" Every muscle in his body was taut and ready for action. Someone had deliberately lured her outside, but why?

"I couldn't say, Mr. Butler, but when I returned to the entry hall to relieve the footman, I caught a glimpse of Lord Westfield outside talking to her."

The earl frowned. "What was the gist of the conversation?"

"I couldn't say, my lord. It was too low, and I was too far away."

"Why the devil would Lord Westfield need to talk to Caroline alone and outside?" The earl shook his head. "It makes no sense." He glanced at John. "Did your father greet you this evening when you arrived?"

"I haven't seen him as yet." Which in and of itself wasn't odd, but...

Brand cleared his throat. "There was no reception line, and we didn't arrive late to have merely missed it."

Everyone looked at Abrams. The butler shrugged. "Lord Westfield said he didn't need one."

Of course he didn't, for he hadn't planned to remain at the

event for long tonight. "Damn it all to hell." Without needing to question the man further, John darted from the room. He sprinted along the corridor, and the sound of pounding footsteps behind him gave him an odd sort of comfort. At least the Stormes were united in this. After nearly knocking the footman down, he wrenched open the front door and then launched out of the house, clearing the few steps in one leap. The wrought iron gate was open, and he shot through, not stopping until he'd gained the curb. "Caroline, where are you?" he whispered into the night air.

By the time Brand and the earl joined him, John was scouring the grass and shrubbery. "Here!" The ivory scrap of paper had lodged against the root of a bush near the brickwork of the house.

Caroline,

Join me on the curb in front of this house. I wish for a stroll with you, for I have something wonderful to tell you.

John

He passed the missive to the earl. "I did *not* write that."
"Who did?"
The damning evidence had been seared onto John's brain. "It's in my father's handwriting. There was no way Caroline could have discerned the difference, for she loathes reading, doesn't like puzzling through it, and even if she didn't, she's not had cause to see my handwriting."
"Why would he do this?" Brand cast a glance about the immediate area. Already, carriages were lining up at the curb, for the party had more or less broken up, and without the host in attendance, there was no point to continue it.
"I don't know." John shoved a hand through his hair. "I knew it was too good to be true that he wanted to wish us well." There'd been no announcement, no toast, no attempt to talk to them both together. "Why the hell would he even go to the trouble of having us return to London?"
"Drew! John!" The hail came from Finn, who was silhouetted

in the open doorway with a piece of paper in his hand. "You need to see this."

"What now?" John led the way back up the walkway to the door, whereupon Finn shoved the paper into his hand. "Where did this come from?"

"Well, that Abrams fellow was rather shifty and uneasy, so while you fellows were out searching, I questioned him further." His eyes twinkled with mischief. "I may have employed a couple of old military tactics on him to… encourage him to talk."

"And I missed it?" Brand fairly hopped up and down as if he were a schoolboy itching for a fight instead of a married man with a new baby at home. "I'll wager it was bully good."

John rolled his eyes and ignored the banter between the brothers. He unfolded the note while the earl read over his shoulder. This note, too, had been penned by his father. "'By now you are aware I have your wife. You may be many things, but you are not stupid. Eventually you would have realized I took her anyway.'" His hand shook as anger rose up to tighten his throat.

The earl yanked the paper from his lax fingers and took up the narrative. "'Lord Hadleigh—for you must have wondered why I invited you to my humble event tonight—unless I receive twenty thousand pounds from you by midnight, I'm afraid you'll find your dear cousin Caroline floating in the Serpentine. The drop point is listed below. Either you come alone or send John. It matters not to me.'"

"Oh, dear God." For the moment, the will to fight leeched from John's bones. He sagged, but Brand was there to lend a supportive shoulder. "The gall of the man!" Though he battled both anger and horror from the situation as well as the betrayal, the overwhelming emotion that swamped him was fear. Never had he been more terrified in a situation, not even while forced to do hand-to-hand combat onboard naval ships. "Perhaps I couldn't keep her safe, after all."

Had it been a mistake to remove her from the earl's care and marry her?

"Poppycock. That's plain rubbish and you know it." Brand gave him a little shake. "Caroline has bloomed since your arrival in her life last Christmastide. She glows and is happier than I've ever seen her."

Tremors played John's spine. Threatening tears stung his eyes, but he wasn't ashamed to show them. "If she dies because of my bugger of a father…"

"She won't." Brand shook him again until their gazes met. "You won't let her."

His heart ached so much he feared it might attack him. John pressed a hand over that organ. "She's only just begun to trust others, and now this." Damnation, but she must be terrified. And she already didn't like his father. "All along she's likened me to a storybook hero, asked that I always come and rescue her."

Finn grinned despite the gravity of the situation. "Then don't disappoint her. When women have a set idea about their men, they rather expect us to come up to the mark."

The earl moved into his line of sight. "Do you wish for a pistol?"

"No." Slowly, John shook his head. Then he straightened to his full height. "I have my fists but know this." He met the earl's gaze. "I *will* kill my father if he's harmed her in any way." The man needed stopped, even if that meant plunging his own life into chaos.

"I believe you, but remember, you can't be a husband to Caroline if your arse is rotting in Newgate for murder."

The irony of the matter wasn't lost on him. John snorted. "There is that."

"Allow me time to secure the funding."

"No!" John glanced at the three Storme brothers, the men he was now related to by marriage. A muscle in his cheek twitched, for he'd clenched his jaw. "We are *not* negotiating with the bastard. I refuse to let him abuse my connections, for if we give in, this won't be the only time he tries something like this. He'll go through that coin in a week."

"He's a desperate man, John."

It was the second time Hadleigh had called him by his Christian name. Perhaps he'd finally been accepted into the fold. "While this is true, I am not. I know what I'm capable of more than he does. All my life he's bullied and beat me to get his way. No more." John curled a hand into a fist. "Any man, regardless of relationship, who threatens my wife will find himself with a large comeuppance."

The earl nodded. "If you're certain?"

"I am." He swallowed heavily in an effort to dislodge the wad of fear stuck in his throat. "I have Caroline's dowry. If it comes to that, I'll offer it to him, run him out of England if I must, but I *will not* allow that man to go forward on this same path."

Brand clapped a hand onto John's shoulder. "I'm coming too. I couldn't help Caroline before, but I sure as hell can now."

How much did he love his best friend's loyalty? John sighed, and his shoulders drooped as he regarded the captain. "I can't guarantee your safety, my friend. You must think of your own little family."

"I'll keep myself intact. Don't you worry about that, but I have been itching to land my fists into something. Miss the action I had in the navy. Your rotted father will do nicely." His eye flashed with anger.

John nodded, but felt rather grim and defeated. "Glad to have you by my side. I think this night will not end well, and I pray we reach Caroline in time." He glanced at Finn then at the earl. "I don't know what I'll do without her," he said in a choked voice.

"Then go out and prove to her that you are her knight in shining armor after all." For the first time since John had married Caroline, the earl grinned. "You'll have marvelous stories to tell your grandchildren. Hell, you might even give Finn or Isobel fuel for future books."

"Thank you. If I might have use of your carriage?"

"Of course." The earl looked at Finn. "Tell that sorry excuse for a butler to have the vehicle brought 'round." Once the other man wheeled himself about, Hadleigh sighed. "You are exactly who Caroline needs in her life, and this might not matter right now, but you are nothing like your reprobate father. Never have I met a more patient or strong person. I… I envy you that."

"Thank you." There was nothing else to say. As a knot of guests appeared in the corridor beyond, he cleared his throat. "We should be going. Do what you can to mitigate the scandal."

Hadleigh snorted. "Isn't there always *something* when a Storme is involved? Let us hope the family as a whole will mellow now that we're all married and settled."

As John made his way to the curb once more, he tamped down hard on the emotions rising in his chest. Above all, he would keep Caroline safe. After that, he could make no promises.

CHAPTER EIGHTEEN

F EAR TURNED CAROLINE'S blood to ice the longer the ride in the hired hack continued. From her position on the floor with her hands tied in front of her—the baron had done that shortly after tossing her into the carriage—she couldn't see the baron's face, but her other senses were on high alert. The pungent odor of horse excrement seeped into the interior of the vehicle. Stale smells of tobacco and wine also proved noxious to her nose. The steady rhythm of the wheels and the slight swaying motion of the carriage provided a bit of a calming effect, but with each *clip clop* of the horse's hooves, the distance between her and John widened.

Would he even know she'd been taken?

The pain in her head and her cheek provided grounding, so she concentrated on that in an effort to prevent succumbing to a faint, but she remained curled on her side, facing the front wall of the cab while the storm inside brewed once more into a frenzy. This man, this baron, thought to kidnap her, hold her for ransom. What did that even mean?

Eventually, curiosity won out over the need to protect herself from further harm. "What want you me from?" She pulled at her bonds, but he'd done his job too well. The length of cloth—was that an old cravat?—remained firmly around her wrists.

"Oh, so the frost queen has decided to speak... if you can call what you do speaking." Heavy sarcasm threaded through the baron's voice. "For a moment there I wondered if you'd decided to sleep through the whole thing."

Frost meant cold. Winter. She frowned. Or standoffish. He assumed she was that due to her reticence for speaking. "I don't like you."

He snorted. "Then we're even, for I don't care for you either." The baron dug the toe of his shoe into her side, laughing when she whimpered. "Either face me when I'm talking to you or shut the hell up. I have little patience for half-wits."

That is not what I am. No, John was nothing like this horrible excuse for a man. With anger churning inside her, Caroline pushed herself into a sitting position on the floorboards. She half-turned toward the baron, and with the movement, the pain in her head intensified. Concentrating on her words, she asked again, "What do you want from me?" Again, she tugged at the bonds, but there were two large knots, and they were tight.

"Since my son has made the egregious error of marrying *you*, I may as well use that to my full advantage. He'll give me the funds I so desperately need."

She frowned. "John has no coin." At least, she didn't think he did. From the way he'd talked about his life in Ipswich, she'd ascertained he wasn't well off. At least not yet, but he was a good man and a hard worker. They would have a good life.

If she could get away from the baron.

"Dear stupid woman, I don't expect my son to pay your ransom. I'm after your cousin's coin. His coffers are quite full." He gazed upon her as if she were the scum one found at the bottom of a pond. "John is useless and a disappointment. He cares naught for my title, a fate which will be his someday. Didn't even have the decency to marry an heiress to bring the lands out of disrepair."

Marry an heiress. What did her husband have use for in that? He put no stock in matters of the *ton*. She shifted her gaze to the window, but it was too dark to guess at their destination. "John likes me as I am."

"Which proves he's as daft as you." The baron spat as if to rid himself of the words, and she jerked aside to avoid the expectoration. "Making him a widower is accomplished easily enough. It's not as if you'll know enough of what's happening to stop it."

Well, she wasn't the village idiot! Caroline gasped. "You will kill me?" Did he truly intend that?

"Not perhaps immediately, for I might wish to exploit Hadleigh one time more before I finally do away with you." His grin sent chills down her spine. "Eventually, John will have no choice but to do as I ask, for his honesty and his sickening wish for family will compel him to take care of everything."

"Has a family he." She was beyond caring about putting her words in the correct order. The longer they were in this stinky carriage, the more her heart pounded with fear. John would come after her, of that she had no doubts, but at what cost? Would this man harm his own son?

"Bah!" The baron shoved at her shoulder with a foot. He laughed when she sprawled over the floorboards due to her tied hands. "He gave his family up for lost years ago. Wanted nothing else to do with either me or his brother. Now he's sacrificed his future to be a part of the Storme family, with an insane wife to boot." He shook his head. "What a shame."

No, the shame lay squarely with this man, this worthless excuse for a baron. John deserved so much better than him. Caroline remained silent for long moments. If the conveyance were to slow long enough, could she manage to open the nearest door and jump out? She had no idea where she was or where they were going, but she would run until she felt safe, despite her immobile hands.

It wouldn't hurt to inquire though. "Where are you taking me?"

"Hyde Park."

Good. She was slightly familiar with the area. "Why? Could have asked Cousin Andrew for blunt at the ball."

"God, you're an idiot." The baron shifted on his bench. "If I'd have done that, his brothers and your husband would have attacked me right there. And making threats against an earl in public would land me in greater trouble. At least this way, you've been separated from the herd, so to speak. They'll give anything to have their precious cousin back, and John... Well, I intend to put a bug in his ear that I can, at any time, threaten your life. For a while he'll dance attendance on me like he should have for the rest of mine, had he been a devoted son."

She frowned. "Devotion is earned. As is respect." The carriage slowed as it prepared to take a turn. Her heartbeat increased. Now was her chance!

"Tradition demands it no matter what, and John broke with that." When Caroline reached for the door handle, the baron pulled a pistol from an interior pocket of his evening jacket. "I would think long and hard about doing something foolish if I were you."

Never in her life had she seen a pistol let alone had one pointed directly at her head. Her pulse rushed so hard through her veins that it echoed in her ears. Chill bumps raced over her arms as she lowered them and rested her hands in her lap. Would it hurt much if he shot her? Would John mourn if she were to perish? She lifted her gaze to his, but the darkness hid whatever emotions were reflected there. "I am no good to yams if I am drunk." *Oh, botheration.* That wasn't close to what she'd wished to say. After a tiny sigh, she tried again. "If you kill me, you won't receive payment."

Above all, he was a greedy man.

He relaxed his finger from the trigger. "True, however, it is not the only thing I want this night."

"What then?" She didn't much care. Her first concern was escape.

"You wouldn't understand. You with your pampered *ton* life and all the luxuries so you'll never want for anything." He fairly spat out the words.

Caroline's eyebrows soared. Surprise temporarily made her forget the fear. She snorted. "I am not that."

"Ha! Cousin to an earl. Daughter of a viscount. Gadding about to a vast country estate following your marriage. Hell, that opal ring you wear would fetch a veritable fortune in a pawn shop." When he looked too long at her engagement ring, she hid her hand in her skirting, for she'd once again neglected to wear gloves. "You have much more than I could ever hope for, even if I have a title."

Oh, it was laughable how wrong he was. Should she tell him of her real history, of what her life had been? Would it have any effect on his current plans?

You are strong, Caroline. You are beautiful and clever. Never let anyone tell you differently. John's words jumped into her mind to buoy her confidence.

She forced a swallow to moisten her dry throat, and carefully, deliberately, she concentrated on her words. "Titles and coin mean nothing when there is no caring or compassion."

"What the devil does that mean?"

"I was sent away as a girl of twelve. My parents assumed I was insane due to my mind." She focused out the window once more. The faint smell of water betrayed the fact that they were nearing the park and the Serpentine. "Twenty years I lived alone. Unwanted. Fearful. Hating myself for being different. Left in an asylum with no future. No one to talk to. Away from my family."

"And?" The baron shrugged. "You're here now, so obviously your circumstances didn't matter. I assume your cousin had enough influence to pull you out of that place."

"Cousin Andrew doesn't abide by anyone's rules." At least, that's what she'd figured merely by watching him interact with others.

"That is his right and comes with privilege"

Caroline shook her head. "No. He is arrogant, rash."

"Every peer is to some extent."

"No." She shook her head. As she thought about John, the

man she'd married, the man she'd come to love and depend upon, tears filled her eyes. "John isn't like that." He was the exact opposite of those men in every conceivable way. She concentrated on her words to make them clear. "He was the one who finally rescued me, saw me. Cousin Andrew held no sway over that decision."

"John is an idiot. He has a responsibility to the title he'll eventually inherit over making some woman with a history of insanity happy."

Her temper flared. "Not insane." The words snapped from her. If he wouldn't listen, there was no hope of changing his mind. "I am different. Not stupid. Not slow. John doesn't want the title." Perhaps she shouldn't have told him that, but dissembling was a waste of time. There was no purpose to it. "He is happy without it."

"There is no such thing as happiness, and the Westfield title is his damned birthright." The baron shifted again as the hired hack slowed to a halt. "There is only the business of living, of trying to survive in a world gone cold, and then there is death. What a man does during that lifetime is his own business."

So much bitterness wove through his voice that it tugged at her heart. "There is also love. And belonging. And feeling safe." All of those things she'd found with John. He'd made her realize she wasn't all the things that had happened to her. She wasn't what everyone thought of her. She was her own person, with unique qualities she should rejoice about instead of try to hide in an effort to be "normal."

"Love is for stupid children who enjoy fairy stories." He grabbed the door handle, yanked on it, and then pushed the door to the cab open so violently, it slammed against the side of the vehicle. "Love doesn't last. It leaves a man weak and vulnerable, but above all, it leaves a man desolate and alone, without purpose or direction. I don't believe in that emotion any longer."

She gasped. "Grieving you are." That would certainly explain his horrid behavior. John hadn't talked about his mother's death, but then most of his focus had been on her. *I need to change that.* "It makes you sad."

"You know nothing about it." There was a bit of a snarl in his tone.

"My mother died recently." Perhaps it was time for her to think about it and determine how she felt about that. No matter that she'd never truly known either of her parents, never again would she hear her mother's voice or see the emotions hidden deep in her eyes. Knowing that this man was like her—grieving, perhaps missing—someone had those emotions pressing in on her. "We have in common that." And with that, they could find balance, but still her chin trembled, for she hadn't been able to tell her mother goodbye, had refused to see her the last time her brother had told her to.

"Don't try to make this personal. I won't fall for it." Before she could say anything else, he'd jumped from the carriage.

"Let's go." When she didn't move, the baron yanked on her arm. In the process of dragging her from the conveyance, the sound of fabric rending echoed in her ears. "If we don't hurry this transaction along, a couple of the men I owe money to will come find me."

She could have forgiven him for his emotional responses, for she was just now learning how to navigate hers, but ripping her beautiful gown went beyond the pale. The second her slippers hit the ground, she shoved at him with her balled fists, catching him off balance. "Ripped you my gown!" A piece of the sparkling fabric embroidered with stars and crescent moons drifted to the ground. "You do not deserve John as your son." With another shove, she bolted away, running along the bridle path that led deeper into Hyde Park. In some distracted part of her brain, she knew they'd disembarked near the Temple Gate. If she could find it, she could access a main road soon after. Wasn't that how she'd arrived in Andrew's carriage the day of the rain when she met John, and everything changed?

Whatever it took, she would prevent the baron from harming

her husband. And at the end, if John decided he didn't love her, she would let him go. She wanted him as happy as he made her. Perhaps he would ask her to go back to Hadleigh Hall, but then she would never lay eyes on the sea. A sob tore from her throat as she ran blindly over the path. The tiny gravel and pebbles bit into the thin soles of her slippers, but she didn't care. The goal was to get away from the baron. He needed to solve his problems instead of thinking someone else could do that for him.

"By Jove, woman, if you don't come back here, I'll start shooting. You won't get far." The baron's call rang in her ears, and again she wondered if it would hurt too terribly much if one of those balls were to lodge in her flesh. "It won't matter to me if I hit you or my son in the process."

That gave her pause. Though her heartbeat ricocheted through her veins, she slowed her pace. She loved John too much to let his father harm him. "If leave him alone you promise to, I'll come with you."

"Caroline!"

She jerked her head up at the sound of her husband's voice. "John! I'm over here!" Moving in the direction where she'd last heard him, she winced each time rocks and pebbles pressed into the tender skin of her feet. Not having the use of her arms made her balance unsteady.

"Don't listen to anything he tells you, Caroline! He's a thief, a liar, and a drunk. I'm coming." Determination echoed in his voice.

Running footsteps from behind warned her that the baron was all too close for her liking. There was bridge up ahead that spanned the narrowest part of the Serpentine. The handsome stone construction of it made it gleam almost white in the moonlight. As soon as she gained the structure, John appeared at the other end. "John!" Relief shot down her spine. "Run! Your father has a pistol."

"Damn interfering wench." Lord Westfield's hand landed heavily on her shoulder. He yanked her backward, pulling her hard against his body. "I asked nicely but won't make the same mistake again." Annoyance rumbled through the whispered words. He pressed the nose of his pistol into her left side while holding her to him with his right arm wrapped about her middle. "Now we'll have to do things the difficult way."

The area was dark, for no gaslights had been installed there. It wasn't a heavily travelled section of the park, especially at night; most people preferred the other end of the Serpentine, where it was wider and more idyllic with fountains and beautiful landscaping. Sounds of carriages rumbling along the main streets and through the park echoed in her ears.

John halted with one foot on the bridge at the opposite side. "Damn it, Father, release my wife immediately."

"Once you've given me the ransom."

Fear twisted up her spine in an effort to steal her breath. "Don't do it. He lies. Said he'll marry can someone kill me so you else." Then because the events of the evening had severally taxed her strength, plus the trauma of realizing her mother was indeed dead continued to plow into her, tears welled in her eyes. They spilled onto her cheeks. Just the sight of her husband made everything better, but they were both in danger. "He thinks me insane but he's hurting with grief." How did her words choose what times to order themselves clear? "Wants you to marry someone else."

How could she go on if she lost him?

"Don't let what he says poison your mind, Caroline." Slowly, John crept forward, step by step as if unsure of what might set his father off. "You know what's right and what's wrong and what is true. I would never hurt you or do anything that wasn't what you wanted. You remember that, right?"

She concentrated on the stark white of his evening shirt and cravat, of the gloves he still wore, remembered the grin he reserved for her, the way his eyes lit whenever he saw her or the way his whispers in the dark made her feel tingly inside. "Yes."

The baron snorted. "He's the one who lies. Do you truly

think any man in his right mind would choose to wed you, to have a life with one of your affliction?"

"John is a good man."

"Yet you are tainted. Broken." There was no mirth in the man's laugh. "You are consigning him to a dark future."

"No." When she attempted to squirm away from the baron, he tightened his grip and dug the nose of the pistol harder into her side.

"Caroline!"

A whimper escaped her. "John!" She threw a panicked glance his direction. "I don't want to die. My is dead mother. I don't want that also."

"I know, sweeting. We shall talk about it in a bit."

Then she understood the baron's motivation as she began to realize that her own anger wasn't merely that; it was *grief*—for her wasted life, the stolen time, the lack of understanding, the deaths of her parents that she couldn't yet process. "I am… sad," she told John, temporarily ignoring his father. "Feel that is what I do." And the baron missed his dead wife—John's mother. Perhaps he mourned for the life he once had as well.

We are not that different at all.

"That makes sense, and I want to hear more about that after this." He nodded, but his expression remained wary. "I won't let you die. That's a promise." His tones were soft, soothing. The sound of the constantly moving water nearly snatched them away.

Forever the dashing hero.

Lord Westfield scoffed. "You make me ill. What sort of man encourages and grows a sensitive side?"

"The kind of man who has seen a lifetime of violence and death during that travesty of a war and wants no more of that." Even from a distance, the hard clench of his jaw was evident. "Or perhaps the sort of man who was abused as a child—both physically and emotionally—by someone who knew better but did it anyway because it was the easy choice, the only choice he knew… a man who only wanted praise and love from his father."

"Bah. You understand nothing of what drove me back then. You know nothing of it now." Yet there was a faint note of fear in those words.

Why?

"It matters not." John took another few steps forward. "There was no effort made by you to apologize, to reconcile, or to even explain. You chose instead to destroy yourself and the title so there's hardly anything left of both. It will take generations to repair what you've done, and that's the worst crime, for that means time I'll have to take away from the things I adore the most. It will harm any children Caroline and I might have."

Her heart squeezed. Did he want that with her?

The baron's body went taut. "Why the hell couldn't you have paid attention to the things *I* enjoyed? Why couldn't you have been a real son?"

John snorted. "When did you give me that choice?"

As his grip went slack for a few seconds, Caroline attempted to dart away, but the baron was quick even if he was distracted. He grabbed a handful of her hair and yanked her backward.

Pain exploded along her scalp. "Please. Let me go. Talk to John."

"No. This interlude has gone on long enough as it is." He pulled tighter, grinning when she whimpered, and tears coursed down her cheeks. "Where is my ransom money, boy? That's my immediate concern. If you don't show it to me within the next few minutes, I swear I'll put a hole through this worthless woman you call wife. And then I'll come after you. My creditors won't care regardless."

Oh, John, please be careful, and if you can't, please walk away so that you can be clear of this desperate, sad man.

CHAPTER NINETEEN

JOHN'S HEART WAS firmly lodged in his throat as his father continued to hold Caroline captive on the Serpentine Bridge. And what was more, her wrists were bound in front of her.

He bristled. The effrontery of that scurvy scum!

The structure served as a boundary between Hyde Park and Kensington Gardens, with the fat part of the Serpentine on one side and narrow Long Water on the other. The more the baron held that pistol trained on her, the more anger roared through his chest. His pulse thudded hard in his ears, and he hoped that Brand would be able to surprise him, for the plan was to have him come up from the rear. John's part was to serve as a distraction, and he'd been remiss thus far.

"I rather doubt you'll kill anyone." It was a gamble, to be sure, for his father was slightly unhinged. How had he come to this pass? And how the devil could he rescue Caroline, untie her, *and* do something about his father at the same time? He hoped Brand had an idea.

"Desperate men are driven to desperate measures." Slowly, his father advanced, pushing Caroline ahead of him until they reached the middle of the bridge. "I want that coin."

So, this was where his father would make his last stand. So be it. After this incident, John wanted no part of the man's life. He was finished trying to make amends. Caroline certainly didn't need that sort of anxiety in addition to what she already carried, and from the moment he'd pledged his life to her, she came first. With a growl, John took another step. He'd meant what he said to the earl. If need be, he'd put a period to his father's life. As he came closer, he caught the unmistakable evidence of bruises forming on the side of Caroline's face.

The bugger will pay for that.

One of his hands curled into a fist. The longer his father mistreated Caroline, the more John's anger grew, filled the whole of his being until he was shaking with it. Perhaps he'd have the whole mess done with tonight.

"Let her go. We'll talk as men."

The baron snorted. "The time has passed for that."

"No." Caroline shook her head. Somehow, she maneuvered herself around so that she could peer at her captor. How could the man not be taken with her looks, her soulful eyes, that mouth that hinted at a smile? "You can *always* talk. John me that taught. Makes you feel better."

Oh, he was so proud of her! She'd come so far with growth since they married. It also humbled the hell out of him that he could help her in that way, but if he didn't do something and soon, he might lose her. *I'm so sorry you're in the middle of this drama.* If he could snatch her away, would his father shoot him in the back? Cold fear shook him. He took another tentative step toward them, for he had to try. "I brought the blunt, but not the sum you specified."

"Damn it! You had one directive, and you've failed." He gestured with the pistol but kept hold of Caroline's hair. "Because of your incompetence, you've as good as signed my death warrant."

John frowned. What the devil did that mean? Then he understood. "Ah, some of your money lenders aren't best pleased you've got pockets to let. Have you sold off everything of value then?" The townhouse had certainly not seemed as if the paintings and décor had been picked through, but that didn't mean it wasn't spoken for after the ball had ended.

"I did what I needed to do."

"Ah, to continue to purchase enough spirits to pickle your liver? One hell of a slow way to meet your Maker." Well, that was his own sorry fault. He'd made that mess all by himself. Perhaps he didn't deserve mercy or a second—twentieth—chance. "I'll wager they won't kill you just yet. Cause you pain, sure, but not death. You're no good to them in a coffin." The sad fact remained there were not enough funds to lay his father out in a vault on the Surrey property with his forebearers. A simple coffin in an unnamed churchyard would be his final resting place.

His emotions were split upon that fact, and it further angered him. Why should he care what happened to this sorry excuse for a man?

"You have no idea how far gone things are." The admission was said in a soft voice. "I am out of options, and quite frankly, I'm tired of fighting."

"Meaning what?" Surely, he didn't wish to end his own life. John's chest tightened, not because he would miss his father; there was no love lost between them, but due to the fact that he wasn't ready to land in the spoiled soup the title represented.

However, if suicide were declared as the cause of death, perhaps the courts would rule the Westfield title and Butler blood "infected" or "corrupt" which would therefore circumnavigate the need to become baron. The title and the debt simply wouldn't pass on.

"Meaning I've made a muck of things and have no idea how to fix it."

"Do you wish to make amends?" That would come as a surprise if so.

"I don't know. I've been miserable for so long…" The words trailed off, and when John assumed he might lower the pistol, he shook his head, narrowing his eyes. "I only know that it will start with the coin you've brought, but I'm still going to demand the ransom I asked for." He jammed the nose of the pistol harder into

Caroline's side. "Perhaps I'll hold her hostage until then."

Her whimpers of alarm went straight to John's heart and squeezed. "Of course you would say that." Everything the man did revolved around money. There was nothing inside him that had compassion for anyone else. "You're quite the selfish bastard, Father. It's good to know you never disappoint in that regard." He didn't trust his father as far as he could throw him. "Did you ever wish to make something of yourself instead of dig a hole around you and the title?"

"Perhaps, at one time, when your mother was alive."

"But you broke her heart along with the rest of us," he said in a low voice. That had been a terrible time in his life. Shortly thereafter, he'd escaped to the navy. John glanced at Caroline as the rhythmic slap of the water below provided background sound. Trembles racked her frame as she clasped her hands together. Tears streaked her face in the moonlight. Portions of her pretty gown had been torn, and the crescent moon pendant she'd worn tonight was missing from around her neck. Whatever he did, he *would* free her from his father. "Mother had so much hope you'd make her proud, but you couldn't manage it. Vices took control. And now, you're holding my wife at pistol point. Such a gentleman." Sarcasm dripped heavily from the statement. The muscles in his belly clenched. How to extricate Caroline without rendering her harm? "It doesn't bode well for the future, does it?"

For one second, he thought that perhaps his father might have had a change of heart, but then his expression hardened, and the baron shook his head. "Our future was decided the day your mother died, and then the days you and Mark walked out on me."

"You gave us no choice!" What did he not understand about that? Why would grown children wish to continue to let someone beat them nearly every day?

"Shame on you, Lord Westfield." Then Caroline gasped.

Oh, no. She'd seen her cousin as he crept up behind the baron.

John couldn't grab her attention with her back to him.

"Brand!" she exclaimed. "Help!"

"You betrayed me." Shock reflected on the baron's face. "I said to come alone." John's father whipped around, taking Caroline with him. He took aim and fired.

Bang!

"No!" The ball released as John launched into motion, but the harm had already been done. By the time he'd reached his father's location, Brand had fallen to the ground not ten feet away. "Bloody hell," he muttered. Save his wife or save his best friend? The critical moment was upon him. In the flash of an instant, he decided. For the moment, Caroline was unharmed, and his father wouldn't leave without the coin, but Brand needed him more.

And there would be hell to pay once he saw to the captain's care.

He ran to where his best friend had gone down while Caroline struggled in the baron's hold. "Brand?" John kneeled at the man's side and gingerly performed a perfunctory examination. When Brand groaned, he uttered a quick prayer, for that meant he was alive. His glove came away stained with dark blood. "Where did he get you?"

"Left shoulder." Brand gasped when John yanked at his clothing in an effort to bare the wound. Blood soaked his fine lawn shirt.

"Damn." John removed his gloves. Then he relieved Brand of his cravat. "First glance says it went clean through in the fleshy part but press this to the wound until I can properly have it examined." He folded the length of cloth and held it to the wound.

"Go." Brand shoved at him with his free hand. "Go rescue Caroline. Oh, and beat the stuffing out of your father while you're at it. The man has some gall to shoot me."

"Right." Though the gravity of the situation wasn't lost on him, John grinned. "I'm ending this tonight." He sprang to his feet. "You'll be all right?"

"Yes, damn it, now go!"

But a cacophony of sound and anguish met his ears before he could start off. "What the deuce?" He glanced toward Caroline's location and then his jaw dropped. His wife currently berated his father, beating him about the head and chest with her tied fists.

"You shot my cousin!" *Thump, thwack!* "No reason for it! You are such a grumpy, sourpuss, you want others to add you be because!"

"I'll be damned." This time, he couldn't make sense of her statement, but it didn't matter. John looked at Brand, who'd struggled into a sitting position. "Caroline is the epitome of a storm's fury, and my father has just been caught in the middle of it."

Brand snorted then bit back a groan. "I'd say he deserves every bit of it."

"Agreed." John shrugged out of the evening jacket. No sense in ruining a perfectly good piece, for he would land his father a facer—or four.

"John is trying to help you, but you snarl and hold him away." *Thump! Thud!* "You hurt me too, and ever do that no gentleman would." *Thwack!* "John is a hero. He makes me happy. Why can you not leave him alone?" *Thump, thump, thud!*

"Enough, you crazy bitch! Since I don't have my money, you have to go." Before John could approach, his father picked Caroline up bodily and then hurled her over the stone railing.

Her raw scream of terror sliced through the silence of the night.

"Damn it to hell and back." He bolted toward his sire with a slight red tinge sliding over his vision. His father had dumped the single most precious person in John's life into the water as if she was nothing more than rubbish. The urge to vomit made itself known. Caroline had only had perhaps two swimming lessons, and her hands were tied besides. That water must be at least seventeen feet, perhaps a bit over from the recent rain, and the current was decent. "Attempted murder now, Father? It would seem your list of crimes is growing." He grabbed hold of the baron's cravat and shoved him into the railing as he loomed over him. For the first time since he'd known his father, fear had gathered in the depths of his eyes. Movement off to the side indicated Brand slowly coming their way. "If she dies, there is nowhere on this earth you can hide." He let him go. "Stay here. We are *not* done, but I'm quite certain Captain Storme will keep watch. But to be fair, you've riled him up, so you might have a bit of a rough go."

Then he scrambled over the wall and dropped into the river below.

Instantly, the cool water closed over his head. After propelling himself to the surface, he wiped the water from his eyes and cast about for his wife. "Caroline!" His voice echoed oddly off the underside of the bridge. "Caroline, where are you?"

A series of splashes reached his ears, somewhere off to his left in the darkness. Then, a weak, "Help!" sent his heart aching anew. "John? I'm sinki—"

Oh, God.

CHAPTER TWENTY

PLEASE LET ME get there in time.

He swam to the area where he thought she might be. "Caroline!" Another series of splashes before the eerie silence engulfed the night. The hell with it. Diving beneath the surface, he swam as best he could with his shoes on. The inky blackness didn't help, but his hand rasped against the filmy fabric of her skirting. With his heart pounding, John reeled her to him, hand over hand, until he was able to wrap an arm about her waist and push them both to the surface.

Once more, his head cleared the water, and he pulled her up with him. Caroline coughed and sputtered as they bobbed along with the current. She gulped in lungsful of air.

"You came." Her words were soft, choked, wheezy.

Oh, dear Lord, his heart would soon explode from the relief of having her still with him. "Didn't I say that I would?" He smoothed the wet shanks of hair from her face. "Good enough so I can get you to the shore?"

"Yes." A shiver racked her shoulders. "I was so frightened." She lifted her arms and then looped her arms about his neck so her tied wrists were at his nape. "Your father lashes out…" She took another gulp of air. "…because grieving he is, like a wounded animal."

"That's not an excuse for trying to kill both Brand and you."

John hardened his heart against his father's plight or his emotional fragility. "But I will say my piece to him. If he's receptive, we'll proceed from there." He swam as best he could with Caroline clinging to his body like a quaking monkey. "Sweeting, we shall talk once the business with my father has concluded."

Precious minutes ticked by while he brought them both to the riverbank against the current. At the back of his mind, he wondered if a patrol would come by, attracted by her scream when she'd gone into the water. Would they agree to take his father into custody even if he was a peer? Doubtful. Men with titles were very seldom arrested or even put to trial. There was absolutely nothing keeping men from being the worst versions of themselves. No consequences meant continued bad behavior.

It needs to stop. For my sake. For Caroline's.

For their future.

Finally, he disentangled his wife's arms from about his neck and then hefted her onto the bank. When he pulled himself out of the water, a chill immediately swept through him, but he ignored it in favor of removing Caroline's bonds, rubbing her wrists. "Are you all right?"

Her teeth chattered but she nodded. "He ruined my gown."

Despite the gravity of the situation, the corners of John's lips twitched. "He has much to answer for, I'm afraid. We'd best have it over and done with. The sooner we do, the sooner we can go home."

"Home." Caroline gave him a tired smile. Then she gasped. "Brand is hurt." Before he could respond, she'd dashed off, moving over the grassy embankment and toward the path that would lead to the bridge.

"I suppose there's no stopping her when she's determined." He followed, but every muscle in his body was taut and overwrought, for there was no easy answer for his father. Catching up with his wife as she approached Brand and the baron, he drew her to a halt. "I want to keep you safe. He's a dangerous man at this point."

She nodded. "Will you punch him?"

"Do you want me to?"

"Yes." She laid a hand on his arm. "But he's your father. Mine is gone; yours is not." Her gaze met John's in the dark. "He is hurting, doesn't be kind know how to, so show him. Then if he rejects that, you have the answer." Her fingers tightened. "Please?"

Perhaps she'd summed up the situation clearly. "I'll do my level best." Residual anger gathered in his gut, pushed into his chest. The crimes against his family—the people he'd chosen to put in his life—still rankled, but Caroline remained by his side, and he was sorely glad for her presence.

The baron stood with his back to the stone railing. Brand waited a few feet away. Even in the inky blackness, it was apparent his face had blanched. Somehow, he'd taken possession of the pistol, but it didn't matter. It was a single barrel weapon, and until it could be reloaded, it was basically useless. Leave it to his father to cling to antiquated pistols like he did ideals.

"I want the coin I was promised." Emotion rendered his father's voice rough. "It will at least mitigate some of the worst creditors."

The gall of him to think he'd be rewarded after the events of the night! In silence, John retrieved his evening jacket. Before handing it to Caroline, he withdrew a small leather pouch from the pocket and tucked it into the waist of his trousers. "Put this on, sweeting, lest you shiver to death. You can tend to Brand after." Then he addressed his father, ignoring the others for the moment. "You are the lowest form of blackheart I can imagine just now." And because the night had already been trying enough, John lashed out with a fist. He caught his father on the chin. The force of the blow sent him flying, crashing to the ground. "That's for what you perpetrated during my formative years."

Damn, that had felt all too good, and he'd wanted to do that for too many years.

When the baron struggled to his feet, he laughed. The bugger actually laughed! "Men all over England regularly beat their children. There is no crime in it, and it's done in the hope of making them into fine gentlemen, strong leaders who don't let the weakness of emotions color their decisions. I learned from my father, and he from his. So on throughout the generations."

"By fear, intimidation, and pain?" He'd had enough of his father's excuses and reasons. He struck again, and this blow glanced off the baron's cheek. Would be a first-rate shiner tomorrow. Yet, the satisfaction he'd gained after that first punch didn't come with this one. "That was for daring to shoot my best friend, the man who is closer to me than my own brother. Thanks to the horrors you inflicted upon us that made us both flee."

When his father staggered back to lean against the bridge wall, he held up a hand. "So I can assume the beating you're giving me is acceptable behavior?" He lifted a hand to his broken lip where a thin trickle of blood had started. "Where is the line, John? Why is this any different from what I did to you and your brother? You who are allegedly so noble and kind and gentle." The mocking tone he'd adopted when he said those words grated across John's nerves. "You would bust me up with your fists and leave me here for the criminals to pick over?"

The truth of it caused his heart to seize. There was no difference, and in continuing to rain blows upon this sorry excuse for a human merely in retaliation, he was exactly like his father. With a gasp, John shoved a hand through his hair instead of landing him another blow for tossing Caroline into the river.

"You're right. It was my mistake, and it won't happen again." His wife had told him time and time again he wasn't the same man as his father, and he needed to continue to believe that, act like it. "But there *is* one difference between you and I." He took a step away. Behind him, Caroline murmured soothing words to Brand, fussed over him as if it were her single mission in life to take care of him. Later, when he had the opportunity, John would marvel over that little bit of growth in his wife, but right now, he needed to clear his future. "I am making a conscious effort to *not* live the whole of my life in your footsteps. I refuse to perpetuate the hurt and coldness I received from you. There are other, more effective ways to teach the next generation, and in doing that, my children will not fear or come to loathe me."

His father scoffed. "You will prove an embarrassment to the title."

"Ah, since you haven't?" John shook his head. This man held no power over him. Not anymore. "It is my right and my decision to deny taking up the title. It can lay empty for all I care. There are more important things to occupy my time and pour my attentions into."

"It's your birthright."

"Perhaps, but from all I've seen, once a man carries a title, he becomes someone else entirely besides the man he was always called to be." John glanced at Caroline, who had ripped panels from her gown and had neatly wrapped them about Brand's arm and shoulder to stem the bleeding. His heart skipped a beat. "I want a simple life, Father, the life I've built for myself that has nothing to do with the *ton* or the drains and stresses of society."

"What of my debts, then? Once I pass on, they'll become yours."

"No, they won't, for you are going to make something of yourself for once in your life." He yanked the pouch from his waistband and tossed it to the ground at his father's feet. "This is Caroline's dowry I received from Lord Hadleigh. I'd wished to buy a cottage and setup housekeeping with it, but I feel the best use for this coin is to purchase you a ticket on the next outbound vessel bound for America."

"What?" The baron gawked at him.

Both Brand and Caroline stared with identical expressions of shock.

John continued. "Leave England. Go start again in America. Perhaps discover truths about yourself and make a fortune. Drink yourself to death, I care not." He shrugged. Long ago he'd lost the ability to care about his father.

"But the title…"

"You'll escape your creditors. Perhaps when enough time has passed without a word from you, I can go through the arduous legal process of having you declared dead." He frowned. "But then, I don't care that much. If word reaches me of your demise, I shall refuse the title. If I have a son, he can decide what he wants to do when he's of age."

"It's my legacy."

"No." John shook his head. "Your legacy is a drunkard, a disappointment, a missing the mark to being the man I needed when I was a boy—or even now." For long moments, he remained silent as he stared at his sire. There was absolutely no affection left for this man. "Mother would be ashamed to see what you've become. I handed you the means to change that. Do her memory proud so you can eventually ask for her for-giveness."

"But what will you do without this money?" The baron stooped to retrieve the pouch. Seconds later it vanished into a pocket of his evening jacket.

"The same thing I have always done. Work hard. Put my back into the labor. Conduct myself with honesty and integrity at the profession I've chosen. I already have everything of value a man could ever need—good, loyal friends, a view of the sea, and a wife who I adore to distraction."

"And don't forget, the power of the whole Storme family behind you, backing you up and giving you whatever reach and assistance you'll need."

John spun about, and his lower jaw dropped. The Earl of Hadleigh approached with a pistol drawn and trained on his father. Behind him was the countess, and Finn in his Bath chair, the Earl of Worchester, as well as Caroline's brother William and his sister Isobel following behind. Seeing all of them decked out in formal clothing while entering this sad and sorry scene both made his chest swell in gratitude and sent tendrils of hilarity through his being.

"What are you doing here?" The statement they made by presenting such a united front humbled him.

The earl shrugged. His expression said John was a nodcock to even ask. "Rendering help to the newest member of the Storme family." Then he stepped around John to address the baron. "Come along, Westfield." He gestured with his pistol. "The best thing for you to do is listen to your son. Let the Americans have at you. We English have had enough."

The baron's expression twisted into a mask of hate. "You have no right, Hadleigh."

"I have every right. You have threatened my family, nearly tried to kill two of them from what I can gather." All the authority of the earl rang in Andrew's voice. "Since you haven't the ballocks to change for yourself, I'm stepping in."

John shot a glance to Brand, who shrugged and then winced. When he turned to face his father once more, his resolve had strengthened. Finally, he'd been accepted into a family on nothing except his own merits. Perhaps he had a bit of the storm inside him as well. The knowledge both brought comfort and panic, but given the alternative, he'd choose them. He stepped close to his father, stared him in the eyes, caught the trace of fear there... and then released it, for his father's fate wasn't his concern any longer.

"Do not think to return to London until you've made deep inroads into turning your fortunes—both personal and financial—around. You are not welcome here." Though his stomach muscles clenched, his father needed the tough truths he was about to find.

"Ah, if I do these things, turn my life about, will you accept me as your father?" The question was asked in a quiet voice, and suddenly the man John had hated over the years shrank, became a fragile shell of himself.

John's heart squeezed. "If you do all of that, make yourself into a respectable member of the *ton*, square with your debts and your drinking, then yes. I'll welcome you back with open arms." He laid a hand on the baron's shoulder. "If you want the reward, you must put in the work. There is no other way."

His father nodded. "I'll prove you wrong."

"I hope you would, and I'll be properly proud. Until then, I wish you the best of luck." Slowly, John backed away. He fought against a wave of emotion, refused to give his father fuel to call him weak. "I can't in good conscience have you in my life or a part of my future until you've changed."

As the earl led him away with Caroline's brother on his father's other side, he said, "Inspector Storme will keep an eye on you until we can arrange passage. I'll gift you with enough coin to see you modestly settled, but that's all you'll extort from the Storme family, and if you threaten one of us again, you shall have the whole of my wrath to reckon with. I don't suffer fools gladly, Westfield."

Bloody hell.

The countess laid a gentle hand on his arm. "You did what is best. Truly. Now go take care of your wife. She looks quite lost."

"I will. Thank you." This night had drained him, both physically and emotionally. Feeling more exhausted than he had in years, John joined the knot of his extended family with a sigh. He found Brand's gaze. "You should let the doctor take a look at that wound."

"We shall do that directly." He sighed. "I want to go home, John. London wears on me."

"I know how you feel. Make the arrangements and I'll be there." Finally, he glanced at Caroline. "I can't wait to show my wife around Ipswich."

Finn rolled his chair over to them. "Since Drew took the smaller carriage, we can all pile into the larger one and put this madness behind us. Perhaps we can convince our brother's butler to put together tea at this late hour."

"I second that idea." Brand nodded. Of course the talk of food would motivate him, whether he was wounded or not. As they moved as one entity toward where John had left the first carriage, Brand frowned at him. "Are you coming?"

John waved a hand. "I'll follow in a hired hack. There are things I would say to Caroline that can't be delayed any longer."

"I understand." A faint grin took possession of his mouth. "We've all been there. I'm happy for you, my friend."

"Thank you." John wrapped an arm about Caroline's waist and led her toward the middle of the bridge. With the faint moonlight shining down to make the ripples on the water's surface sparkle like diamonds, the setting redeemed a portion of the night. "How are you feeling?"

Streaks of blood stained her once beautiful gown. Parts of the skirting hung like rags from where she'd ripped it up. Her damp hair fell about her shoulders and back in heavy ringlets. But she lifted her head and held his gaze. The fear from earlier had vanished, but it was too dark to properly read the emotions that clouded her stormy eyes. "I am fine. Tired, worried about Brand, but fine."

He had so much respect for her. When she'd had every right to dissolve into a shivering heap beset with fright, she'd held her ground, had made strides to help her cousin, had given John advice when he'd needed it the most. Almost speechless with a throat clogged with unshed tears, he encouraged her into a loose embrace. There was no reason to delay further. "I love you so much, Caroline. I can't contemplate life without you in it."

"Oh, John." A frown tugged down the corners of her mouth. "No one has said that to me for so long." She leaned into him, rested her forehead on his chest. When she looked at him again, tears welled in her eyes. "*Why* do you love me?"

Just when he feared his heart couldn't expand any more with affection for her, she'd proved him wrong. It was an honor to say those words to her, continue to show her how valuable and worthy she was. "Why?" That one-word question was said on a choked whisper. As he peered into her eyes, wished for nothing except to lose himself in those blue-gray pools, he sighed. "Why?" Now was the time to confess everything his heart had realized in the last few days. "Because I wasn't fully alive until I met you, for you opened my eyes to so many beautiful things."

Wonder shadowed her face.

"Why?" he continued, almost reckless in his wish to tell her all. "Because you show me every day, I don't need to be of the *ton* to be a good man, a man with honor and a gentle soul, a man who adores working a trade."

A few tears fell to her cheeks as she curled her fingers into his waistcoat.

"Why?" John's voice broke. This was the single most humbling and amazing moment of his life. Tears gathered in his own eyes, and he rejoiced in them. "Because those broken pieces of you that you despise? Well, they fit into the jagged holes in me that are left behind by my own broken pieces. Together, we somehow work; we are perfect for each other." When his tears fell, he let them, wanted her to see that he was a man of feeling instead of holding it back. "I love how your mind works, sweeting, how you see life, how you see me."

Of course, there was every possibility she didn't return his regard, but that was all right. He'd work that much harder to win her heart.

"Oh." Her lips formed an "O" of surprise, of shock, of realization. "So romantic." She trembled in his hold. "My heart is happy, John." The words were slow, deliberate. "You saw me when I was invisible, felt unlovable."

"How could I not? You soul fairly called to mine that day on the snowy lane. And darling, I will rescue you again and again— from whatever dragon plagues you—if you need me to keep showing you how much I adore you."

"John." Another few tears tumbled to her cheeks. Then Caroline moved slightly. She held his face between her hands, lifted onto her toes the better to look into his eyes. "You *are* my hero." Her voice shook from the force of the emotions no doubt battering her—new feelings that had undoubtedly surprised her. "Now, tomorrow, always. I... I..."

"Yes?" He could hardly force out the word, for they balanced on the precipice of a new life.

She smiled, and his world spiraled out of control. "I love you too." When he gasped, she nodded. "I finally understand."

"Understand what?"

"What this feeling for you was, this all-encompassing thing that makes me want to explode and fly from it when I'm with you. I am break from the glory frightened my heart might of it as it grows." The delicate tendons in her neck worked with a hard swallow, and the out-of-order words didn't matter. "I you, John, love."

She loves me!

The dear, jumbled words were so like his dear Caroline that he laughed, and when she joined him, it was the sweetest sound he'd ever heard. Never had a woman said those words to him, and now that they'd come from his wife, he wanted to weep from the sheer joy of knowing he'd won her.

He tugged her into his arms and held her close. All the fear and uncertainty faded away in the face of these new and surprising emotions, shared by them both, born out of trust and patience and understanding. "Ah, Caroline, I am so glad you're my wife. I couldn't imagine anyone better for me than you." Releasing her slightly, he traced a fingertip along the forming bruises at the side of her face. "Will you marry me again?"

"What?" She frowned. "We are already. See?" When she held up her left hand and the opal glimmered in the moonlight, he chuckled. She was a woman of fact.

"I mean for good this time. With love behind it. I want to start our life together anew and for the right reasons. Honestly. As a couple in love should, and especially now that you know what marriage will entail."

Her grin gave him all the affirmation he needed. "I'm so happy."

"As am I. Does that mean you will?"

"Yes." A few more tears fell. "Will you tell Cousin Andrew?"

"I will."

Caroline rested a hand on his chest and then shivered. "We will have a *real* wedding night?"

Heat crept up the back of his neck. "If that's what you want. I can deny you nothing." For the remainder of his life, he would endeavor to keep her in happiness.

"I want you, John." She wiped her streaming nose as well as her tears with the back of her hand. "Only you. It's always been you."

"Oh!" There was nothing more to say, so John crushed his wife in his arms and then proceeded to kiss her soundly, regardless of the fact they were both wet and in a very public place. It mattered not. She was his. He was hers.

Life truly was amazing.

CHAPTER TWENTY-ONE

October 9, 1818

IT HAD BEEN a month since Caroline had married John. Now, she stood flushed and incredibly happy, for she'd married him a second time earlier that day, and the two experiences couldn't have been more different. The first time had given her freedom, but the second! Oh, the second time had given her love, and it was as if all the dreams she'd ever had as a lonely young woman hidden away in the asylum were finally coming true.

She couldn't stop smiling as he escorted her into Hadleigh House. As they handed over their outer garments to the butler, it scarcely felt as if her feet touched the floor. They'd had the ceremony at Cousin Finn's townhouse as well as the breakfast following—since Cousin Brand had been advised to rest as much as he could following his gunshot wound—and the atmosphere had been one of jubilation and celebration instead of the concern and speculation of the first. Now they'd planned to complete her packing, for on the morrow, she and John would accompany Brand on schooner and would travel to Ipswich.

"It was fun marrying you again." Today, she'd worn the old, tarnished tiara her mother had given her long ago. She didn't mind how it looked; it was a piece of her she'd been too angry back then to appreciate. Over the course of the time between professing her love for John until today, she'd made peace with her family, both in person and in her mind to the people who had died. That simple act of forgiveness had further set her free. She didn't have to forget—those memories as well as her time spent at the asylum wouldn't soon leave her alone—but she didn't need to continue wearing them as a heavy mantle of anger and fury about her shoulders.

"I wouldn't have it any other way." He paused at the foot of the staircase in order to nuzzle her neck. "Hadleigh told me as we were leaving that he and Sarah have a social engagement that will keep them away from the house until dinner."

Awareness of him danced along her skin as it did each time he touched her. "Did you wish to converse with them?"

"No, sweeting." John dragged his lips to the spot behind her ear that had the power to drive her mad with sensation. "We could use the privacy to consummate this second marriage. Wasn't that one of your requests should we have another ceremony?"

"Yes." Anticipation buzzed at the base of her spine.

"And as much as I adore that shimmering navy gown, I can't wait to take it off you, do wicked things to you in an effort to show you how much I love you," he whispered, and the warmth of his breath skated over her cheek. "Would you like that?"

"Must you ask?" She met his gaze, offered him the ready grin that felt as if it hadn't left her since that night on the bridge over the Serpentine. "I wanting you will never stop, John."

"It's always good to hear, though." Without warning, he scooped her up into his arms. The folds of her pretty gown draped over them as he climbed the stairs. "Ah, Caroline, we are going to have such fun together. I can't wait to show you everything Ipswich has to offer."

As much as she longed to paint the sea, watch the sun as it set upon that vast expanse of water, for the moment, her mind was overtaken by her husband, and all she wished to do was luxuriate in the safety and protection found in his embrace, surrender to his lovemaking in the hopes he'd make her fly again.

"Right now, I only want you." Since the night on the bridge, they hadn't come together carnally, mostly out of exhaustion and healing, but there had also been much to occupy their time with packing, seeing John's father off, as well as a host of other things.

His chuckle reverberated in her chest. "I don't intend to go anywhere." Then he balanced her in one arm while manipulating the door handle to her rooms with the other. After pushing open the panel with a foot, he carried her over the threshold and let her slide down his body until her feet rested on the floor.

Caroline reached around him to close the door. "Good. Life would be exceedingly debutante without you." Heat jumped into her cheeks when he flashed her a look of confusion. "I meant dull."

"I love you." He framed her head with his big hands. Then he brushed his lips over hers in a tender kiss. "Don't ever change. Not one tiny bit."

Perfectly happy not to commune with him in words, she gave herself up to the embrace. The scrape of his barely there stubble against her neck when he dragged his lips along the column of her throat provoked delicious shivers down her spine. The touch of his fingers at her waist, her ribcage, the sides of her breasts as he explored had flutters filling her belly. Perhaps she *was* insane after all, for wanting this man—needing him—as much as she did wasn't a good thing.

Was it folly to have so much happiness invested in another person that she wished to cry from gladness because he was here?

In the end, Caroline didn't think so. She'd been so starved for love and understanding the bulk of her life that when it had finally come along, she grasped it with both hands and hung on tight. Because of John, her true existence had begun; due to her husband's faithful patience and courage, her future now stretched before her in an array of brilliant color like an oil painting, each one brighter than the last instead of being splashed with shades of gray.

He led her over the floor, with her retreating and him advancing, and with each step, each nip and nibble and play of their lips, he encouraged the tiny buttons from their holes at the back of her gown. By the time they reached the bed, the garment gaped about her breasts and shoulders. It took little effort—one clever tug really—and he had the gown pooling at her feet in a heap of navy silk and sparkling beadwork.

Not to let him have all the fun, she worked at the knot of his cravat. It soon gave away and she slipped it from around his neck. The length of lawn fluttered to the Aubusson carpet, quickly followed by his cuffs and collars. Oh, the scent of him was heavenly! Salt, sand, and the sea, they all teased her nose until she was nearly drunk on him. Her fingers fumbled at the silver buttons on his jacket, but with a giggle, she managed to finish her task.

"I need to see you," Caroline said while she shoved the garment from his broad shoulders.

"Patience, love. There is an art to this." After he'd divested himself of the jacket, his waistcoat followed, and finally his shirt. "Do you want me to stop here, or would you like me fully nude?" That cheeky grin of his said he already knew the answer.

"Clothes, all the way off." Not able to wait for him to comply, she reached for him, but he edged away. "John." There was a decided whine in her voice.

"When did you become managing?" Teasing lined his expression. "I'll be with you in a thrice."

Pouting, she removed her petticoat, then the stays once he'd manipulated the laces, and when she tugged the thin silk shift up and over her head, she let it dangle from a forefinger while he watched, apparently transfixed. "I'm waiting, husband." But oh, he was beautiful standing there with desire and love mixing in his eyes as he looked his fill at her naked body. Heat prickled along her skin. Tremors of need pulsed between her thighs, and he stared with one boot on and one off. Physical relations between them were still new. She barely knew how to ask for what she wanted him to do, so as her nipples tightened into hard, pebbled points and her breasts ached for attention, it was only natural for her to touch them herself, roll them, give one a light pinch. "Oh!" Shivers of pleasure edged down her spine, buried themselves deep into her core as she imagined it was John's hands on her instead.

"Well, damn if that's not the most erotic picture I've ever seen." He completed the remainder of his undress with alacrity. "You never cease to amaze me, sweeting."

One second, she reeled that a simple touch could begin such a cascade of feeling and then in the next second, she was lying on her back in the middle of her bed with John's hard body over the top of hers, and he pressed feather-weighted kisses all over her face.

But she needed so much more than that!

Not wishing to talk, she applied herself to kissing whatever part of him she came into contact with. She ran her palms along the breadth of his shoulders. The power muscles beneath his skin drew her notice, and she traced them down his arms and up his chest. When she came to the tattoo of the North Star, she licked the artwork, pressed her lips to it before moving on in discovery. At one of his flat, pink nipples, she worried it with her index finger until it tightened into a bud. Was it as sensitive as hers?

As best she could, she took it into her mouth, teasing that nubbin with her tongue until he groaned. "Caroline, hold."

But she didn't want to. She'd married this man—twice—and now she wished to enjoy him to her heart's content. Ignoring him, she drew a hand along his torso. Her fingers furrowed through the mat of hair on his chest. As she'd yearned to since seeing him shirtless that first time, she followed the line of hair as it thinned the farther south she went. Her palm skimmed over his nearly flat abdomen and finally, finally, she arrived at his impressively erect shaft.

How well she remembered the feeling of fullness when he employed that equipage, but right now, she wished him at her mercy so she could explore as much as she wished. Quickly, she peered into his eyes. Need had darkened those golden-brown depths and given them a green tinge. "May I?"

"Yes, but don't be surprised if things escalate quickly after that. I haven't had you nearly enough to control the impulse to claim you."

Heat slapped at her cheeks. "I don't mind." It was one of the aspects of coitus she enjoyed the most—that heart-pounding, breath-catching pace and friction that swallowed her whole. Then she curled her fingers around the fat girth of him, and he groaned. Caroline smiled. The feeling of power such an action gave her was indeed heady. With a tiny moan of her own when he fondled her breast and squeezed her aching nipple, she stroked her curved hand up and down his shaft. He was so hard and hot and silky! The breath shuddered from her when she thought of that part of him being inside her moving, thrusting, pushing her closer and closer to that exhilarating edge...

"Caroline!"

She gasped as the first faint contractions fluttered through her core and he'd yet to touch her. "I you need me in now. Please." Releasing his shaft, she looped her arms about his shoulders and crushed her mouth to his. She sought out his tongue, met his in a dance as old as time itself. Yes, perhaps it *was* insane how much she wanted this man but then, when had sanity ever been measured by just one ruler?

"Gladly." He shifted his position, widening her legs with his knee until she was splayed open, vulnerable, waiting for him to claim her.

Love her.

And then the head of his member glanced along her wet channel to pause at her opening. He kissed her as if he had all the leisure time in the world, as if he wasn't ushering in her demise by the flirting, teasing he enacted, and when she uttered a sound halfway between a whimper and a moan, he grinned, nipped her bottom lip, and then with a powerful flex of his hips, he thrust into her body, joining them, and he didn't stop until he was fully seated.

She panted, squirmed beneath him to accept all of him more comfortably. "This is my favorite moment." That initial joining when pleasure streaked through every nerve ending and he filled her so completely it brought tears to her eyes. "You are... You feel... I can't..." There were simply no words.

"I understand." John dropped a kiss to her forehead. "I love you and will count myself fortunate to have rendered assistance to you that day on the snow-covered lane when your coach broke a wheel. You've never been far from my mind since."

"My hero. Always." Caroline wrapped her legs about his waist and locked her ankles at the small of his back. "Want to fly, John."

He apparently needed no other encouragement, for he slowly withdrew only to stroke back inside with the same tenderness as before. Then he gripped her hips in his large hands, lifted them slightly to an angle he preferred, and rising onto his knees, he proceeded to claim her body more thoroughly than he'd ever done before.

Over and over and *over* he drove into her, and just when Caroline thought she would shake apart from the hot pleasure playing through her body, the dear, wicked man changed his pace, slowed it so that he thrust into her gently, lovingly, but even then the angle of his penetration rubbed against the swollen nubbin at her center, and tingles fell down her spine.

"More!" She didn't care if her voice was raised or if any servant passing along the hall could hear her. This was her man and her life, and she was finally enjoying every second of it. "I need more from you."

"One second. You might like this." When she assumed he would increase his rhythm, he slid out of her and then off the bed.

"What—"

"Come here, you wicked wanton of a wife." John grabbed her ankles and pulled her toward where he stood by the side of the bed. As her tailbone balanced on the edge, he encouraged her to bend her legs at the knee, and while he held her hips in his big hands, he once more thrust into her passage with enough force and went so deep her moan blended with his. "Tell me how you like this."

He stroked in and out, and the large length of him hit every sensitive spot she had. Wild, intense pleasure slammed into her, went through her, lifted her up so that she felt as if she weren't on the bed any longer. Over and over, he worked, filling her with everything that he was and taking all that she was in return, until she was crying from need and wonder, and her breath came in quick bursts.

Terrible pressure built and stacked low in her belly. Oh, she wanted to fall over that edge, wished to fly into the brilliant light of the heavens, and while this coupling had nearly gotten her there, she still required a bit extra. Just like she'd touched her nipples earlier, when she slipped a hand between the frenzy of their bodies coming together and rubbed her fingers over the slippery pearl at her center, it was enough for that dam to break.

"John!" Her keening wail would no doubt make the servants talk, but she didn't care. "Yes, yes, yes. Finish me!" The first twinges of contractions began deep in her core, and John thrust harder, went deeper, moved faster, his face a mask of concentration and exquisite pleasure. That's when she broke. Knowing he enjoyed this act as much as she did sent her hurtling over that elusive edge, and then she was flying, free once more, gliding through a vast white nothing with tiny rainbows of light chasing around her and musical notes dancing all around through the storm.

Wild sensation still shivered through her being when John pushed again. He said her name and then a groan swallowed it up. His member pulsed and jerked, pulled hard, followed by that familiar warmth when he spent. He ground his pelvis into hers, presumably to prolong the pleasure, until finally, he collapsed on top of her with his head between her breasts. "Dear God,

Caroline, you wear me out in the best possible way."

His words, coupled with his fleeting breath over her nipple tugged a tired giggle from her. She cradled his head in her hands, stroked his hair back from his forehead, and sighed. "I rather enjoy doing this."

"Good." His chuckle reignited the fires in her blood he'd just put out by sending her flying. "I rather like seeing you undone. Perhaps we can do it again tonight."

"Yes!" Her already flushed skin prickled with renewed anticipation. She shoved at his shoulders until he straightened and met her gaze. "Next time, I want to explore you—all of you—with my mouth." Her attention dropped to his semi-flaccid length. "You will pleasure you like teach me how to that?"

Mottled red color engulfed his face, and it was the dearest thing she'd ever seen. "We shall do anything and everything you've ever dreamed of, sweeting. The world, as well as my regard, is at your feet, breathless for your notice."

"So romantic."

"Only with you." He gave her that cheeky grin that never failed to make her smile. "I look forward to seeing what our life will be like, and I hope you'll never cease to find the wonder in it all."

"As long as you're with me, I will always love everything." Then she tugged on his hand until he joined her on the bed, and with a sigh of pure contentment, she snuggled into his side as his strong arms came around her. "Thank you for seeing past my storms to my truth."

"Thank you for letting me." He pressed a kiss into the top of her head. "There is no one way to see beauty, and the more of a mess it is, the more fulfilling it will be."

Caroline smiled and let her eyes drift closed. A lifetime with this man would never be enough. But for the first time since she was a young girl, she couldn't wait for each new day to begin.

EPILOGUE

November 13, 1818
Ipswich, England

CAROLINE STOOD AT the railing of the sloop John had named *Freedom*, and she sighed. The autumnal sunset had produced vibrant colors in the sky of pinks, purples, and golds. "I can't wait to reproduce this on canvas," she murmured while quickly sketching the various details as the sloop skimmed through the water, moving them swiftly toward the shore.

"If anyone can put one moment in time to canvas, it's you, sweeting," John said from his position behind a highly polished steering wheel.

For the past five weeks, they'd been in Ipswich, and while Cousin Brand had gone home to reunite with his wife and baby, she and John had made do with his rented rooms at the Great White Horse Hotel. There was a tavern on the ground floor, with a handful of private dining rooms, an interesting common room, and then the upper floors hosted rooms for rent. As residences went, the rooms were nothing to provoke excitement, but she'd spruced them up as best she could, using some of her paintings and drawings to decorate the walls.

Besides, a place's trappings mattered not to her, for she had John, and he was more than enough. When they were together, his company was all she needed, and when they were not, he'd thrown himself into making the shipping business he owned with Brand and two other men a success. Which they'd done. It was wildly popular, and all four men were constantly busy with moving goods, services, as well as travelers up and down the coasts.

While he was gone, she'd contented herself with painting and drawing. Two weeks ago, he'd surprised her with the news that one of the shops in the village square would let her sell a few of her paintings on consignment. With alacrity, she'd chosen her best pieces, and to her delight and John's pride, they'd sold within days of putting them in the shop.

She'd put forward the small income with John's, for someday they would purchase a cottage, and the longer he encouraged her to sell the paintings, the closer they'd grow to that dream.

Her fingers slowed on the drawing so she could peer at the colors that painted the sky. The world had proved a marvel to her and continued to do so with each passing day. So much so that the days spent stuck in the asylum were fast becoming faded memories. When moisture rolled down her cheeks, she sucked in a breath to realize they were tears. "Oh, John."

"Why are you crying?" He frowned and gestured at her for her to join him at the wheel. "I thought you were happy just now?"

"I was." She closed the sketchbook. "I am." Once she'd reached his side and he wrapped one strong arm around her, she sighed. "Beautiful area this whole is. Makes me cry out of gratitude. I can't believe I'm here. With you."

John pressed a kiss to her temple. "I know that feeling well."

"Since we've been here, I think… Well, I feel…" It was difficult for her to explain. The more she was with John, the more he helped draw out her emotions, experience them, to recognize them and let them go if need be, but it was difficult. A lifetime of repressing them would take work to accept that it was perfectly fine to feel… everything. A shuddering sigh escaped her. "I feel happy but frightened."

"Why? You are safe here in Ipswich and with me."

She concentrated on her words. "What if everything is suddenly yanked away from me? What if I wake up and find this was all a dream, that I'm not married to you at all, that I'm back in the asylum?" Fright moved down her spine. "I couldn't bear it."

"Listen to me." John rested a finger beneath her chin, tilting her head until their gazes met. "You'll never return to that asylum, and no one will take this life from you." He cupped her cheek, and with a sigh, Caroline nuzzled into his palm. "You are my wife, my partner, the reason I look forward to waking every day. I dare anyone to challenge me for that."

"No one will take you from me either." They'd been married for just over two months and already she couldn't imagine a life without him. He'd always been there, watching, waiting, hovering, encouraging her to spread her wings and take on the world. "I am a Storme."

"Actually, you are a Butler now, but yes. I understand the sentiment," he said with the grin that turned her knees into cooked porridge.

"Yes." She nodded. "Where are we going?" They were nearly to the harbor.

"Home."

"I don't know if I want the evening to end yet by going into that hotel." She lifted an eyebrow. "The taste of beer is off-putting."

John laughed at that, and the corners of his eyes crinkled. Amusement danced in those golden-brown depths. "I suppose it is if you're not used to it. But no, we're not going to the hotel."

"Then where?" Was he keeping secrets from her?

"You'll see." When she offered up another protest, he reeled her closer to his body and then kissed her until she'd forgotten the thread of the conversation.

An hour later, they'd disembarked from the sloop and took a stroll along the harbor road, winding their way through the village proper and farther into the hills.

"If you'll look across the harbor, those townhouses are where the people associated with the *ton* live when they're in the area. Lord Nelson has a residence there."

She didn't know who that was, but there was such excitement in John's voice, he must be someone of importance. "And the cottages on this side?"

"It's where the other people live, the ones who work the harbor and sea, the ones who fill the village and give it life. Ipswich would be nothing without these salt of the earth people." He nudged her elbow and gestured with his chin. "You've been to Brand's cottage often enough since we've arrived. Do you think it's cozy?"

"I thought it adorable. Plenty of room for him and Elizabeth and their baby." Her cousin could even have two more children without making it feel as if the place was crowded.

"Good." John guided her up a well-worn dirt path until he came to a white-washed cottage, dear in its construction, with the upper story windows thrown open to catch the autumnal breeze. "There's a decent garden in the back. Perhaps we can plant a tree or two." He waved a hand at the side of the cottage where mulberry bushes reposed. A rabbit poked its head out of the foliage, stared at them, and then ducked down beneath the branches once more.

"Why?"

"Come." He took her hand, guided her up a short walkway and to the green-painted front door. With a simple touch to the handle, the panel swung open. "Welcome home, Caroline. It's not a castle from the storybooks you adore, but I think we'll pass a happy life here."

"What?" She frowned as confusion clouded her mind. "Our hotel the home is."

"Not any longer."

"This is… Do you mean… House our this is?"

"Yes." His grin was wide. "Are you pleased?"

Another round of tears welled in her eyes. She let them fall unheeded as she pushed further into one of the large rooms. As of yet, there was no furniture to speak of with the exception of a single straight-backed wooden chair, but the floors were clean and the walls tidy, and there was a dear little staircase in the corner that curved tightly to the upper level.

"We'll live here?" It wasn't too far from Cousin Brand. She would have family nearby.

"If you wish it. I took the bulk of our savings and gave it to the man who is our landlord. We shall still need to make payments for a bit, and we're quite near dun territory until I can do a few more jobs, but I think it worth it." He waggled his eyebrows. "If it makes a difference, our bedchamber looks out onto the harbor."

"Oh." She scrubbed at her tears. "It's ours?"

"Yes."

"To live together?"

"Yes."

"And you won't leave me, go to sea without me?"

"Absolutely not. I plan to grow old here, sweeting, with you by my side." An expression of vulnerability crossed his face. Uncertainty shadowed his eyes. "Unless you don't care for it."

"Already, I adore it, and it's perfect for me—for us." Overcome with emotion, Caroline threw herself into his arms. She rained kisses all over his face, his neck, and once she'd loosened his cravat, she pressed them to that exposed skin as well. "I love you. So, so much."

Home. She finally had a home where love and affection would fill the rooms, and kindness and gentleness would guide their days. Perhaps if she and John had children someday, he would teach them how to be good men like him. *Home.* A place where she belonged without condition or restriction.

"I love you too." He slipped his arms around her and pulled her close. Into her ear, he said, "There is, however, a bed upstairs. The rest of the furniture we'll procure as time goes on. Perhaps by Christmas, we can invite Brand and his wife to dinner."

Awareness of him prickled over her skin. "Then let us consecrate making use of that bed our new home by."

John picked her up into his arms, chuckling when she squealed. "I adore how your mind works, which is fortunate, since your mind was what made me remember you, convinced me to take you away from the earl."

"And I've been yours ever since." She slipped a hand around his nape and tugged his head to hers, which made him pause at the base of the stairs. With a sigh, she kissed her husband, took her time with exploring his mouth, until the teasing little licks and nibbles introduced too much heat and urgency to that one meeting. When she wrenched away, a shaky laugh escaped. "I can't wait to see what life gives us." It was her turn to wink. "Perhaps a babe like Brand's."

John's eyes widened. "You want children?"

"Yes. Want them to be like you." She kissed him again then concentrated on speaking her next words. "Give me a baby, John, since you've already given me everything else."

With a whoop of pure masculine victory, he carried her the rest of the way up the stairs.

Caroline smiled. There was nothing else she wanted from her life. The future indeed beckoned with gorgeous color, danced like the music she adored, and all because this large, protective man had first treated her with kindness and understanding that grew into the love she'd always hoped for.

Everything else was like sparkles on a pretty gown.

The End

About the Author

Sandra Sookoo is a *USA Today* bestselling author who firmly believes every person deserves acceptance and a happy ending. Most days you can find her creating scandal and mischief in the Regency-era, serendipity and happenstance in Victorian America or snarky, sweet humor in the contemporary world. Most recently she's moved into infusing her books with mystery and intrigue. Reading is a lot like eating fine chocolates—you can't just have one. Good thing books don't have calories!

When she's not wearing out computer keyboards, Sandra spends time with her real-life Prince Charming in central Indiana where she's been known to goof off and make moments count because the key to life is laughter. A Disney fan since the age of ten, when her soul gets bogged down and her imagination flags, a trip to Walt Disney World is in order. Nothing fuels her dreams more than the land of eternal happy endings, hope and love stories.

Stay in Touch

Sign up for Sandra's bi-monthly newsletter and you'll be given exclusive excerpts, cover reveals before the general public as well as opportunities to enter contests you won't find anywhere else.

Just send an email to sandrasookoo@yahoo.com with SUB-SCRIBE in the subject line.

Or follow/friend her on social media:
Facebook: facebook.com/sandra.sookoo
Facebook Author Page: facebook.com/sandrasookooauthor
Pinterest: pinterest.com/sandrasookoo
Instagram: instagram.com/sandrasookoo
BookBub Page: bookbub.com/authors/sandra-sookoo